The Wedding Kiss

The Wedding Kiss

Hannah Alexander

summerside
PRESS™

Summerside Press™
Minneapolis 55337
www.summersidepress.com

The Wedding Kiss
© 2011 by Hannah Alexander

ISBN 978-1-60936-308-6

Scripture references are from the following source: The Holy Bible, King James Version (KJV).

All characters are fictional. Any resemblances to actual people are purely coincidental.

Cover design by Lookout Design | www.lookoutdesign.com
Cover photo by Veronica Gradinariu, Trevillion Images
Interior design by Müllerhaus Publishing Group | www.mullerhaus.net

Summerside Press™ is an inspirational publisher offering fresh, irresistible books to uplift the heart and engage the mind.

Printed in USA.

Dedication

With many thanks to my excellent Summerside editors
and staff for a beautiful cover and flowing prose.
It takes a team to make a good novel.

Hannah Alexander

One

A meadowlark's song lingered in the chilly spring air as Keara McBride's boots squished through a wet field of new wheat. She tried to let the song soothe her and the warm sunlight take the chill from her bones, but the beauty that seldom failed to settle her heart was failing today. Betrayal and shock and rage warred within her with such force they nearly outshouted the fear that trembled deep inside her bones.

These past two years since Ma's death, Keara had defended her grieving pa's antics to anyone who complained, but if Brute McBride was standing in front of her right now, she'd blast him with more words than any of the neighbors had ever dared speak to her against her bullheaded father.

The perfume of honeysuckle reached her, but she didn't turn to enjoy its beauty along the split rail fence today as she usually did. The splash and roar of White River filled her heart, loud and fast after the rains, like the storm that had whipped up inside her when she discovered how much she had lost, and what she must do to survive. All because of Pa.

She loved this land whittled from the forest around it by hard, backbreaking labor. The nearby resort city of Eureka Springs, with its gardens, healing springs, and steep, winding hillside streets, could not compare to the beauty of this Arkansas countryside. The thought of living and working there away from the ones she loved made her shiver, but if this plan didn't work, what choice would she have?

Stepping over the rise with legs that felt shaky, she saw the peaked roof of her neighbor's home. Smoke drifted from two of the three chimneys. She stopped, and for a moment she couldn't catch her breath. The sky appeared to blacken with clouds, but there were no clouds, only blue that stretched from the ridge of hills in the east all the way to the end of the world in the west.

The end of the world…of *her* world.

Bite the bullet, Keara.

She marched like a soldier down the rise through White River Hollow, her gaze set on the big house, painted like a brilliant butterfly, its multiple colors chosen with care, its gingerbread trim carved by the hands of a man who'd willingly indulged his wife's whimsy. It was put together strong to last, like the man who'd built it, with the help of his relatives and other neighbors who lived comfortably spaced from one another along the hollow.

A porch, gilded with yellow and lavender railings, skirted the front and east side of the house, and a kitchen garden greened the yard where the rock fence protected the crop from many rooting and foraging animals.

Eight-year-old Britte and six-year-old Rolfe were proud of the garden they had helped Keara plant. She could close her eyes and see their beautiful faces—Britte so much like her mother, and Rolfe like his father. Thoughts of them gave her strength to keep walking. This was for Gloria's children.

Keara inhaled the scent of the fruit tree blossoms in the orchard as she drew near, the pink and white blooms looking like pastel clouds. Her mouth usually watered when she thought about the peaches and apples, plums and pears that would come from those trees—a few of which still had not reached full bloom. Today her mouth tasted of dust.

She looked for signs of the children in the yard or playing under the trees. No one was in sight.

By the time Keara stepped up to the broad porch, she was winded and shaking, and not from the half-mile walk. She rang the cowbell Elam had hung next to the door for Gloria. The clanging echoed in her ears.

After a moment the wooden door with navy and sky-blue trim opened and Elam's tall, strong frame filled the doorway. His familiar dark brown eyes lit with welcome. "Keara."

She caught her breath, but the steadiness of his voice calmed her. She had come to know Elam Jensen well over the winter—knew the burden he carried after Gloria's gruesome death late last summer.

"I thought I'd check to see how Cash is doing on the goat's milk and corn gruel." *Liars go to hell, Keara McBride.* But truly, they'd had a time weaning the baby since his Cherokee wet nurse moved on to the Oklahoma Territory with her family.

"I think it's going to work." Elam moved aside and gestured for Keara to step into the great room, which was warmed by one of the new iron stoves he'd bought last year for Gloria. He'd also built the cushioned chairs and sofa, the wood glowing golden from the same log beams that held the house in a sturdy embrace beneath its charmingly decorated exterior.

Nearly the whole valley along the White River had come to see the Jensens' comfortable new furnishings, several relatives riding the five miles from Eureka Springs—any reason for a get-together since the recent entry into the twentieth century. The all-night party had been one to remember. Elam's sisters, sisters-in-law, and cousins had helped Gloria and Keara keep the refreshments flowing while the men talked about their animals and the young ones raised a ruckus in the barn with their dancing and singing.

Only weeks later, those same neighbors, family, and friends had returned with food and prayers of mourning for one of the most generous and kind women in the county. A hapless tourist, seeking relief in the healing waters, had unknowingly brought smallpox to Eureka Springs, even after the vaccines across the countryside had long ago promised protection. Gloria—with her trips to town to deliver meals for the sick and their caretakers—had been caught in the disaster.

Keara stepped past Elam into the large front room. She glanced toward the stairway with its fancy railings and slats painted the color of cream and butter. "Where are the children?"

"David and Penelope stopped by this morning on their way to the swimming hole for the day. They invited Rolfe and Britte to go with their cousins."

"On a Monday?"

"You know Pen now that she's expecting again. I just put Cash down for his nap." Elam's deep voice filled the room. His whole presence filled the house as it occupied Keara's thoughts.

Keara still ached with the loss of her dearest friend. Caring for Gloria's children, keeping her family fed and clothed, and teaching Rolfe and Britte their letters and numbers over the winter had helped fill the emptiness Gloria's death had left in Keara's life; she hoped it had made a difference in theirs.

Elam touched her shoulder. She jerked before she realized he was only taking her shawl to hang it close to the stove. *Get hold of yourself, woman! Do what needs to be done.*

He frowned at her. "Keara? You're as skittery as our new foal. What happened? Did you see a baby snake on the way here?" He spread the handmade woolen covering over the hall tree Keara's own father had made for the housewarming.

She blinked up at Elam as his words registered. Was that a teasing note she heard in his voice? He'd barely cracked a smile since Gloria's passing. Elam Jensen was once known for a good sense of humor, and though he was never mean, he used to like to tease. He knew she hated snakes.

"No." *Tell him, Keara.* "I guess I am a touch jumpy lately, what with having the whole house to myself since Pa went to jail."

Elam glanced at the floor. "Come have a seat. We need to get those dry."

She looked down and discovered she'd tracked mud across the floor. "Oh, jiggers. Where has my mind gone?" She skinned off her boots. "I'll clean this mess—"

"Not today. Something's bothering you." Elam reached out to ease her onto the sofa. She was glad he didn't know her skin tingled wherever he touched it.

He took the boots, set them near the stove, and sat down across from her, close enough for her to believe she could feel the physical warmth of his body reaching her. There was a strength about him that calmed her.

"Is everything okay at the farm?" he asked.

"No." Keara took a breath and met his gaze. "Pa gambled it away." This morning, after the banker left, she'd sat stunned on the front porch for probably two hours. Her lifelong home...gone.

Elam shook his head as if he had water in his ears. "I don't understand."

"I said it plain, Elam. Pa got into a card game two months ago and gambled away the whole farm. All I've got left is the livestock. At least he didn't gamble the horses, cattle, and hogs away."

Elam leaned forward, a frown deepening along the suntanned lines around his eyes. "Who told you this? Is someone trying to take advantage of you because you're alone?"

"The bank president himself came out this morning before the bank opened and showed me where Pa had signed the place away." She swallowed back tears, shaking her head. "Mr. Simon even went to the jailhouse and asked Pa directly if he did it. I knew he'd gotten up to all kinds of tomfoolery since Ma died, but this? This is... it's devilish!"

"He kind of lost his mind." Elam's voice held knowledge and compassion. "I know how it feels, but—"

"But you didn't suddenly turn into a drunken gambler or a hothead," Keara snapped. "You were here for your children. You kept working, kept going no matter what. Pa's been up to this for two years, just as if the boys and I weren't there. And he's not even around to help me. But I'd never have thought he'd end up in jail."

"You and I both know he's not a killer," Elam said gently.

"If he hadn't been in that bar, he'd not have been caught in the fight. Even so, I sure never saw this coming. My home, Elam. The whole farm!"

Elam reached for her hand and held it in both his own. "You were busy with the planting and the stock and coming here every day. I let you come when you were needed at home. I'm sorry."

Keara suddenly lost her ability to think as she stared at their clasped hands. She started breathing again when Elam released her. Here she was, losing her home, and she was behaving like a lovestruck girl. But could this mean he might care enough to help her the way she needed to be helped? Would he see reason?

"Sean and Morris shouldn't have left you there alone," he said.

Keara leaned back on the sofa and closed her burning eyes for a moment. Her younger brothers had never wanted to farm. They'd never understood her love of the land. "What were we supposed to do, tie them up in the barn?" At seventeen and eighteen, they were of age. They'd asked Keara to travel west with them after they helped with the planting earlier this spring, but she had no interest in riding a train west. She suspected they'd planned to catch their rides on freight cars, not wasting their means on passenger tickets to California.

With Ma paralyzed the last ten years of her life, Keara had shouldered most of the load. Now all she'd worked for was gone.

She looked at Elam and straightened. Time to get this over with. "I have a week to move out."

The muscles clenched along Elam's jawline and his eyes narrowed. "That long." His tone suggested he might be thinking the same things Keara had about Brute McBride. "So the winner of the bet waited until you got all the spring planting done before he decided to make his claim."

"You helped. Even Britte and Rolfe got blisters on their little fingers helping me. It was your hard work, as well, that's been frittered away."

"Who is this squatter?"

"Drifter by the name of Rod Snyder, comes from up in Missouri. Thinks he wants to 'settle down' here. I've not met him, but Mr. Simon says I don't want to mess with him."

A new, unfamiliar glint entered Elam's eyes. "Then maybe I will."

The threat in his voice warmed Keara's heart, but it startled her too. "You don't want to rile a cuss like him, living so close."

"He won't live close if he never moves in."

"Elam, the children come first, especially now. We don't know what this man's capable of. From the sound of him, he might try to hurt them." She had never mentioned to Elam what she'd overheard from others—that Gloria should have considered her own children before placing her life at risk by having contact with the suffering victims. Elam couldn't put his children's lives at risk for her. "You've got to think of them first."

Elam got up and paced to the stove. "This should be illegal."

"Mr. Simon says it isn't. Pa signed the papers." Unable to sit still, she also got up. She walked to the side window to gaze out over the new green of trees that encircled the south twenty. "That's why I need to talk to you."

For a man so big, Elam's footsteps were quiet as he followed her to the window. "I'll help any way I can."

"I've got to marry."

There was a silence behind her.

She didn't want to turn around and see his reaction. "It's my only hope of staying in White River Hollow," she said. "There's nothing for me among folks in Eureka Springs. Who'd hire the daughter of a jailbird?"

"Nobody thinks of Brute McBride as a jailbird. He's well respected as a hardworking…" Elam's voice wavered to a stop. "Did you receive a proposal?"

She pressed her fingers against the windowsill. Was it so hard to believe that she would? "That isn't what—"

"Keara McBride, don't jump into marriage with just anyone because you're desperate."

She turned at last and found herself nearly jabbing her nose into his chest. "Desperate?" A desperate woman. That dug in and clawed at her.

He took her by the elbows and squeezed until she looked up into his gentle, haunted brown eyes. "You know I didn't mean you're a woman desperate for a man. I mean you're in a bad place, and you can't make rash decisions. Eureka Springs is crawling with strangers, sick folk dreaming the water can make them well. You never know what kind of man you might meet amongst the crowds of tourists."

She swallowed and wet her lips. *Say it, Keara. Say it now, or you'll never have the nerve.* "You need to marry me."

The crack-snap of fire reached them from the stove. Elam froze, still holding her. He didn't move or speak. She looked up into a well-chiseled face that had turned to astonished granite, lips parted.

"I'm not expecting a marriage like the one you had with Gloria," she rushed to explain. "It would be strictly a friend-type arrangement. I know you've not been looking for anyone to take Gloria's place, and I'll never find another friend so true, but you still need help here, and now I need a home."

Elam released her and took a step backward, his mouth working silently.

What was going through his mind? She hoped he wasn't feeling ill.

"I haven't lost my wits, you know," she said. "I'll never be the kind of woman Gloria was. There's never going to be anybody else like her, and I never had time to learn how to snare a man." She'd been too busy running after Sean and Morris and caring for all Ma's needs while keeping up with the household and the farm.

She could see sympathy forming in Elam's eyes. Poor, plain Keara McBride, twenty-six and never had a beau. Sure, he wouldn't say it, but she knew most folks thought it.

"I never regretted taking care of Ma and raising my brothers." She'd assured herself of that many times. "I always told myself there was time for courtin' later. But now is too much later." She forced a smile to hide her desperation.

"You have neighbors, Keara," he said gently. "You know I have family all up and down the hollow. Let your neighbors help you."

"Your brothers and sisters have children bursting out of their lofts. There's no place for me, and I can't stay with a man who isn't married. Pa's not going to be able to help support me from a jail cell."

She held her breath and waited. She knew her appearance—her shapeless, threadbare dresses, her hopelessly untidy hair, her habit of getting dirt on her face from the garden or the field—didn't draw the admiration of men, but she had borne witness to Elam's devotion to Gloria's memory and had quietly fallen in love over these past months. How wonderful it would be to have him love her that much. As if that would ever happen. She'd have to take what she could get.

How awful it felt to be unwanted.

"What would you be willing to sacrifice for your children?" Her throat was dry. She was begging now; he couldn't help hearing it in her voice, could he?

During Sunday meetings, for the sake of the children, Keara had checked out the women who'd set their bonnets for Elam. They might be pretty, but they weren't kindhearted. Raylene Harper suddenly considered herself too proper to get a little dirty, and her friends were even worse. Living here on a horse ranch, one couldn't be too prissy.

"Gloria and I talked about marriage before Cash was born," Keara said. "We weren't talking about me. We were talking about you."

Elam grew still, and his attention focused on her with uncanny intensity. She hesitated, entranced by the air of expectancy in those dark eyes as he awaited a new word from his wife, still loving her past the veil of death.

"She told me that if anything happened to her during childbirth she didn't want you and the children to hide out here alone on the farm. I've come to you because of Britte and Rolfe and Cash." It was true. Keara wouldn't have the courage to be here if it weren't for the sake of the children. "Helping you raise them is something I could do to honor Gloria's memory."

Elam's gaze traveled over her face, as if considering her proposal—or wondering if she had lost her mind. "You were always so good to Gloria." His voice was gentle, almost indulgent. "You're Auntie Keara to the children."

"I can help you as you can help me. I may be small, but I'm a strong hand...and I don't get sick. It would be a good partnership."

He grimaced and turned away. "That isn't what a marriage should be."

"Oh, don't get all particular on me. Marriage can be all kinds of things, but it surely is a partnership. Lots of folk marry without all the hearts and flowers and romantic trappings. I could sleep in Cash's room while he's little, or sleep with Britte. Whatever animals I don't sell I can bring with me. Buster is strong, and you know he's broken to wagon and saddle." She'd never sell her beloved chestnut gelding.

It wasn't until Elam reached out, took her by the shoulders, and gently nudged her backward that she realized she'd been advancing on him like one of those sirens in town. Heat traveled from her face to her toes.

He released her. "Don't throw away the chance for love because you can't see any other way out right this minute."

"And where do you figure I'll live while I wait? A tree in the woods? Who knows when Sean and Morris will return from California? I heard tell there's good work to be found out there for strong men. Right now, I feel like I do when Buster startles at a snake and nearly jumps out from under me when I'm riding him."

Elam took a heavy breath. The lines of sadness that had haunted him over the winter appeared to deepen. He gave her a look of total understanding. "You've just had your life yanked out from under you, and that's no time for quick decisions."

"My decisions have to be quick, Elam, don't you see?"

"You've got a lot of friends here. We'll parcel out your things and animals and hold them, and you, until you find a place to settle."

His words burned into her heart. All she felt was the rejection. What should she have expected?

"I guess my idea was as crazy as I feared," she said. "Of course you wouldn't marry a jailbird's daughter."

"That isn't what I mean, Keara."

"The Jensens and Pettits might not even want Brute McBride's daughter near them for fear Pa might kick up a ruckus if he ever did get released from jail."

"You know better. They all remember the kind of man Brute was when your mother was alive."

"Your children will need a mother," Keara said. "I can't come out this far from Eureka Springs every day, even if I do manage to scrounge a job there, serving at one of the bathhouses or cooking food under a tent."

"You won't have to—"

"I may not even be able to find a job there." She avoided him as he reached for her. "And you will need someone to keep house and help you on the farm. Don't try to take it all on yourself, and don't dump it all onto Britte's little shoulders." She stepped around him and gathered her boots and shawl. She had tried and failed.

Elam reached for her again. "Please, Keara, I'll help you settle—"

She drew away. "I've done for myself all these years and I suppose I'll keep it up." She would not be handed along to the neighbors like an unwanted orphan. *Parceled,* he'd called it. What a horrible word. Like a hot potato nobody wanted to handle. Well, she could camp out in the woods if need be. She had a wagon and plenty of food. She could sell the animals to neighbors and—

"Keara, I won't let you leave like this. We can work it out." He put an arm in front of her. She stepped around him, refusing to listen, ignoring him as she moved through the room.

It wasn't until she'd stepped out into the sunlight that she felt the first tears trickling down her face. Really, what was she going to do?

Two

Late on Monday afternoon, Keara McBride's voice continued to haunt Elam Jensen as he brushed the haunches of his two-year-old gray filly, Freda Mae. She was coming along, took to the saddle like a catfish to the river bottom. A few more weeks and he wouldn't be afraid to allow Britte to ride her.

The only problem was that the filly's hooves grew too fast. He had to trim them twice as often as he did the others, but she could run like the wind itself. She was worth the extra time it took to care for her, if only he had that time to spare.

Time was in short supply, and it promised to become shorter without Keara. "Lord, how am I going to keep up?"

The only thing that stopped the worried circle of his thoughts was the rattle of wagon sideboards.

He waved toward the Pettits when the wagon pulled up to the front of the house. Britte and Rolfe jumped off the back, sun-touched and laughing, the way he loved to see them. His sister and brother-in-law waved and continued on with their brood of six healthy, rambunctious saplings. David and Penelope would want to be home long before nightfall to get their chores done.

Britte dropped her picnic basket in the grass and ran to the enclosure Elam had built so he could watch Cash while working the horses. Britte doted on her baby brother. She was so like her mother, headstrong and sure of what she wanted, with eyes that had begun, once again, to shine with life just short of mischief, and long hair a tangled mess from her day at the river.

"Papa!"

Elam turned to find Rolfe running toward him with arms open wide for a hug. Elam swung him up and held him close. Rolfe had not recovered from his mother's death as quickly as his sister had, and Elam worried about him, especially now, if they were going to lose Keara's comforting presence.

Had Elam ever wondered why God intended for children to have both a mother and a father, he'd have discovered that answer this past winter. He would never forget the kindness the Cherokee family had shown by camping and hunting nearby throughout the autumn and winter so Ayanna could be Cash's wet nurse. The horses he'd given them in exchange had been far too small a payment, and he'd had to insist to get them to accept even that.

As for Keara's help...all the horses he owned would not be enough pay for the loving care she'd given his family. And him. He had to admit that, because of her, he'd had time to grieve deeply.

A heavy spirit had vexed him since her visit today. He'd let her down. After all she'd done to help him and the children, he had refused her request when she was in cruel need.

But what could he do? Marriage less than a year after Gloria's death would be a travesty to her memory. Making vows to a woman he did not love would mock all he knew marriage to be, and it would rob her of finding the kind of love he'd known.

He would be swift to invite Keara to stay with them and continue to care for the children, but one of the more troublemaking younger women in town had already accused Keara behind her back of impropriety for the hours she'd been spending with Elam and the children.

He knew the gossip would hurt her if it reached her ears, especially the murmurings in the church about some wanting to speak to the pastor. If that happened, he wondered if Keara could bear it. She would be devastated if the church expelled her for a sin she'd never committed.

Elam was disappointed in Raylene Harper. He'd known her since she was a friendly little girl with a big heart for stray animals. She'd grown into a sneering young woman with a bite in every word. What was it about some females when they grew up?

"Look, Papa!" Britte walked behind Cash as he crawled through the uneven grass. "He's racing me!"

Cash squealed with laughter when Britte caught up with him and tickled his belly.

The evening sun made their black hair glow. They both resembled their mother, and a tug of familiar pain made Elam wince. At eight, Britte needed time to grow and time to play. Without Keara to care for the children, much of the housework, gardening, and cooking would fall on Britte. She was too young to take the whole load.

Rolfe pushed against his arm. "Papa, you're squeezing me."

With a soft apology, Elam set his son on the ground. Rolfe was the child most like him, who had his papa's nature of feeling too deeply. Rolfe, too, would be forced to grow up too soon without Keara here to help tend to things.

"I'm hungry," Britte said. "We swam a lot! What did Auntie Keara leave for us today?"

"We have cracklin' cornbread and head cheese." Elam led his family toward the house. Brute McBride had butchered a hog only three days before he was jailed for a crime Elam was convinced he had not committed. Keara had seen to it that the Jensen family would not want for tasty food. Elam and his children ate well.

"Auntie Keara will come home tomorrow, won't she?" Rolfe asked.

Elam looked down and laid a hand on his son's dark head. To them, this colorfully painted home—which had been Gloria's dream since she was a child—was now Keara's home as much as theirs, though until now she'd continued to live and work on her own family farm as well. "I…am not sure."

Both Britte and Rolfe looked up at him. "But why wouldn't she?" Britte asked.

"She has things to see to at her house."

"We can go help her," Rolfe said. "She says we're good helpers."

"You are good helpers, but I don't think she needs a garden planted or her cow milked today. She has other things on her mind." Elam swung Cash up into his arms and felt a wet bottom. The thoughts of getting dinner and caring for the children, checking on the horses and cattle, seeing to breakfast tomorrow, and keeping Britte, Rolfe, and Cash safe while he worked the farm were enough to stagger him.

But wouldn't it be selfish of him to marry Keara so she could become a servant in his house? She deserved better than a lifetime of labor without love.

He stepped onto the porch as Britte and Rolfe charged through the front door ahead of him, but his steps slowed before he entered the house. "She deserves much better than she's received all her life, but will she get it, Lord?" As she'd told him, she'd had no time for meeting beaus. "Where will she go?"

David and Penelope were so crowded that their oldest two boys slept in the barn. Kellen and Jael weren't much better off, and though both families had plans to add rooms, they hadn't built them yet.

What would a single woman do alone in the world? Some

kindhearted older lady in town might take her in out of pity or loneliness. Keara might even set up a tent for selling containers of the healing spring waters to the hordes of visitors, and add to that the herbs and teas she collected in the forest. But there were hard-hearted businessmen in the swiftly built town, and Keara was not as wise to the ways of the world as she wanted to think.

Elam reached the table, stacked with freshly washed nappies. Keara, again, had taken care of washing. What would he do without her? But how selfish could a man be?

He reached for a napkin and laid Cash down on the much-used table Gloria had always used for changing her babies. "Children, Auntie Keara may not be able to come see us so often."

Even Cash grew still, his chubby, kicking legs stopping in mid-air as Britte and Rolfe turned shocked looks on Elam.

"Papa, why?" The whisper that was forced from Britte's lips betrayed a tremor in her voice. Her wide blue eyes filled with a renewal of the loss that had haunted her so often since Gloria's death.

Rolfe's face puckered in an attempt not to cry. Already, he showed signs of the deep, abiding love he would have for his own family someday.

They loved Keara. They had known her all their lives, and she was the closest thing to a mother they now had. They were both capable of doing their chores, and Britte could cook and help care for her brothers, but they needed Keara in a deeper way.

He changed Cash into a dry cloth and carried him to the sofa with a cup of goat's milk and corn mush warmed in a kettle of water over the stove. As if afraid to get too far away after the news about Keara—as if suddenly afraid they might lose their father as well—Britte and Rolfe tucked themselves closely on each side of him.

They watched in silence as Elam spooned gruel from the cup

into Cash's mouth. Their fear touched him in a way no argument from Keara could have done.

How much could he tell them?

"Papa?" Britte said.

Rolfe swallowed hard. "Papa, doesn't Auntie Keara want to see us again?"

"She does," he said. "Yes, she does. Never doubt she loves you. But a mean person has caused her to lose her farm, and she may not be able to be near us when she has to move out."

"But she can stay here with us!" Rolfe said. "Remember when Britte was sick, and Auntie Keara stayed to take care of her? Why can't she stay here?"

Elam couldn't explain to a six-year-old about the nastiness of gossip and unfair judgment that had spread like hot grease on a griddle after that prolonged visit. He nudged the spoon to Cash's lips only to have him push it away with his tongue. He'd been warned that weaning Cash this suddenly would not be an easy task.

"Papa?" Britte was more insistent than her brother.

"If Keara were to move in with us," Elam told them, "she would have to become your stepmother."

"You mean she'd become wicked, like in the fairytales she's been reading us?" Rolfe's eyes rounded.

"No, Rolfie," Britte said. "Auntie Keara isn't wicked."

"But then why would she have to become a wicked stepmother?" Rolfe asked.

"I didn't say she'd be a *wicked* stepmother." Elam sighed and looked at Britte. He'd have to speak to Keara about those stories.

"If Auntie Keara moved in with us and took care of us, people would say nasty things about her that aren't true," Britte said. "She would have to become Papa's wife so no one would say those things."

Rolfe glared at his sister in confusion. "You aren't making any sense."

"Grownups don't always make sense," Elam said in an attempt to derail this train of thought. "But there are rules people must follow, and this would be one of them. I'd have to marry Auntie Keara." He prayed silently that Rolfe would ask no more questions and that Britte wasn't actually as wise in the ways of the world as she suddenly seemed to be. He had too many other thoughts to ponder.

The silence stretched. God answered his prayer. The children questioned him no more, though he could see them from the corner of his eye as they exchanged long, meaningful looks. He could imagine that later Britte would tell her younger brother a few more things about the facts of life than Elam wanted his son to grasp quite yet.

He continued to feed Cash as he reconsidered Keara's predicament. He didn't wish to imprison her in a loveless marriage. They both believed in the permanence of wedding vows.

Cash took a bite of the gruel, and then another. Maybe this would work after all, though he ate much more willingly when Keara fed him.

Keara was the only mother Cash had ever known.

Cash took another bite then pushed the spoon away with his tongue when his mouth got too full.

The marriage wouldn't be loveless for Keara. The children loved her, and she them. She also loved the land and farming and working the horses. She would dry up and die like a plucked elderflower if she was forced to move into town.

Elam leaned back and wiped Cash's chin, realizing at last what had been the cause of the despair in Keara's eyes today. She knew nothing but farm life, and she had thrived on it for twenty-six years, capable as either of her younger brothers, and nearly as strong for her size.

It was the despair that worried him. Keara wasn't one to be

hasty, but she was being given no choice. What would prevent her from marrying the first farmer she met who was looking for a household servant? There were rough men in this area, and Elam had seen evidence that some of the wives received only cruelty in their marriages.

Cash gave a loud burp and a satisfied grin. Britte took him from Elam's lap and Rolfe took the cup. Keara had taught them well. Even without her, he knew he would fare better than she would.

Keara had been Gloria's dear friend ever since Elam brought Gloria here from Pennsylvania after their fancy wedding. She'd been their beloved neighbor, Elam's rescuer, his children's teacher and loving auntie. She was a good woman. What did it matter that she lacked many feminine graces that came naturally for other women? He'd heard her snort like a foal when she laughed. She'd roughhoused with her brothers and his own children and nieces and nephews like one of them and had helped Elam saddle break more than one horse.

Marrying Keara McBride would be like marrying a farmhand, but watching his children while brooding on Keara's predicament, he realized he had no choice. There would be friendship between himself and Keara. He'd seen many marriages worse off. And besides, he had never expected to enjoy another love as fine as the one he'd shared with Gloria.

He could live a celibate life for the remainder of his days, and in Keara he would always have a friend.

Marrying Keara McBride was the right thing to do.

Three

Keara's fingers dug deeply into the knot of ribbons that bound a small bouquet of blossoms from Elam's fruit trees. She found herself struggling for each breath against the stiffness of her stays.

Elam's sisters, Penelope and Jael, married to the Pettit brothers, *said* they were happy about this marriage. Truly, they'd seemed so this past week as they rushed to prepare a wedding celebration after the marriage announcement. But this? In Eureka Springs? With a crowd?

Of course, Elam and Keara's sudden decision had stunned the community all the way to town, but their local neighbors along White River Hollow had shown nothing but excitement, even relief.

But did Penelope and Jael intend for her to faint from oxygen starvation before the vows could be spoken? How did they expect her to have enough breath to say a word? She could span her cinched waist with her own two hands, and she didn't have huge hands.

"You're beautiful," Jael whispered, her russet hair caught up in an elegant chignon. "Don't fidget so, Keara, or your veil will fall."

Penelope, with hair as dark as her brother Elam's, and dark brown eyes as calming, brushed a loose petal from Keara's arm. "Remember to walk straight and proud down the aisle, for you have much to be proud of. And hold the bouquet out to show off your tiny waist."

"So everyone can get a good look at it," Jael added.

"So everyone will know I'm not in the family way," Keara muttered.

"Nonsense, my dear," Penelope said. "Your reputation is above reproach, no matter what one or two jealous women may attempt to imply." She cast a cool sidelong glance in the direction of Raylene Harper, Cynthia Lindstrom, and friends.

"And smile at Elam," Jael said. "Keep your eyes on him. Let everyone see how you feel about him."

"And don't trip over your train," Jael said.

Keara groaned. "I may lose my breakfast."

"No!" both of her future sisters-in-law cried in unison.

"It's being shoved out by these stays."

Before they could ply her with more instructions, the first chords of the huge organ filled the church with…a lot of noise.

Keara would've preferred the meadowlarks and a private ceremony far from Eureka Springs—one of the largest cities in the state of Arkansas, thanks to the railway system that brought travelers to this place for the benefits of the healing waters.

This past week, Keara had often blessed Penelope and Jael for their support, despite their wrong-headed efforts to prepare for this wedding. They were, at heart, romantics who'd seen too much of their brother's grief and wished only for his happiness—and that of the children.

That they believed Keara could bring the family happiness touched her deeply and made her want to please them, even if it meant going through with this dreadful, fancy service.

Why had she ever doubted their friendship in her darkest hours last week? They were much like the rest of the White River Hollow neighbors, and though they descended from a class of settlers who felt comfortable rubbing shoulders with the upper crust of Eureka Springs society on East Mountain above the bustle of Mud Street, they cherished many of the same things Keara did—the open fields, deep forests, and rushing waters that made up their true home.

Keara peered from the back of the church at the crowd and nearly swooned again. She'd barely recognized herself in the mirror when the sisters were preparing her. The pale blue dress that Mother wore for her own wedding twenty-seven years ago had been altered for Keara's smaller form—and in Keara's opinion, Penelope had been a little heavy-handed with the thread. Had she twined it with steel? The material refused to give.

"You will take his breath away." Penelope tugged at Keara's blond hair beneath her veil.

"You mean like mine's been taken," Keara grumbled.

"I've wanted to get my hands on you for the longest time," Penelope said, "but I couldn't drag you out of the fields or the garden or Elam's horse paddock long enough to do anything about it. We can bet he's never seen you looking like this before."

Jael patted her sister's protruding belly. "You've done a perfect job, despite your morning sickness, Pen."

"And I appreciate it," Keara said. "I do. Sorry I'm jittery as a katydid. You're both…you're so good to me."

"It's about time someone was good to you." Jael grimaced and nibbled on her lip. "Sorry, Keara, I mean no disrespect to your family or others"—another glare toward Raylene—"but your time for happiness is long overdue. We know our brother. He can make you happy."

Keara felt worse every second. They didn't realize, did they, that this wasn't going to be the marriage they expected?

"And now she'll be closer," Penelope said. "We can teach her a few things her mother never wanted her to know." The sisters exchanged a long look, which left Keara wondering.

The music changed. Penelope whispered last-minute instructions to Keara as Jael turned with graceful serenity and proceeded down the middle aisle of the church.

"I know you didn't have time to practice this, but just do what the minister tells you to do, and when it comes time for the groom to kiss the bride, *you're* the bride." Penelope's dark eyes sparkled with teasing lights. "I bet you and my brother haven't even kissed, have you?"

Keara gasped for a deep breath and couldn't quite fill her lungs. The tight stays and at least fifteen pounds of undergarments made her feel buried alive. "How do you—"

"Never mind, just raise your face to his and let him do the rest. He's got three children, so believe me when I tell you he knows how to kiss you…and much more, besides." Penelope gave her a sly wink as she turned to proceed down the aisle behind her sister, her head turned toward the love-filled gaze of her husband, David, who walked to the front of the church from a side door.

Wedding services had taken on a whole new set of rules since Mother and Pa married. Keara remembered listening to her mother tell about the wedding celebration in their home, with just a few friends and family looking on when the circuit preacher reached the hollow on his monthly rounds. As for what happened after the wedding ceremony, Mother had never seen fit to share the basics with her daughter. Only the ceremony itself, which sounded idyllic.

But Eureka Springs was a different world, where the self-appointed proper citizens had developed their own ideas about etiquette from back East. Keara didn't belong here.

Today, though, she had to pretend. From what she saw in the mirror—that stranger who had her eyes, her firm chin, her widow's peak, but who appeared to have stepped from one of Jael's fashion magazines—she only had to follow the lead of her future sisters-in-law for a few hours and all would be over. Then she could go home to Elam's ranch, settle her things in Britte's bedroom, and carry on as usual. All that mattered was that she would have a roof over her head, and she would be with the ones she loved most. Gloria's children.

And Elam.

Keara closed her eyes and moaned softly. Why couldn't they have jumped in the wagon and ridden to town, hunted down a justice of the peace, and then announced the marriage to all after the fact? Why this huge show for a union that wasn't...well...could never be the real thing?

The music changed again. Penelope and Jael nodded toward Keara, who had no one to walk her down the aisle. She would walk alone, as she had done for a long, long time. She followed the trail her friends had blazed, holding her bouquet out away from her waist to show how tightly they had drawn the binding.

Of all the nerve, for Raylene to start a rumor that Keara was pregnant! Elam didn't know, and if Jael or Penelope had anything to do with it, he never would, but Penelope had warned Keara about it just yesterday.

If Keara blacked out from lack of oxygen, she could blame nasty gossip for forcing her to go to this much trouble to prove the gossips wrong. Tiny waist, indeed!

To endure it all, Keara sought for a glimpse of the children as she stepped down the aisle, keeping time with the music in the wedding march. She found Britte's angelic face in the crush of guests near the front, looking so much like her mother.

Keara winked. Britte grinned back, eyes alight with excitement, as were Rolfe's. They both waved with great enthusiasm, and she returned the greeting. A couple of women tittered.

Who cared if this type of thing wasn't done in polite society? Polite society could go dump themselves in White River for all she cared, so long as they didn't contaminate the water for the citizens of the hollow.

Then, in the midst of all her rebellious thoughts, she saw Elam step from the same door that had released David and Kellen a moment ago.

Keara's steps faltered. In a thrill of private pleasure, she couldn't help soaking in the male lines of the man, his serious, dark gaze on her. He was without a doubt the most handsome man in the church—in all of Eureka Springs. She loved him not because of that, but because of his steadfast love for his wife, which spoke to Keara of his ability to love.

She would never forget his solid support of Gloria. He was a man who could always be counted on to do the right thing for a friend in need—even to the point of giving up any thought of remarriage to a more attractive and socially acceptable mate.

To Keara's chagrin, she discovered she was enjoying the fact that the rumormongers must be feeling rubbed raw from watching the most eligible man in all of Eureka Springs and the surrounding countryside marry a woman they seemed to despise. In fact, it felt wonderful.

Awful to feel such satisfaction. Even worse, awful to feel no compunction. Raylene Harper had caused her enough trouble, and it was time for a reckoning. Why was the girl even here? To make sure she didn't miss a single slip-up she could gossip about later?

Stop it, Keara McBride. Mind your thoughts. Remember your Christian charity. It must extend to her enemies as well as her friends.

And Raylene hadn't always been her enemy.

Keara's toe rammed something hard, and she realized she'd wedding-marched into the step leading up to the raised dais. The pain shot along her foot, but she refused to show a response.

She forced a smile for Elam through gritted teeth, and she saw the amusement in the gleam of brown eyes. He'd seen the stumble. She suppressed a nervous giggle, horrified that she might suddenly laugh out loud and snort like Buster when he rolled in the dirt after a hard ride.

Jael and Penelope both nodded with encouragement—but did she see the barest hint of worry in their expressions?

She stepped up and joined Elam, so very glad she wouldn't have to turn and face the crowd just yet. Not that she should care. This day stood as a testimony to her future—one filled with strength and support from Elam, and love for the children. What others believed about her shouldn't affect her.

Jael placed a hand on her arm and gently retrieved the bouquet then nudged Keara closer to Elam's side. His smile drew her in, and his strength held her steady. For a tiny slip of a moment she allowed her eyes to close as she relived the time last week, only a few hours after her humiliation at his house, when he rode his stallion to her farm and asked for her hand in marriage. As he'd explained, Gloria would never forgive him for turning her best friend away in her time of need.

It wasn't the kind of proposal she'd dreamed about as a girl, but she continued to bask in the relief she'd felt that day. Her hero. He'd saved her life—at least, the only kind of life she'd ever known.

The minister began his memorized lines, and Keara opened her eyes, listening with care so she would know what to do and when to do it. Elam had a ring for her. He'd wrapped a string around her finger three days ago to measure for a fit and then ridden into Eureka Springs. The solid gold band was etched deeply with filigree, and already she worried that she would wear down the delicate etching with her constant work around the ranch.

She repeated the words the minister fed her, finding it difficult to meet Elam's gaze as the ceremony grew more serious. She promised to love him and then listened for the slightest hesitation as he made the same promise to her. There was none. She looked up at him as he continued his promise to honor and cherish her and felt warmth flow through her as he held her gaze, speaking to her as if they were the only two people in the sanctuary. He spoke as if he meant every word. He was vowing to be a good and loving husband to her.

She knew it couldn't be the kind of love she'd dreamed of and longed for since she was a young teen, but it was love all the same. He performed acts of love by placing a roof over her head and supporting her. Those things showed the character of the man she would share her life with. This would be the only time she would hear these words from him, and she would savor them as long as she lived.

At the minister's prompt, Elam pulled out the ring for Keara's finger, and when she held out her hand, to her alarm, it shook. Elam caught it in his own, squeezing to reassure her as he slipped on the ring. He caught both of her hands in his and held them steady, smiling down at her with gentleness. And then the minister's words registered as he pronounced them man and wife and told Elam, "You may kiss the bride."

Keara raised her face to his and shut her eyes, feeling as if she might be bracing for a slap. She prayed it didn't appear that way to the rest of the congregation. The scent of soap and bay rum reached her as warm lips—Elam's lips—found a perfect fit against hers.

The stays beneath her fitted dress seemed to tighten yet again, and her head roared with the impact of the intimate caress. If not for his arms drawing her close and holding her securely, she would have toppled to the floor.

Oh my...

This changed everything.

* * * * *

A thousand thoughts and emotions attacked Elam through the softness of Keara McBride's—no, make that Keara Jensen's—lips. He felt as if he'd been stuck in sand up to his waist. For a moment, he couldn't move except to grip Keara's arms more tightly. As his head continued to reel from the vision of Keara adorned as a woman prepared for marriage—a real, flesh and blood, beautiful woman whose appearance could put any other woman in the county to shame—he could barely catch his breath.

He'd never seen her look so…womanly. He'd never dreamed that the touch of her lips, the taste of them against his, could make him feel this way.

This wasn't supposed to happen.

It was wrong. Dead wrong. It took all he had to not jerk away and bolt. He was still married to Gloria. His wife, his beloved, still lived in his heart, in his dreams, followed him wherever he went. He no longer saw her as clearly as before in his mind, but he kept her picture beside his bed. How could he claim to be doing this for Gloria's sake—marrying her best friend—when this made him feel like a dirty, rotten cheater?

And Keara. Until she walked down that aisle, had he ever before read this message she seemed to be sharing with him from her eyes—a message of more than a simple friendship? Was this his imagination?

He couldn't help remembering the pain in her eyes the day she'd first asked him to marry her and he'd turned her down. Was that more than simple desperation? Hadn't he seen a hurt that went more deeply than fear for her future?

And hadn't that expression touched something deep within him, despite all?

Strange how a man's mind could recall a moment with more clarity a week later.

Guilt—no, shame—battled with a lightness in his spirit; a shaft of hope thrust through the darkness that had pressed down on him all these months. This was too soon. All wrong.

Keara's kiss captured him, spread through him with a power that he'd not anticipated. Not at all. He felt caught off guard, stripped bare before a crowd of onlookers. Why had he not been braced for this?

The woman he held in his arms was not Gloria. The fit wasn't the same, the slender shoulders felt more fragile than Gloria's—though he knew they were anything but fragile. The scent of spice replaced the honeysuckle and roses of Gloria...and the scent of death that had clung to her during those final days of the nightmare.

The most powerful impact of Keara's kiss, however, was the reminder of comfort and hope Elam had felt in her presence throughout the bleak winter, and the connection she gave him to Gloria in her love for the children.

Connection to Gloria. That was it. He responded to Keara because she brought him closer to the love of his life.

But much was different. Keara spoke a language Gloria never knew. She was a horse enthusiast, she loved to garden, and she could shovel out a stall and teach the children common, down-to-earth practicality, whereas Gloria had wanted a more cultured life for her offspring. Still, Keara's devoted friendship had been Elam's solid rock when Gloria died.

That had to be what drew him to Keara now, what enveloped him in the kiss, the warmth of her skin, and the power that emanated from her very being. He couldn't betray Gloria's memory by indulging in the sweetness of Keara's lips or the sway of her loving gaze.

And yet, in this moment, as he released her and turned to face the congregation, in their eyes he could read that they believed all was well. As it should be.

How firm a foundation God had given him—and Britte, Rolfe, and Cash—today, in the person of Keara Jensen.

He allowed reality to rush in—the crowd before him could believe what they wished. But he knew the truth. So did Keara. Theirs was a marriage born of desperation.

He would do all that was within his power to make sure Gloria would look down on him from heaven and approve of his kindness to her dearest friend. Beyond that, the wedding kiss would have to be his only betrayal of the love he would always have for Gloria.

Four

"Chivaree?" Keara fingered the beautiful new band on her finger, relished the warmth of her new husband sitting close beside her, and pondered the kiss that changed everything for her—that frightened her and held her in its wonder and pierced her heart as it challenged the decision that theirs was not to be a marriage of romantic love.

"It's when friends and neighbors tease the newly married couple with partying and merrymaking and—"

"I know what a chivaree is, even if I never took part in one." Mother had needed much care in the final ten years of her life, and the boys had needed a firm hand. Anytime Keara had attended a wedding in the past, she'd always rushed home to see to her family's needs. But this evening, word had spread that there would be a chivaree for her and Elam.

As if this whole day had not been awkward enough—with Cynthia Lindstrom's little innuendoes and Raylene Harper's attempts to attract the groom with her laughter and manipulative wiles during the formal reception at the Crescent Hotel—someone had decided a chivaree would be fun.

But maybe it wouldn't be so bad. It wasn't as if they would have an audience when Keara made herself comfortable in Britte's bed after the commotion died and she and Elam were left alone, able to carry on as before.

She couldn't ignore the quiet question deep inside that asked whether or not they would ever be able to do that—carry on as before. That kiss, hadn't he felt it, as well? Or was she behaving like a silly adolescent? After all, what did she know about the romantic side of marriage? Men were said to respond much differently than women when it came to affairs of...amour.

Penelope and David were taking the children for the night, and so Britte, Rolfe, and Cash had ridden off with them in their wagon. Now, as Elam urged the horses toward home in the buggy he'd prepared for the special occasion, Keara was dismayed by the lack of comfortable banter that she and Elam had always enjoyed—about the children, the ranch, the horses, especially frisky young Freda Mae. Many times this past winter they had shared memories of Gloria...

But tonight was different, as if speaking about normal things would break the spell. Tomorrow she would awake in Britte's room and begin her new life with little fanfare, but today was her fairytale day, and she didn't want it to end with talk of horses and breeding and what needed planting next week. And she felt awkward bringing up Gloria's name on the night of marrying that wonderful woman's husband.

Elam, though seldom taciturn, also seemed introspective as they rode to the ranch. Keara couldn't help wondering about the regrets that must be plowing through his mind.

She glanced over at him to find him watching her. "I guess thanking you again would be silly," she murmured. "For all this. For—for rescuing me."

"You've thanked me at least three times a day for the past week." His voice was gentle, almost tender.

"But now the deed is done. You followed it through. You can't know how relieved I am."

"Surely you knew I would not go back on my word."

"Of course I did, but unless you've been in my place you could never understand how indebted I feel."

For a moment, he didn't speak, just watched her. And then a smile passed his lips—brief, with a shake of his head. "Nearly every day since Gloria first got sick, you've been seeing to her family. I'm the one who should be thanking you. I believe she's in heaven now, watching us and approving."

Keara swallowed, then before she could stop herself, she blurted, "You think she saw the kiss and everything?"

Elam remained silent while warmth crept across Keara's face.

"I don't think she'd have turned her head to avoid it," he said, his tone thoughtful. "It's normal to kiss in a marriage." He held her gaze for a long moment. "Many things are normal in marriage, between husband and wife. You told me yourself that Gloria wanted me to remarry."

"I reckon I never thought about Gloria up there in heaven watching us all the time."

"The Bible says there's no marriage in heaven, and that remarriage here on earth after a death is true and right."

"Still, it kind of makes me rethink a lot of things. Do people feel jealousy in heaven? Do they feel betrayal?"

He didn't reply for a moment, and as the sky darkened into night, she couldn't read his thoughts in his expression the way she'd learned to do these past months.

"We aren't betraying anyone," he said at last, his voice almost a whisper.

"Then why do I feel like we are?"

"Because you loved her too." He shook his head, looked at Keara. "I didn't expect you to come down that aisle the way you did, looking like a princess."

Her breathing stopped just for a second as she allowed those words to echo in her heart. A princess? He thought she looked like a princess? All thoughts of Gloria vanished, and the kiss—the feel of his lips, the strength in the arms that had held her, the passion of his gaze when he straightened from that kiss...that wonderful, beautiful kiss that seemed to come from heaven—filled her thoughts.

She knew she could not let them linger there.

"I've never had a stylist's art worked on me before," Keara said dryly. "Penelope and Jael are talented."

"They aren't the only ones with talent." He cleared his throat, looked toward her. "You have a way with Britte and Rolfe and Cash."

She realized he was distracting her from the subject of Gloria, as if he also felt like a betrayer. But why would he feel that way unless he, too, had experienced more than easy companionship between them during their kiss?

"We both know they need constancy, and I can give them that," she said.

"And you, Keara?" His voice was quiet, solemn, and she heard a concern in it that disturbed her. "What do you need? When you were a little girl, did you ever dream that you'd spend your whole life taking care of other people, raising another woman's children?"

She lingered for just a moment on the deep rumble of his voice, the...intimacy of it that warmed her in ways she'd never felt warmed. "Why not? If that's my calling in life, then that's where I'll feel my finest satisfaction."

"Just because caring for others is all you've been allowed to do these past years doesn't mean it's all you could do."

"Maybe God's placed me right where He wants me."

She was still pondering his words and her own reply when the deep neigh of a horse reached them from ahead.

"Did you leave Freda Mae out in the corral?" Keara searched for a sign of the animal but could see little in the deepening gloom.

"No, and Buster and Moondance are in the barn as well."

"That didn't sound like any of them," she said. "Do you think the chivaree crowd has beaten us to the house?"

Elam urged the muscular stock horse forward with a flick of the reins. "I don't know. That call was unfamiliar to me, and it wasn't coming from the corral."

This perked Keara's attention. Elam knew the voice of each horse in the territory. If he didn't recognize the call, it was a strange horse not from these parts...and perhaps a strange rider?

By the time they reached the house, they sighted a dark shadow that blended with the overhang of the porch. Another whinny. They scrambled from the buggy to find a large and beautiful black mare, fully saddled, standing with head lowered, nuzzling at a still form on the steps. A human form.

A soft, feminine groan reached them as the horse continued to nudge.

Elam and Keara rushed forward. The lingering light from the last glimmer of sunset showed the glow of long, dark hair and a woman lying as if she'd fallen there.

Keara saw the outline of the woman's face and went cold to the bone. She heard Elam's quick intake of breath. It couldn't be. Her eyes were playing tricks. She saw the broken and bleeding body of Gloria Jensen.

* * * * *

Elam felt the world stop revolving. The only sound he heard was the pounding of his heart and the quickening of his breaths. His mind flashed to his last vision of Gloria, ravaged by smallpox, pleading with him to stay away from her, not to look at her, to care for the children.

She could not be lying on the steps of her own home, with her face clear and white.

He fell to his knees beside the fallen form. Not Gloria. Of course it wasn't. He'd buried her, had watched the earth slowly cover her grave, had visited and watched the grass grow and the leaves fall and the snow drift over the gravestone. And yet the hair, the face in the gloom…even the soft moan of pain, were so familiar.

He touched the woman's face, and she groaned again, tried to sit up, cried out, and fell back against the steps. The sense of unreality scattered into the gloom. He recognized her.

"Elam?" Keara's voice held a note of shock.

"It isn't Gloria."

"But who—"

"Susanna. This is Gloria's sister."

Elam couldn't move. For a moment, he couldn't think. Not Gloria…but so like her…

"Elam Jensen, get moving!" Keara snapped, shocking him from his idiocy.

He reached for the woman who was not Gloria, and when his hand touched her left shoulder, she cried out. He felt something sticky and realized that the scent lingering in the air was the coppery smell of blood.

"Elam?" The woman's voice was weak. "I'm here? I made it?" She looked up at him as Keara reached for a lantern on the porch and lit it.

"Yes, it's me. You've made it." As the woman's face glowed in the lantern light, he pushed away thoughts of Gloria. "Susanna, what's happened? What are you doing here?"

"I'm in trouble." Her eyes slid shut. "Hide me," she whispered. "Hide Duchess. No one must see her. Help me. A man tried to kill me. He'll finish the job if he can."

Keara set the lantern on the porch and inspected the bloody wound in Susanna's shoulder.

"Let's get her inside," Elam said.

"She needs a doctor now, Elam. She needs more help than I can give her. The buggy—"

"No quack from Eureka Springs," Susanna said, her voice weak but determined. "I didn't come to Arkansas for those so-called healing waters."

"But you're hurt," Keara said.

"Hide me." Susanna went limp.

"But Elam," Keara said, her voice trembling, "she needs medical care quickly. Look at the blood."

He examined the injury. "First, we do as she says." He lifted his sister-in-law into his arms. "We'll put her in Britte's room for now. No one will be going in there tonight. We can keep her concealed."

"What? Look at her! She must be out of her mind if she thinks—"

He turned to Keara. "What if she isn't? Don't forget the telegram I received last month."

Keara caught her breath. "Nathaniel. But the telegram said it was an accidental shooting."

"I know what it said, but—"

"You think Susanna's husband was murdered?"

"I don't know, but what if he was? We can't take chances with her."

"She's still got to have a doctor."

"You're as close as we're getting tonight." He kept his voice firm, though Keara's fear was obvious, and he shared it mightily. Still…he knew this was the right thing to do. He'd learned in his marriage to Gloria that if she feared something, it was to be feared. He suspected the rest of her family was the same way.

"But we can't just shove her away in a back room when she's—"

"You heard her, Keara." He kept his voice gentle, feeling badly that, for the time being, his new bride would be responsible for treating Susanna's injuries. On her wedding night. "Would you please get the door?"

Despite her protests, Keara did as he asked, and the scent of cedar wafted out to greet them. "This is crazy, Elam."

"Not if she's in danger." And it had been hovering for a while, if Elam's guess was right. Too many past events made him wonder....

"Her life's also in danger if we don't get her to a doctor."

"Keara."

She stopped, eyes widening at what he knew was an unusual sharpness to his tone.

"Listen to me," he said more gently. "You can treat her. I've seen you work miracles on people and horses. It's time for another one, because if we take a buggy into town, or if one of us rides back for the doctor in Eureka Springs, everyone in the county will know about it by morning because of the guests on their way out here now. We can't take that chance."

Keara held the lantern high as she ascended the stairs ahead of him. "You put too much faith in me, Elam. I'm not a doctor. Susanna's the doctor, and she doesn't look to be in any shape to tell me what to do or how to do it."

"You get her back amongst the living and she'll be glad to tell you all about it," he said dryly. From Gloria's own lips, he knew that her sister always did have a mind of her own and was never afraid to speak it. Much like Gloria herself.

As soon as he'd laid Susanna's slender body on Britte's bed, he grabbed the lantern in the room and lit it. They needed lots of light in here. "Get out those poultices and herbs of yours. My bottle of whiskey is in the top cupboard in the kitchen. I'm going to put the mare in the barn. Susanna's sure to have brought her doctor's bag with her so I'll bring you whatever medical supplies I can find."

"But I don't know how to use them."

"You'll have to use what you can, and just do what you do best."

"The others will be coming any minute."

"Then we'll have to hurry."

"We can't keep this quiet for long."

Keara was right. He thought for a moment while adjusting the flame in the lantern. "You're going to have to suddenly take ill," he said. "The way you've been breathing in that torture device my sisters rigged up, that shouldn't be too hard. We'll have to call the chivaree short tonight."

With a quick release of her breath, Keara sagged for a second against the dresser. "Lord, give us wisdom," she murmured.

Each time Elam glanced at Susanna, he had more questions. In the flickering lantern light, Susanna's face half in shadow, the room seemed surreal to him, her body in motion instead of quiet repose. If only she would awaken with answers, show them how to help her.

"If she came here, and if she told us to keep her secret," he said, "there's a reason for it."

Keara pushed away from the dresser. She leaned over Susanna and studied the bloody shoulder. "That's a fresh wound."

"Exactly."

"It must have happened nearby."

"Which emphasizes her need for secrecy." Elam stepped to the bureau they had moved into Britte's room for Keara's use. He pulled out the top drawer and gestured to the dried leaves, roots, and herbs she'd brought from her home yesterday. "You stopped the bleeding in Freda Mae's flank and kept it from infection."

"Susanna's not a horse."

"She's flesh and blood. Remember what we were talking about on the way here? You have a healing touch. Use it."

He spared another lingering glance toward the woman who looked so much like her older sister. Longing and loss streamed through him in a fresh current, and he turned away quickly.

The children must not see her or their loss would be freshened in them, as well. He would ask David and Penelope if they would keep the children for another day or two, at least until he decided what to do about Susanna.

The smell of coal oil blended with the cedar as he rushed back down the stairway and out the front door. Droplets of blood stained the steps, but not too many. God willing, Susanna hadn't bled too much, but Keara would be the judge of that.

Much as Elam felt the need to stay close and help Keara, he was controlled by the sense of urgency he'd heard in Susanna's voice.

As he grasped the mare's bridle and turned to lead her to the barn, he couldn't help pondering what might have happened. The biggest conflict in these parts had been the extension of the railroad into Harrison, Arkansas, straight from Seligman, Missouri. Eureka Springs was no longer the end of the line, and therefore would no longer be such a center of commerce.

The population was already dropping as folks followed the money trail, and fortunes were being lost—not all, because tourists and the ill still came here for the waters—but trouble still brewed in Eureka Springs. He'd seen bouts of violence as a result of the losses. Some of the new breed of tourists—only a handful, but too many, in his opinion—were troublemakers.

But what would events in Arkansas have to do with a couple of married doctors all the way back east in Pennsylvania?

Elam needed to talk with Susanna as soon as she roused.

Duchess was a huge, eye-catching animal with a spirited step, despite the dried sweat and mud on her coat. Her mane and tail had been clipped exceedingly short. He wished he could read the thoughts behind those large, dark eyes.

He was guiding her into the roomiest stall in the barn when he heard the rattle of a wagon and the calls of hopeful partiers. He sighed and patted the horse's neck then pulled off the huge saddle and reached for a curry comb. This night promised to extend into forever.

Five

Keara tried to ignore the voices outside the window, the laughter and catcalls, as she poured a small amount of whiskey into the wound on Susanna's shoulder. Only a low moan escaped Susanna's lips, but it was encouraging. At least she wasn't so far gone that she could feel nothing. The whiskey would burn like fire, but like fire, it would help cleanse the torn flesh.

To Keara's regret, the bullet—if indeed this was a bullet wound, and it sure did look like one—had obviously not gone through the backside of the shoulder. This meant that sooner or later Keara would have to remove it. Susanna moaned again. It could be done later.

Eyes the blue of a summer sky opened and studied Keara. They narrowed. "Who are you?"

"I'm...a friend. Don't worry, Elam's out hiding your horse in the barn."

The gaze went to the window. "I hear voices."

"Friends and family. There's been a wedding, and..." Keara raised her arm and noted she'd stained the lacy sleeve of her mother's beautiful wedding dress with Susanna's blood.

Susanna's gaze sharpened, and she lifted her head. "You're the bride?"

"That's not important right now. Did you bring medical supplies with you? Are you hurt anywhere besides your shoulder? It doesn't appear you've lost a whole lot of blood. You were shot?"

Susanna nodded.

"I'm worried about trying to remove the bullet, and I'll need your help if I'm to use your supplies."

Susanna's eyes glazed over as she laid her head back against the pillow and winced.

Belatedly, Keara saw a patch of blood on the pillow. Oh, jiggers, what had she missed? "Susanna, I think you hit your head. I'm going to have to check you out and see if there are any other injuries."

A loud whoop reached them from downstairs, and Susanna tensed.

"It's okay," Keara said. "Elam won't tell them you're here."

"I did come to the right house, didn't I?"

"You're at Elam Jensen's house."

"You arrived with him." Susanna closed her eyes, squeezing them tightly against obvious pain.

"Don't worry about that right now. You don't want anyone to know you're here, and I'm the only thing close to a doc around without calling one from town." Keara didn't want to touch that head wound, but she moistened another cloth with the whiskey and dabbed at a weeping lump the size of a hen's egg on the left side of Susanna's scalp.

This time Susanna cried out, and once more she lost consciousness.

* * * * *

Elam stepped from the shadows of the barn, hating that many of the wedding attendees from town had ridden the five miles from Eureka Springs to join in the fun. This hadn't been the plan. Not at all. Raylene Harper and her parents were part of the crowd—friends of the family. He and Ray had done a lot of business together over the years.

Carl Lindstrom had driven his sister Cynthia in their parents' buggy. The Lindstroms had moved to Eureka Springs from back East not long after Gloria's death last year, so therefore Elam, in his time of mourning, had spent little time becoming acquainted with the newcomers. Though he didn't know Carl well, his sister had made it clear to anyone who would listen that she despised the state of Arkansas, despised the people in it, and she despised Eureka Springs most of all. Perhaps the reason Raylene Harper befriended her was because she behaved so much like a wounded animal.

Before Elam could cross from the barn to the house, Raylene sighted him and came running from the bonfire that had been built since he'd crossed the clearing to the barn. Though nineteen, she still behaved like someone much younger, as if she were still just a child in a woman's body, who didn't quite know what had happened. And her choice of friends, after she'd been so sheltered at home, was not helping.

She sidled up, nudged him with her elbow, and pointed toward the lighted window upstairs. "Is your shy bride afraid to come down and join the fun? Jacob Minor's already rosining his fiddle bow." Others were setting up lanterns between the yard fence and the corral as the ladies set up a makeshift table for outdoor refreshments.

"Keara will likely join the party later." Elam stepped aside, the medical saddlebags slung over his shoulder.

"Dibs on a dance." Raylene nearly danced a jig in his wake.

"I'm sorry," he said gently, "but I'm dancing with only my bride tonight. If you will excuse me, I have a gift to deliver."

Raylene tapped her fingers on the saddlebags he carried. "A gift? Oh, come on, Elam, Keara may know a few things about plants and such, but a doctor's saddlebags?"

He ignored a prickle of annoyance and reminded himself to speak to her as if she were a child. "Raylene, the gifts I give to my bride are of no one's concern but mine and hers. Now, I'd like a few moments alone with her."

He ignored her protest, not worried about offending her father by snubbing her. Ray tolerated his only daughter's recent behavior with loving indulgence, but he knew Elam's stock would bring top dollar to buyers all over the country.

Three more people interrupted Elam's progress before he could make it to the front door of the house. He only prayed no one would try to follow him up the stairs. He would have to confide in Kellen and Jael, at least, about Susanna as soon as they arrived. His sister and brother-in-law were steadfast and could help form a shield for him and Keara. He only wished David and Penelope had planned to attend, as well, but Pen insisted on extra rest with another little one on its way.

Problem was, Kellen and Jael were nowhere to be seen. It had taken Elam longer than he expected to unsaddle that big mare of Susanna's and cool her down. She'd been ridden hard and long, and though the mud had dried, it had taken him awhile to comb it from her hide. Where, along that ride, had Susanna run into trouble?

In the medical bags, besides medical instruments, he'd found a sheathed knife and a Colt .44 revolver that had been shot recently. Susanna Luther knew how to protect herself, as had Gloria and the rest of their eleven siblings, having been raised on a farm at the foothills of the Appalachians. But all that knowledge hadn't protected Gloria from death. It was yet to be seen whether Susanna had been able to protect her own life.

* * * * *

Keara heard her name being called by men and laughing women from below the window. Fiddle music reached her, and the scent of roasting meats drifted up the stairwell and beneath the door. Someone had brought the party into the house. She heard the tromping of footsteps on the wooden floor and the booming laughter of men who may have already had a little too much to drink. For a moment she doubted Elam's ability to keep everyone out of Britte's room.

She checked Susanna's breathing and heart rate. They were both steady for now, but she'd seen things change quickly with Mother near the end.

This was not the end for Susanna! Mustn't even think that way.

Keara needed cool cloths from the springhouse to place against Susanna's head and reduce the swelling—even ice, if a block had been brought from town. She needed everyone out of the house so she could at least do what needed to be done—and forget this secrecy. If Keara couldn't take action quickly, all the secrecy in the world might not save Susanna.

Keara was halfway down the stairs, bracing herself for the crowd, when a familiar voice reached her. Jael. She was obviously commandeering the kitchen. As Keara entered the large front room, several neighbor women and ladies from the church looked up from their laying out of food they had brought, enough to feed the whole population of Eureka Springs, it appeared. This would be a long night.

"Surprise!" Jael said, looking up at Keara. "I've been roasting this hog all day, and our friends brought desserts and potatoes. You won't have to do a…" Her gaze fell to Keara's arm, and she gasped. "Honey, what happened to you?"

Too late, Keara remembered the blood on her sleeve. Too much happening, too many distractions.

As Jael rushed toward her, Keara backed away. "Just an accident, nothing to worry about. I'll be okay." It was totally true. "I was on my way out to the springhouse for a pitcher of cold water. I don't guess anybody brought ice?"

"On its way from town," Mrs. Harper assured her. "Sugar, did you hurt your arm?"

"Oh no, my arm's fine. This is just a…stain from…another injury."

"But this is a lot of blood." Jael reached for Keara. "You need to let me take a look at it. How did you do it?"

"Silly accident. I had my mind on other things, wasn't paying attention." Keara hesitated only a second. Her problem was solved. "Now that you mention it, I am feeling a bit shaky." It was no lie. "Would you come with me back up the stairs? I could use help with bandaging."

One of the ladies—trim and tiny Clydene Brown—volunteered to help fetch the cold water, while another asked if Keara had her "doctoring stuff" with her.

Keara reassured them over her shoulder as she urged Jael up the steps to Britte's bedroom.

When the door opened, Jael caught sight of Susanna and gasped.

"Shush!" Keara drew Jael inside and closed the door behind them. Thank goodness Elam had built these doors so thick.

"Keara, she looks like—"

"It's Gloria's sister."

Jael leaned closer and studied the pale face by the light of the lantern then sighed and nodded. "Of course. Susanna. I remember her now. What could I have been thinking?"

"Pretty much what Elam and I first thought. They could've been twins."

"But what's she doing here? And what's wrong with her?"

"She's been shot."

Jael gasped.

"She told me so herself."

Jael pressed her hand to her chest. "Goodness, Keara, who on earth would have shot her?"

Keara checked Susanna's pulse and breathing again. "She told us a man tried to kill her. She was desperate that nobody finds out she's here. You'll help us keep this quiet, won't you?"

"Of course I will." Jael leaned more closely over the woman, fingered the long strands of dark hair that had fallen across the edge of the mattress. "How terrifying, Keara!"

"It never set right with Elam that Nathaniel Luther could've had a shooting accident while cleaning his own hunting rifles in his own office, and I agree."

Jael straightened, her eyes black in contrast to the sudden paleness of her skin. "Murder," she whispered. "We're talking about someone attempting to murder her right here in the hollow."

Keara felt a shiver. There'd been no time to dwell on what had happened. "Sure looks that way."

"She rode a horse here in this condition?" Jael gave a shake of her head, as if in awe of Susanna Luther. "Tell me what I can do to help. She'll need a doctor."

"Elam says no."

Jael looked at Keara, eyes widening. "Oh, my dear, you're having quite a day of it."

"I need you and Kellen to help us."

Jael took a deep breath and nodded. "Gloria always did say her baby sister was indomitable. Sort of like Gloria, I always supposed, but Gloria never got herself shot at."

"She made it to the front steps, where we found her. She must have fallen and hit her head there. Elam took the mare to the barn."

Jael paced to the window and looked down on the yard then

paced back to the bed. "Lots of people down there, even folks from town we barely know, tourists from out of state, for Pete's sake, hoping to see what hillbillies from Arkansas do for a good time."

Keara knew what she meant. Oftentimes the locals felt as if they were on display for the entertainment of the sightseers.

"Show me what to do and I'll do it," Jael said. "Did she at least say who did this?"

"No. She's not been awake enough to answer many of my questions."

"Well, if this isn't your blood on your sleeve, get this dress off and pull on another. I can distract the ladies with the stain while you see to Susanna, otherwise half of them will soon come barging in here to see if they can help."

Keara silently blessed her new sister-in-law for her grasp of the situation, as well as for the immense relief of loosened stays. While Jael pulled one of Keara's high-necked church dresses from the bureau, Keara rechecked Susanna's heart rate and breathing, raising her eyelids to see if her eyes looked okay. They did.

When someone knocked on the door, it took all of Keara's self-control not to yelp.

"Coming!" Jael called. "Need a little privacy." She rushed to the door and cracked it just enough to slide the wedding dress out.

"Clydene brought in the water, cold as can be. Here you go." It was Mrs. Harper's voice.

"Wonderful. Thank you. Cold water is also just the thing to stop the stain from setting in the dress."

"Is everything okay?" Mrs. Harper's voice was filled with concern.

"Oh, she'll be good as new in no time," Jael said, voice softening. "It's unfortunately in a rather…delicate area, so you can understand why she won't want the whole party to come clomping into the room to check on her. Would you mind keeping everyone downstairs for us while I help her clean up?"

"Oh my." Mrs. Harper's voice dropped to match Jael's. "It isn't that time of—"

"No, not at all. Everything will be okay if you'll see to it her dress isn't permanently stained. It has a lot of sentimental value for her, it being her mother's wedding dress."

"Why, uh, certainly, if you don't think you could use help. I've doctored many a wound with all my boys over the years. Granted, our little caboose, Raylene, wasn't nearly as feisty as her brothers, but she's had her scrapes with all the little critters she brought home. I'm surprised she didn't get rabies."

Keara nodded to herself. Raylene's five older brothers were all out on their own now. They weren't there to keep an eye on her. A pity she didn't have little brothers to keep her occupied, like Keara did. Maybe Raylene had spent so much time with her critters over the years that when it came time to make friends, she didn't know how to choose properly.

While Jael assured Mrs. Harper that all would be well, Keara quickly buttoned her fresh dress.

"Isn't this a shame?" Mrs. Harper continued, obviously reluctant to skedaddle as quickly as Keara would like. "And on her wedding night."

Jael agreed with Mrs. Harper that it was, indeed, an awful shame and finally closed the door and leaned against it. "How are we going to keep her unnoticed through the night?" she whispered.

Susanna moaned again. Her face pulled into a grimace of pain, and then her eyes opened wide in the lantern light. She spared a look specifically for Keara.

The echo of footsteps receded down the stairs, and they could hear the muffled voice of Mrs. Harper explaining the situation to the others. There was a gaggle of female voices, but the door blocked a great deal of noise. Thank goodness. They would be kept busy for at least a few minutes discussing the best way to take the stain from the material.

"Susanna Luther," Keara said, despite the woman's continuous stern look, "this is Jael Pettit, Elam's sister. You can trust her as well as you can trust Elam, and I need her help."

"Susanna, you look so much like your beautiful sister, I took you for her at first," Jael said, motioning for Keara to open her drawer of bandages and poultices. "It gave me quite a shock. I met you once, at your sister's wedding."

"You mean Gloria's?"

"That's right."

Susanna nodded, obviously attempting to be polite for a moment in spite of her pain. "Then she was your sister-in-law." Her alto voice was soft enough to not be heard downstairs, but stiff enough to cause a chill when her gaze returned to Keara's face.

Jael placed a hand on Susanna's arm. "We need to help you, and quickly. Keara says you were shot."

Susanna's fierce look grew less intimidating as she turned it on Jael. She nodded.

"That's a nasty lump on your scalp, and Keara will need to treat it."

Susanna sniffed then wrinkled her nose. "Whiskey?"

"It's all I had to clean the wound," Keara said.

Susanna nodded, winced. Another moan, and she was out again.

"What are we going to do?" Jael asked.

"All I know to do is watch her." Keara reached for bandages and soaked them with the water that had been brought up. "The bleeding's stopped. Let's wring these out and place them on her head. I need ice if it gets here." A quick check told her the egg-shaped swelling had not grown, but there was no way of knowing how hard Susanna may have hit her head, nor if the swelling might go inward.

"I'll go check to see if it's arrived," Jael said.

"If only we could call for a doctor."

When Jael stepped out and shut the door behind her, Keara placed a cold, wet bandage over the lump. She took Susanna's hand in her own and squeezed. The woman was obviously thinking straight enough to guess about the wedding. Any woman would be disturbed—angry, furious—if her dead sister's husband was to up and marry someone else not even a year after the passing of his wife.

"Lord," she whispered, "let Susanna wake up again so she can ream me out good." It could mean she'd live through this night.

Susanna moaned again.

"It's okay," Keara assured her. "I'm going to do all I can to get you through this."

Susanna's mouth moved, and the bare breath came out in whispered words that were too soft for Keara to hear.

Keara leaned forward until her ear was close to Susanna's lips. "What can I do for you?"

"Don't trust…"

At first Keara took Susanna's words to express distrust of her. But then the woman moaned again, and in an even softer whisper, she said, "Don't trust anyone."

"We're keeping your arrival quiet. You can trust me, and you can trust Elam and his family."

Susanna's hand tightened on Keara's.

"Obviously, Jael's already seen you," Keara said, "but she's tight-lipped. Nobody'll get a hint from her. She's like her brother. Her husband, Kellen, comes from good stock. He'll protect your secret, as well."

Susanna opened her eyes again, trying to withdraw her hand from Keara's grasp. "You married Elam?"

Keara held the woman's gaze for a moment then nodded.

"So…soon."

Anger was a good sign. It meant she might be strong enough to fight this thing—if she didn't spend all her energy fighting Keara.

"Gloria was my best friend," Keara said. "She told me all about you. She was so proud of you, and when she…when she was taken from us, Elam needed help with the children and the farm. When I recently lost my home, we decided it was practical to help each other in this way."

The words obviously didn't register. Susanna had lost consciousness once more.

Six

"Elam Jensen, you sly fox!" The deep voice of bearlike Ray Harper came from the front porch, where several men had congregated, obviously to enjoy the smells of warm food coming from the kitchen.

"Sure thing," another called. "Folks never learn. Teach a man to fish, feed him for life. Teach a woman to catch a man, and he'll learn how to fish just to get out of the house."

Several men chuckled at the joke, which showed who'd been hitting their private stashes.

Ray stepped forward, grabbed Elam's hand, and patted him on the back with a couple of hard claps of thunder. "You got yourself a mighty fine gal, that's for sure. She not only breaks horses and plows fields, but she can raise your kids."

Elam caught sight of Ray's daughter, still lingering too close for comfort. He wondered if Ray knew about Raylene's attempts to despoil Keara's reputation. David had mentioned the rumor just yesterday. Another disappointment. Why was Raylene behaving with such spite all of a sudden?

Without slowing to exchange pleasantries with the other men from town, Elam plowed his way past the unexpected crowd in the house. Several more men tried to stop him, calling out warnings about the horrors of matrimony—as if they could convince him there was horror in matrimony to the right woman—and kidding him about his new young bride with references he was glad Keara couldn't hear.

Until this past week, he'd never seen her blush. In all the years he'd known her, all the hours they'd put in together working the horses while Gloria was alive—and even more hours together after Gloria's death—Keara had been capable of discussing every manner of animal or human behavior with nary a pink cheek. He'd discovered this week that Keara could, after all, embarrass easily with the right subject.

As the fifth man he encountered met him with a drink and a loud congratulations, Elam declined the drink and caught sight of his sister rushing through the kitchen and up the stairs.

In the kitchen huddled a clutch of women with their heads together, fussing over a dress the color of a robin's egg—looked like Keara's wedding gown was the center of attention for the moment, though he couldn't get a good enough look at it to know for sure. Finally disconnecting from the nearly impenetrable wall of well-wishers, he circled the fretting women and ran up the stairs.

Friends were good to have. Elam had always appreciated the strength that came from good ties with family and trustworthy allies. The problem tonight was this blasted crowd.

He knocked at Britte's door and listened. If Keara's dress was downstairs, he didn't want to walk in on her uncovered and—

"We're occupied for the moment, Mrs. Harper." Jael's voice. "Has the ice arrived?"

He slid the saddlebags from his shoulder and knocked again. "It's Elam."

"Oh! Thank goodness." His sister opened the door in a rush, grabbed his arm, and dragged him inside, her dark eyes filled with a combination of relief and distress. "Where have you been?"

He peered past her to find that Keara was fully clothed. Otherwise she would be red as a beefsteak. "Looking for you and Kellen and getting these." He held up the bags. "How's Susanna?"

"In and out," Keara said. "So far, I think she's okay, but she's still upset about the crowd...among other things. I promised her Jael and Kellen were trustworthy."

"Where's Kellen?"

"He's unloading more wood for the bonfire." Jael grabbed Elam's arm and leaned close. "We didn't see hide nor hair of either of you when we arrived, just the buggy out in front. We both figured since this was your wedding night, it wasn't any concern of ours where you were, so we just set to work." There was a teasing note in her voice, and Elam saw Keara's face redden. It was pretty on her, and the fact that he noticed startled him more than the blush.

"Can't we cancel this party tonight?" he grumbled. "This isn't a good time."

His sister laughed. "A chivaree never takes place at a good time. Remember the pranks you pulled on Kellen and me? Nobody's going to listen if you try to slink out of payback. You and Kellen better control the masses while I help Keara take care of this mess."

Elam held out the bags to Keara.

She stared at them as if they were a bundle of snakes before taking them from him and setting them on the dresser. "Susanna's not awake to tell me what to do with any of her medicines."

"You don't have to be a doctor, Keara," he told her gently. "Just look through them to see if there's anything you can use. If not, put them aside. So Susanna has awakened enough to be aware of what's going on, obviously."

"She's overheard vital information about our wedding."

"She'll handle it. Try to keep her talking when she's awake."

Keara looked up and met his gaze. His gut clenched at the look of fear in her golden-brown eyes. After all she'd gone through this past week, now this. But he knew Keara. For all her delicate looks, she was feisty and strong. She could handle this.

"I'm going to have to remove the bullet." Keara blanched as white as the bridal bouquet she'd been holding earlier today.

"There may be utensils in those bags that'll help you at least get it out. Just do your best." He reached out and took her left hand—the one with the wedding ring on it. He squeezed it gently then released her. He turned to Jael. "How'd you keep everyone downstairs?"

"Susanna's blood."

He felt horse-kicked. "They know Susanna's here?"

"Oh, don't overreact. They think it's Keara's, and that the injury was in a delicate area, so no one will have the temerity to ask too many questions."

He nodded. He could trust his sweetly scheming sister to come up with something. Hadn't she and Penelope spearheaded this wedding shindig—one that neither he nor Keara had expected or wanted—in a week? She could work magic. Too bad she didn't know how to extract a bullet.

Keara turned up the lamplight and pulled utensils and medicines from the bags, one by one, handling them with care…or fear and awe.

Elam had a sudden urge to take her hand again or squeeze her shoulders or take her in his arms and remind her she was no longer alone. He'd had the urge several times this past week. Mostly, he'd resisted it. But they were married now. He hadn't expected that to change anything, but now—

"She's got a head wound," Keara said, pointing toward Susanna's bloodied black hair and the water dripping from folded bandages onto the pillow. "That lump's got me worried."

"You think that's why she's unconscious now?"

"Well, it's not from blood loss. Heaven only knows what else I'll find on her, but there's not much blood on her clothing. My worry about removing the bullet is that it may be blocking a vein or artery. Unblock it, and the blood loss could be bad." Keara gave Jael a beseeching look. "You're going to stay and help?"

"That's what sisters-in-law are for."

Elam cast another glance at Susanna and felt a clench in his stomach at the familiarity of that face, the raven hair.

"Strong family resemblance," Jael said, reading his expression perfectly. Her voice betrayed her sympathy.

Jael had never questioned his sudden decision to marry Keara. No one, yet, had heard about Keara's dad losing her farm to a gambler from Missouri. Surprising, the way word spread in these parts, that no one had mentioned it. The bank president, however, was not one for gossip, and Keara could be as tight-lipped as a Baptist preacher.

"Now out," Jael said, shoving Elam toward the door. "We've got work to do, and unless you change your mind about riding into the Springs for a doctor—"

"I haven't."

"And unless you can bring us ice from town—there's supposed to be a block coming—then Keara will do her best. I'll help. Go entertain our friends and neighbors." She grimaced. "And try to lock Raylene Harper in the smokehouse, if you can."

Elam glanced down at Keara, was once again touched by her fear, and he reached out and took her by the shoulders. There was a frailty in her he'd not seen before. If only there was more he could do to keep her from fretting. He knew she wanted to call a doctor and ignore Susanna's pleas for secrecy, he could see it in her eyes.

"I've seen you handle worse than this, Keara Jensen."

Her eyes widened, most likely at his use of her new married name. She met his gaze and seemed to gather strength from his touch. "But she's...Gloria's sister, Elam." Her voice wobbled with emotion. "It's almost like I'm trying to save Gloria's life all over again." Tears sprang to her eyes, and her chin quivered.

Despite the pain her words caused him, he felt closer to Keara at that moment than he ever had before. She shared this haunting with him just as she'd shared in the pain of Gloria's death. Almost without thought, he drew her into his arms, feeling the fineness of her small frame, this woman who could run a farm single-handedly and win the love and respect of three motherless children.

He looked over Keara's shoulder and saw that Susanna's eyes were again open, though only for a second before they closed and she appeared to retreat into unconsciousness.

He glanced at Jael and found understanding and love. He would be teased again, mercilessly, as soon as he returned downstairs, and there would be many ribald comments about his marrying so quickly, but he was a man to face down anyone who wanted to take him on. His brothers-in-law, Kellen and David, and his brothers, Hans and Delmar, would support him.

With a final squeeze, he released Keara and left her in his sister's care. He could think of no more stalwart friend for her right now. As he retraced his steps down the stairwell and the raucous sounds of the party enveloped him, he kept a picture in his mind of Gloria, through the sight of Susanna's lithe form and beautiful face.

He also continued to feel the tender compassion and connection to Keara that was so new to him. His late wife, lost to him, his new wife, real to him. Both suddenly bonded together in his heart because of Keara's love for Gloria.

This was right. He knew it. But he would have a struggle to blend his love for Gloria into this new and awkward marriage. His new wife deserved it. His children deserved it. They should be a real family.

* * * * *

Keara felt as if the air was sucked from the room when Elam walked out. She hadn't realized how much she'd come to depend on him these past months.

She looked up from the utensils and medicine vials she had laid out on the bureau top. Jael hovered with eyes wide, focused, ready to assist.

"You met Susanna before," Keara said. "Was she like Gloria in manner? She favors her so much, and Gloria spoke often of her baby sister with great affection."

Jael stepped back from the bed and rinsed a cloth in the water basin. "When I first met Susanna, I thought she and Gloria might be twins."

"They were that much alike?" A thought began to vex Keara that she couldn't dismiss. "With only two years' difference between them—"

"I can't say what they may have been like growing up," Jael said, "but when I met them they'd been separated from one another for several years already. When Susanna was sent to her aunt's in Philadelphia, it well nigh broke both their hearts."

"I remember Gloria telling me that."

"The societal influence, combined with their aunt's tight control, made an obvious impact on Susanna," Jael said, her voice softening, as if afraid Susanna might be listening behind those closed eyes. "She was given the introduction into a world Gloria had always longed for."

Keara knew what Jael meant. Though Gloria could only read about modern styles and customs from books and magazines, Susanna had been given that life, the education.

"I can understand how it must have wrenched the two sisters apart," Jael said. "I'd hate to be separated from Penelope. But in such a large family, a wealthy maiden aunt was the only way for Susanna to receive higher education. She showed so much promise."

Another check of Susanna's breathing and pulse told Keara she was still stable. If her eyes weren't closed, Keara would think she was listening to the conversation. If only she would open those eyes again, and keep them open.

"Gloria was smart too," Keara said. "She told me once that she had considered staying in the city near her sister, but Elam changed all that." Since Susanna had married a man of consequence, Gloria might also have been counted among the more elite of Philadelphia.

Keara would do all she could to save this woman's life—but what if she couldn't? It would be like losing Gloria all over again. It was easy to imagine Gloria looking down from heaven and watching, waiting for Keara to do something grand to save her sister.

Keara didn't know anything grand.

She didn't know anything.

"We do what we can." Jael placed her hand on Keara's shoulder.

Keara looked again at Jael. Their eyes met.

"It's all you can do." Jael offered a smile and a nod. "Believe me, that's plenty. I never saw another person so in tune with those injured and in pain."

Keara knew Jael meant that as encouragement, but all she felt was the pressure to perform a miracle, and she didn't exist in a world of miracles, only plodding, grasping, praying, and mixing herbs and concoctions that some folks in these parts derided as witches' brews.

What hog slop. Witchcraft? They called the herbs and medicines supplied by God witchcraft. That was just plain evil.

"So are you going to remove the bullet while she's unconscious?" Jael asked. "Or will you wait until she's fully awake and able to feel the awful pain?"

Keara caught her breath. "Leave it to you to put it that way."

Jael shrugged. "That's how I see it. Get to it. Make me proud."

Keara studied her patient then did something she'd learned from her mother before the accident that rendered her paralyzed. She pressed her knuckles against the center of Susanna's chest and rubbed. Hard. If Susanna didn't awaken from that pain, she would be less likely to revive to the pain when Keara removed the bullet from her shoulder.

A low moan, nothing more.

"Let's do it," Keara said. "You see that tool that looks like a pair of scissors, but with connecting handles? It's called a hemostat, if I'm not mistaken. If I can dig down deeply enough, maybe I can grasp the bullet and remove it without too much more blood loss. If we only had more light in here."

"I can fix that," Jael said. "You know how Kellen is always the first one to jump on any newfangled invention that passes through town? Well, maybe now one of his harebrained ideas will help us this time. You ever heard of battery lights?"

"You mean that crazy thing he attached to your wagon so you can work outside at night?"

"That's the one. Well, we've got it tonight, and I think I can convince Kellen to bring it up here without a whole lot of attention."

"And just how do you plan to do that?"

"All I need to do is find him and talk to him and explain to everyone else that this so-called delicate injury of yours will need sewing with a good light."

"And if they want to see the handiwork?"

Jael gave Keara a sly grin.

Keara took a deep breath and held Jael's gaze. "Delicate area. Right. I'm glad we're related now."

"So am I. Now let's get these wounds healed."

Seven

One loud shriek, a trickle of blood, and Keara pulled the slug of lead from Susanna's shoulder. The sounds of laughter and talk dwindled to hushed whispers that Keara could barely hear. She knew all eyes outside were trained upward on this bedroom window and the bright light from Kellen's battery lantern.

Jael's soft, comforting chatter seemed to soothe Susanna, and those haunting blue eyes closed, the harsh breathing softened, and a quiet moan accompanied her back to her world of unconsciousness.

Jael switched attention from their patient to Keara. "Your teeth are chattering."

For the second time in this long, long day, Keara felt as if she might lose her last meal—which now that she thought of it, had been breakfast. No wonder she was lightheaded.

"She'll be okay." Jael put a firm arm around Keara's shoulders. "You did fine. Do you need me to get you anything?"

Keara took a strengthening breath and braced herself. "Hand me the whiskey and get ready for another scream. Can't take any chances with—"

There was a loud knock on the door. "Lands, Jael, are you killing the poor bride in there?" It was Clydene Brown, church organist, church founder, and proprietress of her own bathhouse in Eureka Springs—a force to be reckoned with, and one who had always taken a special liking to Keara.

"I'm f–fine," Keara called. "Everything will be…okay. Just keep the party going, will you? Oh, and Clydene, would you bring us a pitcher of tea? Chamomile. I've got it cooled in the springhouse." She'd discovered years ago that the water from the natural spring that flowed through the springhouse here had as many healing properties as the water used in Eureka Springs.

There was a sound of sniffing. "My smeller may be off," Clydene said, "but if I'm not mistaken, you've already got whiskey in there. Whatd'ya need with chamomile?"

"The liquor's medicinal only."

"What you need is a good dose of laudanum, if you're hurting that badly."

"Why, Clydene, it's her wedding night," Jael called, winking at Keara. "You wouldn't want her to be unconscious for it, would you?"

Keara gave her sister-in-law a warning glare.

"Chamomile tea coming up," Clydene called.

As the footsteps receded, Keara wiped her bloody hands on the damp cloth and tried to calm down. "This is madness. Pure madness," she whispered under her breath.

Jael finished cleaning up after Keara and turned off the bright light. The contrast made it hard for them to see for a few seconds with nothing more than the oil lantern. "What now?"

"Now we clean it, bandage it, and wait. Nothing else we can do until we get ice for that head. Tomorrow I'll get a poultice on her wound to keep it from getting infected."

"Then I suggest you show your face out there to your admiring partiers and get me off the hook. I can clean and bandage. You've taught me that much. They need to know I didn't really kill you in here."

Keara cast a glance over Susanna's pale features. "I have to make sure she's going to be okay."

"Then you have time for another change of clothing." Jael nodded at the full skirt of the green plaid she'd given Keara to put on in place of the stained wedding dress. This dress, too, was now stained with blood. "It's good I know you so well, Mrs. Jensen. I didn't pull out your most elegant gown for you to ruin."

Keara eyed her fashionable sister-in-law.

"I think the red satin will look beautiful with that long, blond hair of yours," Jael said, "when I comb out that chignon. You'll have to promise not to go roughhousing with the children tonight. You're supposed to be injured, remember?"

"I'd rather take a nap," Keara muttered. Of course, she was too keyed-up to sleep.

"I have a feeling there won't be a lot of time for that for a while. Let's get you changed. And then you need to trust me with Susanna long enough for you to enjoy your wedding party."

Keara met Jael's gaze through the gloom and felt the heaviness of compunction. "You and Penelope have worked so hard to put all this together, and I haven't properly thanked you."

Jael gave an uncharacteristic snort. "Only about a dozen times this past week."

"But you don't really know what's…you know your brother wouldn't—"

"I do know my brother." Jael reached down and squeezed Keara's hand with gentle pressure, leaning close enough for Keara to catch a scent of that sassafras bark Jael often swore kept her teeth white and free of pain. "He knows his own mind. He's a good, good man, and you're a blessed woman. I also know he's a blessed man to have had you as a friend, and now as his beloved wife."

"But Gloria was his—"

"Gloria's in heaven now. You're here. She would bless this union as God did today in the sight of a church full of witnesses. I think you've debated the subject to death in your mind. It's time to move forward."

The soft, reassuring voice released—at least for a little while— the taut thrum that had held Keara's stomach in knots this day. The sudden pressure of Jael's hands on hers relayed a wealth of kind acceptance. For the first time in a week, Keara felt as if she could breathe freely. Somehow, surely this would all turn out well.

* * * * *

Elam unharnessed Elijah from the buggy, fed him a scoop of oats mixed with molasses, and had picked up a curry comb for a delayed grooming when he heard the sound of feminine voices on the other side of the barn door.

He stiffened and glanced toward the next stall. Duchess loomed there in full view of anyone who happened to walk in. It was darker inside, of course, but enough reflection from the bonfire glowed through the open upper door that he had light to work—and visitors who snooped too closely would be able to see.

The voices drew closer.

"Face it, she beat you. That tiny little tomboy beat you to the man." It was Cynthia Lindstrom's voice, if he wasn't mistaken. "The wedding's over. You'd better set your cap for Elam's little brother before Delmar gets away as well."

There was a soft sigh. "It isn't as if I can switch affection from one man to another with a snap of my fingers." It was Raylene's voice. "And Delmar's a child."

"He's twenty. Older than you by a year, and he likes you, I can tell."

"He cut off half my braid in school. He was always so ornery. He's nothing like his brother."

"Then maybe he won't be so likely to put a young lady in the family way and have to marry her."

"Don't be spiteful. Elam wouldn't do that."

"Mark my words, Raylene, that woman tricked Elam into this marriage and she'll make a poor man of him."

There was another sigh. "You could show respect for her now that she's his wife."

"Respect," Cynthia muttered. "She was never anything but a servant girl, even in her own family."

"Didn't look like a servant today, did she?" Raylene asked. "She didn't look to be in the family way either."

"I wonder about her injury, though," Cynthia said as the barn door squeaked open and the voices and footsteps drew nearer. "You could tell those stays were tight enough to cut off her breathing. You don't suppose she actually *was* in the family way and—"

There was a gasp. "Cynthia!"

"Well? I just wonder about that so-called delicate injury of hers. I wouldn't put it past her to trap the man, then—"

"You remember that sermon Pastor preached about bitterness and envy last Sunday?" Raylene asked. "It's an ugly thing in a pretty girl. Why do you hate her so?"

"Me? What about you? She took your man."

"There are other men in town. Lots of them. Why, I saw Timothy Skerit hanging around with some of the other men outside the saloon on Mud Street before the wedding today. Don't think he didn't give me a second look when I sauntered past." Raylene laughed. "Now there's a good man."

"Still working on his daddy's farm," Cynthia snapped. "He doesn't have the Jensen money, that's for sure."

Elam felt something ease inside him. Those words, spoken with such venom, told him Raylene wasn't the one causing Keara all the grief.

There was a long silence. "I think you're more jealous of Keara Jensen than I am, Cynthia."

"Don't you dare suggest I'm envious of that greedy little peahen!"

"Greedy?" Raylene laughed. "What makes you think she's greedy?"

"She married a wealthy horse rancher."

"Wealthy?"

"She sold that farm of hers, did you know that? Soon as her father was in jail, she sold it right out from under him then pocketed the money, left him to rot, and hitched up to the wealthiest rancher in the hollow."

Raylene giggled. "Where do you get these stories of yours? Elam's not wealthy, he's just a hardworking man who raises horses." She sighed. "It is a shame. We could have made such a good match. Daddy's always admired Elam and his sense for good horse stock."

"Everyone wonders why he remarried so quickly." Cynthia's voice was too close to the stall door. "I think it's because she's cheap labor."

"Cynthia, you're so hateful."

Elam heard a soft crack and realized he'd squeezed the curry comb so hard he'd split the handle. He eased up on his grip. He'd become so protective of Keara lately. Still, he was relieved to find that Cynthia's venom hadn't infected Raylene as much as he'd feared.

There was a nicker in the next stall. Elam was just about to step from the darkness, usher the two women from the barn, and bolt the doors.

"Raylene?" This was Delmar's voice from outside the barn. "You out here?"

Elam bit back a groan. Soon the whole party would be in the barn with him.

"Well, well, here's that handsome man we were just talking about," Cynthia said.

"Oh hush. You were the one talking about him."

"Delmar, you need to take my friend dancing before she pines away."

Elam waited for his shy younger brother to say something...say *anything*.

"Well, okay," Cynthia said, her footsteps moving away at last. "If you don't want to dance with Raylene, dance with me. She was just out here wondering why on earth your brother would marry Keara McBride."

Delmar cleared his throat as his footsteps joined hers. "I'm sorry?"

"Well, everyone knows Keara's from a rough family. She knows nothing about the gentle life, and your niece and nephews may now grow up to be half wild. What was Elam thinking?"

"Raylene said that?" Delmar exclaimed, his sharp outrage reaching the stall clearly.

"No, I didn't!" Raylene exclaimed.

"Honestly, Delmar, mark my words," Cynthia said. "You watch and see if Keara Jensen doesn't become a simple servant in your brother's home, and nothing more."

There was a gasp nearby, and Elam realized Raylene had not joined the other two as they walked away.

There was another nicker as skirts rustled. Elam was about to move when he heard footsteps along the dirt floor that connected the stalls. The steps halted at the next stall over. Where Duchess had grown restless.

Raylene caught a sharp breath. "Hey, who do you belong to?"

Elam waited, silent, not wishing to be subjected to any questions. Raylene turned and rushed from the barn.

With a heavy sigh of dread, Elam put away the curry comb with the cracked handle, walked from the barn, and bolted it so that no one else could enter tonight. He should have been more watchful. Raylene knew horses, and she was sharp enough to notice the unusual size and shape of Susanna's regal Duchess. He could only hope it was too dark in the barn for her to have seen much beyond that.

Elam would have to warn his younger brother, once again, of the dangers of womanly wiles, especially the wiles of Cynthia Lindstrom.

What Elam had overheard, however, had served a good purpose. It warned him that if he didn't show proper appreciation before tonight's crowd of witnesses, rumors could spread that he had married Keara for the cheap labor Cynthia had insinuated. Keara deserved more respect from the people of Eureka Springs. She already had it from their friends, family, and neighbors along the hollow.

He brushed off his clothing. Time to seek out his wife.

* * * * *

The party noise died again as Keara went down the steps to the kitchen. Upon her appearance, several of the women gasped and surged toward her with exclamations of concern.

Clydene Brown beat everyone to Keara's side. "Honey, should you be up and around? That scream awhile ago like to've clotted my blood." She held out the cold chamomile tea. "We thought you were dying."

Keara forced a smile and placed an arm around her friend as she took the tea. "You know I'm not one to tolerate pain."

Clydene laughed out loud. "Now you're joshing with me. I remember how brave you were when that old mean bull of your pa's gored your leg. You were white with pain when they brought you to town but nobody ever heard a word of complaint."

Keara bit her lip. "Thank you for the tea. Do you like my dress?" She took a large swallow of the honey-sweetened brew then set down the glass and held her arms out to show off her gown.

Clydene and the other ladies were suitably distracted, and Keara warned herself to be more cautious about what she said for the rest of the night.

"I love the lines of this beautiful red satin," Clydene said. "I always knew it would look better on you than my aunt Hilda. Your skin and hair are perfect for bold colors."

"It's always been my favorite. Thank you for giving it to me." Keara noted that the party had once more picked up the pace—and the noise.

"You don't look any the worse for wear, I must admit," Clydene said as the other ladies returned to serving the food. "So glad you took off those hideous stays. You've got more color in your face." She glanced toward the front door, which stood open, allowing smoke to drift in from the bonfire.

The scent of roasted meats on the food-laden table made Keara's stomach complain. She was suddenly starving.

"Hmm." Clydene touched Keara's arm and gestured toward the silhouette of Raylene Harper, who was drawing her father from the crowd. "She seems intent on some kind of business, don't you think?"

"Maybe she's asking to go home." One could hope.

"Dream on, honey. She'll stay all night if she thinks she can get any attention at all from that fine husband of yours. Oh, there I go again, foaming at the mouth with gossip. But is it gossip if it's the truth? That girl, I swan, she didn't get those ways from her mother's side of the family. No two women could be less alike. I think she's fallen into bad company since their family moved closer to town."

Before Keara could reply, Elam came through the front door, filled a plate at the table that had been set up along the wall, and glanced in her direction.

"Oh, here he comes now," Clydene said. "Knew he wouldn't be able to stay away from you for long tonight. You're like a trumpet flower to a hummingbird."

Despite the many men who called to Elam, he politely made his way toward Keara without stopping for small talk, holding the plate high to protect it.

When he reached her, he leaned close. "Have I told you how beautiful you are tonight?"

At his words, several of the partiers turned knowing gazes toward the two of them.

"I—uh—think you did." She felt her cheeks grow warm. "Thank you."

He put the plate in her hands and touched her arm to draw her aside.

She looked from the food to him, surprised he wasn't joining friends on the front porch.

He stepped back and raised his brows as he looked at the dress she wore then nodded in approval and placed a warm hand on her shoulder. He leaned close again—so close she could barely focus on the food she'd craved seconds ago.

Rowdy laughter reached them from the front of the great room, and Richard Brown called out, "Looks like Elam's ready for this party to end!"

"You have no idea how much," Elam called back, joining the laughter.

Keara tried to swallow a bite of beef, but it didn't want to go down. She tried again as the laughter surrounded her. Elam's arm tightened. To her great relief, Clydene picked up the glass of cold chamomile, took the plate, and handed the glass to Keara.

"Drink, honey. Don't pay any mind to those bawdy men. They're as jealous as all creation that Elam Jensen once more landed the most beautiful girl in the county."

"That's no more than the truth." Elam leaned down and placed a warm kiss on Keara's hot cheek. She tried to keep her eyes from bugging, but really!

And yet, it felt so very, very good. She could enjoy it a whole lot more if not for the crowd. But if not for the crowd, would he be holding her like this…saying these things…kissing her?

With a chuckle, Clydene set Keara's plate beside the stove. "This'll be here when you get your breath back."

When Keara downed the contents of her glass, Mrs. Harper refilled it, leaning close. "Sweetheart, hold your head up high," she murmured softly enough that no one else could hear. "You've landed yourself a goldmine, and I'm not talking money. I've seen how gentle he is with the livestock. You can trust him to be gentle with you."

Keara thanked Mrs. Harper and gulped more chamomile. Now she was being given wedding night advice by Raylene's own mother. This day felt like one of the fairytales she read to the children—only embarrassing.

As the well-wishers grew louder and the party atmosphere engulfed them, Keara gave herself up to the joy of the moment in spite of the embarrassment. She could pretend. Those stories she read weren't real, but she and Britte and Rolfe loved them anyway.

She could dream that the warm touch of Elam's hand on her arm, his closeness and attentive behavior—the eyes that told her he was interested in only her company tonight—were real. Couldn't she?

He leaned closer. "Everything okay?" he asked, his voice soft, almost…intimate.

She looked up, forced herself to hold his gaze, forced her lips to quirk into a smile. She wondered if he could tell that, no matter what he was feeling tonight, she was honestly, quietly loving him from deep down inside, and that her love wasn't going to go away with the light of the sunrise tomorrow. It would never go away.

Despite the three glasses of tea she'd already swallowed, her throat was too dry to speak, so she only nodded.

He held his lips near her ear again. "You're doing fine."

She hesitated, then nodded. Of course, that was what he was doing. They were both supposed to be putting on an act for the crowd. Her smile began to harden like tree sap. The sudden tightness in her face reached all the way to her heart. She took a deep breath to once again thank him, but she couldn't say the words. Not another time. She felt like a beggar.

A movement attracted her attention from the stairs, and she glanced up to see Jael motioning toward her. She appeared calm, but her eyes flicked with fear.

Keara stepped from Elam's embrace with the excuse that she was feeling peaked. It was the truth now. As she joined Jael on the stairs, she looked back down at the party and saw Raylene and her father making their way through the crowd toward Elam.

"Susanna is demanding to talk to you," Jael whispered.

Keara turned and ran up the stairs. Elam was on his own.

Eight

Elam watched his bride follow his sister up the stairs and wished he could go with them. Something was up, he could tell by Jael's expression.

He turned to find Raylene beading in on him. Again. The child had been popping up all day like weeds in a garden, and this time she held her father's arm and tugged him through the crowd.

"Last time you had a party, Elam Jensen," she said as they drew near, "you opened the barn for dancing. Won't there be barn dancing tonight?"

"Of course there will. I hear the fiddler already."

"But not in the barn?" she asked.

"Why dance in a dirty old barn when you can dance by the light of the bonfire?"

"I think it's because of that mare you're hiding." Raylene released her father's arm and stood with hands on her hips as the conversation around them grew quiet.

"I have a mare foaling," Elam said, and it was true, though that mare was in a smaller stable behind the house. "Forgive me if I'm not prepared to host a complete party tonight, but with my wife's...difficulties and the animals and barn unprepared—"

"Raylene." Ray Harper turned to his daughter. "Why don't you find Delmar and see if you can convince him to dance with you."

Elam wasn't surprised when she folded her arms over her chest

89

and set her chin. "He's dancing with someone else right now. And I'm the one who saw the horse—"

"Raylene, this is man talk. You mentioned you wanted to dance, so dance." Ray took Elam's arm and urged him away from the main din of the crowd. Raylene tagged along behind.

"You've married a fine woman, Elam Jensen," Ray said, nodding toward the stairs that Keara had so recently ascended. "She's turned out to be quite a beauty."

"Yes, she has."

"Those late bloomers tend to be worth the wait. Your family seems taken with her, as well. Good to marry a neighbor so nearby. I take it the extra land will help you grow your brood stock."

Elam hesitated. It would soon become obvious to everyone that the McBride farm had passed hands, and though he didn't want to be the one to spread the news, he also didn't want yet another rumor to be spread as to the why of his marrying Keara.

"Keara and I will have more than enough land without adding her family's property," he told Ray. "Brute's name will be cleared soon, I'm sure."

Ray nodded with approval. "Spoken like a loyal son-in-law."

"I just happen to know Brute McBride is not a killer."

"Not even when he's drunk?" Raylene asked.

Ray turned to his daughter, caught her by the shoulders, and swung her toward the front entrance to the house. "Child, out the door with you. Find a dance partner or ride back to town with the Johnstons. They're leaving in a few minutes."

With a loud sigh, Raylene left at last, and Elam watched with relief as she made her way through the crowd to the front door.

Ray cleared his throat. "Don't mind my girl. She's just a little surprised about the wedding." He leaned close. "Guess she might've fancied herself a contender, though her mother and I both warned her, you know. Girl barely nineteen taking on a full-fledged family?"

Elam nodded and met Ray's gaze. The slate-green eyes were kind, the skin around them weathered from long hours of work and astute business dealings. The Harpers were a good family, Ray and Rosetta having raised five strong sons who were pillars of the town. Elam had once overheard Rosetta lamenting to Clydene Brown that she had always tried to instill good manners in their strong-willed daughter, but that she was obviously better at raising boys than girls. At nineteen, many young women were already settled with a family.

"Raylene can speak too much of her mind," Ray said, "but even though she's spent most of her time these past couple of years trying to learn how to be a young lady instead of a tomboy, she still knows horses." Ray kept his voice softer than usual, eyeing those closest to them. "Strange she couldn't place the mare she saw in your barn tonight. When she dragged me out with her, the door was barred."

Elam adopted a look of mild interest. Raylene had, indeed, noticed a difference in Duchess, even in that dark stall, and her father was an astute businessman; he knew how to read people.

"You wouldn't be breeding new stock, would you, Elam?" Ray asked.

"Your daughter may have seen the mare I'm boarding for a friend, but she certainly saw no new property of mine. With the fine horse stock I have already, especially with Freda Mae so promising as a racer, why would I want to switch midstream?"

Ray gazed around the room. "So you're not holding out on me? I wouldn't happen to know this friend, would I?"

"Someone from out of town."

Richard Brown, Clydene's husband, slipped up beside them. "Speaking of new horses, you should've seen the mare I saw out at the edge of town this morning. Fine specimen, like nothing I ever saw before, prancing along Dairy Hollow Road like she was carrying royalty." He leaned closer. "Strangest thing wasn't the horse. What caught my eye was the rider. If I didn't know better, I could've sworn it was…Gloria Jensen." He looked away, cleared his throat. "Sorry, Elam, but I couldn't believe my eyes. Could've been a trick of light. Curious thing, is all I'm saying. All this is kind of like one of those hauntings folks talk about."

Clydene joined her husband and took a firm grip on his arm. "Fellas, this is a wedding party, not a business meeting or boys' night at the saloon. Now, Ray, it's time for a dance. Elam, I think your bride might not mind having her husband at her side right now. Why don't you run upstairs and see how she's doing?"

Elam could have hugged Clydene as he excused himself and made his way toward the stairs.

* * * * *

"It's called trephining." Susanna's voice was weaker than before, her face pulled down, eyes dull.

Had she screamed the words, though, they'd have had no greater effect on Keara. "I don't care what it's called, there's no way I'm going to bore a hole in your skull." The woman was crazy. Obviously, the hit on the head had knocked her brains loose.

"Then if I pass out and don't wake up again, in your hands be it."

"If I have to, I'll take you to a doctor."

Susanna closed her eyes. "What will he do, pour his magic water on me? Trust no doctor. Trust no one in town, in this state."

The door opened, and Keara jerked around to find Elam slipping inside. He caught Keara's gaze then nodded toward Susanna.

"Elam, she's awake and telling me to drill into her head," Keara told him. "I can't convince her I'm not a doctor!"

"My Duchess." Susanna's eyes remained closed. "Elam, your new young bride wants to betray me by riding to town. Tell me that my horse, at least, is concealed."

He didn't reply but held Keara's gaze. "The barn is bolted shut. She's been brushed down, she's dry and unhurt."

"But?" Susanna demanded.

Keara glanced back to see Susanna's blue-eyed gaze locked on Elam with suspicion.

"What aren't you saying?" Susanna asked. "Has someone seen her? If they have—"

"Susanna Luther, you're just like your older sister," Elam said, sinking to his knees beside the bed and laying a hand on her arm.

"You mean the sister who died less than a year ago?"

Keara winced at the cold plink of the words against her heart.

"She was independent and willful when we first married," Elam said.

"I don't care to have my sister talked about in such a fashion."

"I'm merely speaking the truth. Gloria was often at a loss if she could not see to the arrangements of every precise detail herself. She eventually learned to trust me, to trust our neighbors and family, and especially trust the outcome of her life to God. That's what you're going to have to do."

Susanna moved her arm from contact with Elam's touch. "I didn't realize my sister married a preacher."

"She married a rancher."

"And then after she died you married a doctor?"

Elam paused and shook his head. "I married a neighbor."

"Your sister has been telling me bedtime stories then, I presume. To hear Jael tell it, your new bride needs only a medical degree and she could be a full-fledged doctor."

"Jael is biased." Keara shot her sister-in-law a look of caution.

"She has the kindest touch I've ever known," Jael told Susanna. "But she can't be expected to perform a procedure she's not been taught."

"Then, Mrs. Jensen, if you're as smart as Jael says, you'll hear my words, and hear them well tonight," Susanna said. "It seems I'll need to teach you a few things while I'm conscious." She paused, closed her eyes, opened them again. "You took the utensils from my bag, I see. I also need you to search through those bags for the books. Do you have any cookbooks, Mrs. Jensen?"

"Yes, I do, but—"

"Good, then you can read."

Keara pressed her lips together, recalling Gloria's behavior when she first arrived in the community. She, too, had been outspoken and occasionally demanding. Susanna obviously liked to give orders the way her sister once had, but this was one time her orders were not going to be followed.

"You'll find a book that describes the procedure, step by step. My life may depend on this," Susanna said. "There are adequate utensils for you to operate. All you need do is follow the instructions." For the first time, Susanna found and held Keara's gaze, and her blue eyes softened. The disapproval slid away. "All I need you to do is tell me you'll try." She swallowed and took a shaky breath. "If you don't at least try, I could slip into a coma and never revive, and I cannot afford to do that. Not yet."

Keara was not a good liar, and when she took Susanna's hand and squeezed and nodded, she was not lying. Not exactly. She was praying that God would not allow Susanna to slip into a coma on this night.

Nine

On Tuesday morning, Elam ran his hand down the warm, muscular neck of Regal Duchess of Blackmoor—her full name, if Susanna was actually in her right mind when she'd told it to Jael about midnight. It was about the same time Susanna had made the decision, of her own accord, that it would not be necessary for Keara to drill a hole in her skull—though she'd warned that she still wasn't out of danger.

He grinned and shook his head as he recalled the relief he'd felt—and which he'd seen reflected in Keara's eyes. Keara may have gone through with the procedure had she thought it necessary. She'd sat beside Susanna all night, studying the textbooks by the glow of Kellen's battery lamp as long as it lasted, then continued with lantern light. There was no doubt that, were she ever required to drill into someone's skull to save a life, she could do it.

The mare snorted, distracting him from his thoughts. Her black coat glowed in the morning sun as he gave her another scoop of oats, but she snuffled at the food then raised her head and looked directly at Elam, her big eyes dark. Could he be imagining her thoughts? Was she speaking to him in the only way she knew how?

"Lost your appetite?" he murmured as he rubbed her short-cropped mane. "Can't blame you for that. Yesterday must have been a nasty time for you."

She was a beauty, no doubt about it. Gloria had told him long ago that Nathaniel and Susanna Luther had always been good judges of horseflesh.

Elam recalled Richard Brown's remark last night about Gloria and ghosts. Obviously, Susanna had been in Eureka Springs yesterday, which meant she had not yet been shot at that time. The only reason she would be in Arkansas, so far from home, must have been to see him. He and the children were the only family she had here. But why would she come without sending word of her arrival? And who, in the five miles between Eureka Springs and here, may have been the likely shooter?

He shook his head, gave Duchess another pat, and turned toward the house. Duchess followed, snorted, nudged his shoulder, her huge feet coming within inches of his.

"Don't push me, Duchess, my friend. I only allowed you into the paddock because you threatened to kick down the stall door."

She lowered her head and pressed her forelock against his chest.

The mare was a big, loveable pet. "I think your mistress is going to be okay." Elam had gathered from snatches of conversation he'd heard from Susanna in the wee hours that Duchess could take credit for saving her life. His sister-in-law and her mighty horse had a bond he understood. "I do believe Keara will see to it."

He hugged the big head and released her then climbed the fence, hoping she wouldn't attempt to plow through it. He wasn't sure the logs would hold her.

At the house, bacon scented the doorway, and he stepped inside to see his sister presiding over breakfast preparations. Solid slices of cooked grits crackled beside the bacon on the griddle, while a pot of chicken broth bubbled alongside—Susanna's breakfast, most likely, if she had awakened.

Elam was glad Kellen and Jael had three strong boys in their teens who could be counted on to take care of the farm in their parents' absence, because his sister and brother-in-law had been desperately needed here this past night.

Kellen met Elam in the kitchen with a cup of coffee. A tall, raw-boned man with pale blond hair and blue eyes, Kellen had proven himself a steady friend, a true brother, over the years.

"Keara was down earlier," he told Elam, his deep voice raw from lack of sleep. "Said Susanna's restless, seems to have a touch of fever, but otherwise she's not shown signs of the coma we feared."

Jael looked over her shoulder from her activity at the stove. "Oh, good, Elam, would you take over breakfast? I don't trust Kellen within three feet of your fancy cook stove, and I need to go help Keara with Susanna. We'll need to bathe her to get her temperature down. You men help yourselves to the food when it's ready. No telling how long we'll be."

With her economy of movement, she passed along her chores to Elam the way she used to when they lived under the same roof, and as she did so, her gaze caught and held his. "You going to be okay, little brother?"

He gave her a friendly scowl. "I'll be fine. Susanna's the one we need to worry about. Has she taken any tea? Soup?"

"We were able to get about half a cup of Keara's weed tea down her."

Elam grinned at his sister's term for Keara's concoctions. "Herbs, Jael. Not weeds, herbs."

"Call it what you want. Oh, not weeds, you're right. This tea was made from the bark of a willow tree. As long as it gets the job done, fine by me. I'd trust Keara to feed me a dose of poison if she said it was going to heal me. We were just rejoicing over answered prayer about the coma when the fever started. Keara made a poultice for the shoulder this morning, so we'll see how that works." She grabbed a cup of the chicken broth, towels, and a bowl of ice chipped from the block they'd carried into the springhouse after last night's party.

Before she started up the stairs, Elam took the bowl of soup from her hands and followed her. She'd just turned the bacon, and the grits would take longer to cook. He wanted to assure himself everything was okay, even though he knew his family had everything well in hand.

Jael pushed open Britte's door and slipped inside then turned to give Elam a warning glance. She mouthed the word, "Quiet."

He nodded as his gaze strayed to the bed. Susanna's skin was glowing red in the early morning light, and Keara sat on a chair beside the bed, bent at the waist, her head resting in her arms on the mattress. Her hair, tumbling in a swathe of blond next to Susanna's black tangles, contrasted so dramatically that Elam stared at the sight for a moment. Neither woman awakened.

Jael took the soup from his hands and set it on the dresser then dipped a towel in the bowl of ice water. She wrung out the towel and placed it neatly across Susanna's face. It didn't awaken the patient or Keara.

Jael looked at Elam and nodded toward the door.

He hesitated. Bacon spattered downstairs. It would burn if he didn't go down and rescue it, because Kellen would either try to turn it and toss it onto the floor or spill hot bacon grease on himself.

Elam stepped back into the hallway, and his sister followed. "I think I'll ride over to David and Pen's after breakfast," Elam said. "See if they'll keep the kids a couple more nights."

Jael sighed. "You don't want them to see Susanna."

He shook his head.

"You can't protect them forever."

"Maybe not, but we need Britte's bed. She and Rolfe love their cousins."

"And after all the excitement this week already, they could use a break before another surprise is shoved onto them," Jael said.

He nodded. "Gloria was my first thought when I saw Susanna last night on the porch."

"I know it's hard for you. Just remember that it's also hard for Keara. Not only did she see Gloria last night, but she has been treating a woman who mistrusts her and may see her as the enemy."

"Susanna will learn otherwise."

"That may take some doing. She has to be wondering why you two married so quickly."

Elam paused. His sister knew him well, but there were so many things he had not told her. He couldn't betray Keara's confidence. If Keara chose to reveal their situation, it would be her choice, not his. As for Susanna, he might need to tell her a little more, if necessary, to keep her from getting too riled and saying something that could hurt Keara.

"Susanna will soon learn to love Keara as Gloria did."

Jael's lightly arched eyebrows rose. "And as you do?"

He held her gaze and then he smiled. "Not in the same way, no."

Her grin answered his. "Very good. Why don't you let Kellen bring Cash home?"

He thought about that for a moment. "Yes, Kellen can do that. Cash won't see his mother in Susanna's eyes."

"I don't believe Britte or Rolfe will see their mother there, either, but seeing their aunt in such distress would upset them. I'm sure David and Pen will be glad to keep Britte and Rolfe. Do you want Kellen to explain the whole situation to them?"

"Susanna asked for silence."

"Susanna doesn't know your family the way you and Keara know us. She's going to have to trust us." Jael placed a firm hand on his arm. "See to the bacon before it burns, but remember that you are the man of this household. You always have been. Just because you were gentle and patient with Gloria early in your marriage does not mean you need to treat Susanna in the same manner you treated her sister. Susanna has a decidedly strong will, which may see her through this crisis, but she must not be allowed to take over and run things around here."

He chuckled. "You mean the way Gloria first tried to run things?"

"Exactly."

He rushed down the stairs to rescue the bacon. Keara and Jael weren't the only ones who remembered his early years with Gloria. His beloved, departed wife had taught him a lot about standing up to her. Susanna would learn the basics as she recovered.

* * * * *

A droplet of water spattered Keara on the cheek and she jerked awake, her eyes encountering a beam of sunlight coming straight through the window. A shadow hovered over her, and she recognized

Jael's back, the long hair only half caught up in a bun. More water splashed, and Keara straightened from the bed.

"Why did you let me sleep so long?" She stretched to get the kinks from her back.

Jael turned with a smile. "Because I slept for at least four hours while you sat in here and allowed Susanna to lecture you every time she awakened."

Keara pressed her hand against Susanna's flushed face. "The fever hasn't gone down yet. How long have I been asleep?"

"Only a couple of hours, since Susanna grew quieter."

Even as Jael spoke, the subject of their conversation opened her eyes. "Am I still running a fever?" She sounded weaker than before.

"I'm afraid so." Keara pulled the warmed towel from Susanna's face and placed it in the bowl beside the bed. "I think we'll need to bathe you more thoroughly if the fever continues to rise."

"Exactly what I would do," Susanna said.

"I have more willow bark tea I want you to drink for me."

Susanna made a face. "Is my shoulder seeping?"

"No, and I've placed a poultice on it."

"I guess it couldn't hurt then. I don't think it's helping except for the additional fluid. You could at least sweeten it with honey this time."

Keara smiled. "I will."

"But first I want to talk to Elam, and I want to be clothed when I see him. You can do your worst afterward."

Keara looked at Jael. Though Susanna sounded weaker, she was still more lucid than when they'd found her last night.

"I'll get Elam while you get your weed tea," Jael said with a teasing light in her eyes.

Keara nodded then followed her to the door. But after Jael left, Keara hesitated. She turned to look back at Susanna, lying nearly helpless in Britte's bed. The woman was beautiful despite her illness, with long hair the color of a stormy night, eyes the color of the noonday sky, face flushed with fever.

Since last night, Keara had begun to feel an uncomfortable gnawing in her belly she'd never felt before, and she hated how it affected her thoughts, made her question each action she took to help Susanna heal.

Gloria would have wanted her sister to be treated with kindness, and Keara despised herself for wishing Susanna had never come here. The children would see a lot of their mother's traits in Susanna.

Even Elam saw Gloria in Susanna's face and form. How could he not? Susanna was as near a reincarnation of her sister as they would see this side of heaven.

Susanna looked up at her. She was so helpless, unable to care for herself in even the most basic functions, and Keara was here to care for her. She was as sure of that as she was sure she'd been meant to care for her own mother, her brothers, this family. That was what God had called her to do, and it was what she would do.

A gentle hand touched Keara's arm and she looked up into Elam's tired, troubled eyes. She'd seen the sadness recover its hold over the strong lines of his face throughout the past night.

She nodded to him and left him to talk to Susanna, closing the door behind her so he could have privacy while she went to fetch and carry for their visitor.

Jael was standing at the foot of the stairs with a cup in her hands. She gave it to Keara. "I've chilled it and sweetened it with honey. She should probably swallow some as soon as possible, and as you told me earlier this morning, the more she drinks, the better the prognosis. I'll take it up to her while you take a much-needed break."

Keara hugged Jael impulsively, taking the mug from Jael as she did so. "You slept little more than I did last night. You're a blessing to me, but one doesn't want to wear out her blessings." With a tired smile at her sister-in-law, she retraced her steps up to Britte's room.

When she reached the door, it stood half open. No matter how often she told Elam that in order to lower a temperature one must keep the patient cool, Elam tended to want warmth in every room. He must have opened the door to allow the heat inside from the downstairs stoves.

Keara reached for the door to step inside, but Susanna's voice stilled her movements.

"You cannot imagine my shock when I found out last night that you'd just come from your wedding. Yours and Keara's." The voice was soft but fortified with steel.

"That's right," Elam said. "Keara is my wife now, but you are still family, and she will treat you like a sister."

"Have you forgotten my sister so quickly?"

For a moment he didn't speak, and Keara knew she should step in and interrupt.

"Gloria is always in my heart." Elam's voice grew tender and wavered, as it often did when he spoke of his lost wife. "I see her every time I look at Britte, and now, as I look at you. But she would not have forgiven me for turning my back on her best friend and leaving her homeless."

Keara winced and closed her eyes. Why was she surprised by his words? Of course she knew he still loved Gloria. He had never stopped. It was why she loved him. Of course it was, so why should she expect to hear different from him this morning?

Why did his words feel like a stab in her heart?

The kiss.

"Homeless?" Susanna asked. "I don't understand."

"There are a lot of things you don't understand." Elam had a hint of steel in his own voice now. "We will care for you here like family, and we will keep the secret of your presence here as well as we can, but most of your care will come from Keara. My wife. I would ask that you treat her with the respect she deserves."

Keara gave the door a brisk knock and stepped through. "Time for your nasty tea, Susanna. I believe we may want to bathe you again to bring the fever back down if the tea doesn't work for us."

As Elam turned to leave, he caught Keara's gaze, and in his eyes once again she could see his sorrow and longing resurge for the loss they'd endured. It was perfectly natural.

Tears stung her eyes as she watched him leave, and she blinked them away to turn and face Susanna.

"You love him." Gone was the steel in Susanna's voice. A strange combination of pity and accusation replaced it.

"Right now, we have a fever to fight," Keara said. "And I'm too tired to fight both the fever and you. You choose what you want from me, because it appears you believe I'm here at your command, mistress."

Susanna's eyes narrowed and she watched thoughtfully while Keara placed the tea on the table next to the bed and then gently helped her sit up enough to sip from the cup. She didn't say another word about the marriage, which was a relief. Last night, Keara had hoped Susanna would rouse enough to become angry. Well, it had happened. If only she would now keep her thoughts to herself.

As Keara listened to Susanna's instructions and worked to battle whatever infection had entered the woman's body, she chastised herself for being so transparent. She would be more careful in the future.

How could she have been so silly as to think one kiss could have changed Elam's heart? Just because she'd imagined more than friendship in his eyes yesterday—just because he'd told her she was beautiful—didn't mean anything had changed for her. For them. As he'd told Susanna, he was giving Keara a roof over her head.

That one kiss was the end of it, and the sooner she accepted that fact, the easier it would be for all of them.

Ten

Barely an hour after the sun rose on Wednesday, Elam sat in the wooden rocker on the front porch and held his burping son up to take a look at the orchard beside the house. Cash loved colors. As the morning sunlight dazzled the blooms of the trees and flowers Keara had planted along the rock wall, Cash gazed at the beauty with wonder.

A nicker reached them from the corral, where Duchess and Freda Mae stood with heads over the fence, waiting for Elam to come feed them. Later in the afternoon, the two new friends would probably stand head-to-backside, swatting flies from one another's faces with their tails, as they had done yesterday.

It was a good thing for Freda Mae that flies weren't as bad now as they would be when summer came; Duchess's tail had been trimmed with almost as much aggressiveness as her mane, and Elam had begun to suspect that she also had feathering along her fetlocks, which had been intentionally cut. This was definitely an unfamiliar breed.

He'd been glad of the short hair when he had to clean the caked mud from her legs and withers, but why anyone would cut away the additional beauty of the midnight dark horse was a mystery to him. Susanna, however, was still much of a mystery.

Cash burped again, and a door slammed in the house. Elam heard Keara in the kitchen, muttering under her breath.

With a sigh, he stood up and reached for the screen door as Cash gurgled with joy at the sound of his stepmother's voice, unhappy as it sounded to Elam.

"Weeds, my foot," Keara murmured. "I'm having a talk with Jael next time I see her." With a sniff and a quick glance at Cash, Keara grimaced at Elam, reached for a nappy, and tossed it to him.

He caught it, confused, then looked down at his son. How could she know about a soiled nappie when Elam hadn't even noticed it right next to him? Until he sniffed.

He placed Cash on the changing table. "Jael doesn't mean anything by the things she says about your teas." He unfastened the dirty napkin and was glad for his strong constitution. Pen and David had six children with another on the way. They were similarly strong.

"I know Jael doesn't," Keara said, "but now she seems to have Susanna convinced I'm a crazy witch doctor trying to poison her with my brews."

"My sister said that?"

"No, but Susanna thinks I've got everyone fooled around these parts. She hates me."

"She told you that?"

Keara lit a burner and heaved a huge kettle of water over the flames. "She didn't have to. I can see how she looks at me and how she sniffs at the tea every time I take her a cup, like she mistrusts me."

"But she's drinking it."

Keara stirred her small pot of willow bark tea as the steam began to rise then added honey and tasted it with a spoon. "So far."

"I think in time she'll come around. She'll see in you what everyone else sees."

Keara worried her lower lip with her tongue. "If she lives through this. Her temperature keeps going back up, no matter what I give her, in spite of the poultices I apply."

"Keara, look at me." He waited until she raised her gaze to his and read the message in his eyes—gentleness...affection. He hoped. "Your teas and poultices and loving care have worked many times in the past, and it's not even been two full days since her injuries. You've battled these things before. Stop doubting yourself."

She put the spoon down and stepped around the counter to help with Cash.

Since Susanna's arrival, the only time Elam had seen Keara smile—or even a light fill her eyes—was when she settled her gaze on Cash. Elam stepped back with the dirty nappy and allowed Keara to complete the task, not because he didn't want to do it, but because he knew Cash had a way of setting Keara's mind at ease.

Something Keara said Monday night rang true. She seemed created to care for children...for people. It was when she took care of others— even horses in the field—that the color of her eyes seemed to lighten and glow golden with satisfaction. Her whole attitude changed.

"I'm going to bring Britte and Rolfe home this afternoon." Elam spoke the decision aloud without meaning to.

It wasn't until Keara glanced up at him, eyes widened, that he realized he probably should have consulted her. More children would mean even more work for her.

"It's obviously going to take longer than a few days for Susanna to heal," he said. "We can't keep the children away for weeks on end."

"You think she'll be here that long?"

Elam didn't mention that his first thought was for her. "She needs your help, Keara." And Keara needed Britte and Rolfe. Something in her had changed and darkened since Monday, and he didn't know if it was the wedding or Susanna's arrival, but he did know that before Susanna had arrived on the front porch steps, he'd seen no darkness in his new wife. Change, maybe, but it had not been a dark change. It had been a hopeful change. For both of them.

"Children don't keep secrets well." Keara cleaned and wrapped Cash expertly. "Susanna hasn't told us anything about the shooting yet."

"Britte and Rolfe won't be going anywhere for a while now that they've had a nice long visit with their cousins, so we won't need to worry about word spreading. Don't worry, it will work out."

"But if they see her—"

"I'll warn them about what to expect."

Keara finished dressing Cash and tucked him onto her hip. She looked up at Elam, started to speak, but the sound of a horse coming toward the house at a fast trot drew her attention to the front window.

Elam saw the change in her expression as her eyes narrowed, her blond brows drew together, and Cash began to fuss.

"Whoa, Lass!" came a bold, deep voice outside as the dust flew and a red roan whinnied at the front gate.

Elam joined Keara at the window as a robust, black-haired man with full beard and well-worn work clothes slid from his mount with a growl.

"Hello the house!" Brute McBride called, his guttural roar typical of past visits.

"Pa," Keara whispered.

"Elam Jensen," Brute called from beyond the front gate. "My friend, are you here?"

At the sight of Keara's darkening expression, Elam reached for Cash just as the baby began to howl, as if Keara's mood had traveled through her skin and into his.

"Keara," Elam warned quietly, "he's your father."

The daggers she shot Elam nearly ripped a hole in him, and he stepped back.

"That's right, he's *my* father."

"But he's my father-in-law, and I will offer him hospitality in my home."

"Then I will talk to him outside of *your* home."

As she stepped to the front door and wrenched it open, Elam stood gaping after her like a landed trout, wishing he could recall his words. He'd invited Keara to make this her home. How must that have sounded to her? His home.

Cash wriggled in his arms as Keara stepped out the door. Elam had to trust poor Brute to the tender care of his angry, misused daughter.

* * * * *

At Keara's first step onto the wooden porch, her father's head came around the side of his mare. His eyes widened at the sight of her.

"So it's true?" he asked. "You're here with Elam Jensen?"

She clenched her hands at her sides and glared into his eyes as she stepped from the porch. "What would you have had me do, Pa? Join you in jail, maybe? Beg on the streets of Eureka Springs? Not a lot of money flowing there right now, with so many leaving with the extension of the railroad."

She heard the anger in her voice and knew he could hear it too. Brute McBride had always had a gentle spot for his wife and his only daughter, and he didn't bristle as he would have with anyone else. Instead, he looked abashed.

"Why are you out of jail?" Her words sounded more like an accusation than a question, though she didn't honestly intend to be so mean.

He took his old felt hat from his head and dusted it against the denim stretched tight across his thigh. He suddenly couldn't meet her gaze. "I was acquitted."

She remained on the bottom step of the porch, making no move toward him, though part of her wanted to run to him and jump into his arms. Her father's arms. She'd been so worried…

Once, those arms had been a safe place from the harshness of the world when life became too filled with burdens and cares. Now all she allowed herself to see was the man who had left her helpless and homeless because he'd thought only of himself when he drank himself into a sodden mess. He'd willingly thrown away her life as well as his own.

"How were you acquitted?" she asked, warning with her voice and her eyes that he was not to come closer.

"I plain didn't do it, Keara. I don't go around killing people. That man jumped me when he lost a game. He pulled a knife. I told you all this when you visited last. It's been over a week since I saw you."

She clenched her fists at the reproach in his voice. "How did you prove your innocence?"

"A fella and his son saw it happen. Thomas and Timothy Skerit, from down by Clifty. They could see I was only defending myself. Problem was, they didn't know I was arrested, and they've been out tending their crops. They came in Monday and heard the news."

She felt relief but refused to let him see it. Her pa was innocent. In her heart she'd known it, but hurt and anger had clouded her thinking. She took only a single step toward him. "Sheriff believed them?"

"Judge did too. Sheriff Nolan wired him. Honest truth, Keara. I'm a free man." There was jubilation in his voice as he stepped forward, arms coming out as they so often did.

She felt a burning in her eyes and she gritted her teeth. She stepped back, anger and relief warring in her belly. The anger won. "And did the sheriff also believe you were innocent of gambling the farm away?"

The words halted him midstep. A heavy sadness drew down the dark, still-handsome features of his face. "Keara."

She wanted to cry, but she'd done too much crying these past days, too much fretting and tending to a woman who had set up a haunting in the house, who haunted Elam with memories of his dead Gloria.

"Did you think of me when you went into that bar in the first place?" Keara asked Pa then winced inwardly as he winced outwardly. "Did you think of me when you went to that card game and gambled everything away, leaving us all without a home? The boys won't have a farm to come to if they ever do return here."

Pa leaned against the stone post of the gateway. Lines of weariness attested to the way he'd abused his body over the past two years of grieving. "Keara, child, I've had a lot of time to think about what I've put you through since your mother…since she was taken. All a fella has to do in that jail most of the time is think."

"It would have been nice if you'd thought long enough to warn me that I was going to be kicked from the only home I ever knew, that I'd be dependent on the kindness of neighbors to take me in." She felt her chest swell with a bout of tears that had grown familiar to her—which she'd seldom given vent to until the horrors of the past days. How could he have done this to her?

He stood watching her as if he might be standing over a coiled snake, wondering about her next move…her next words.

She raised her chin, distracted by the sound of Cash indoors, still crying. In fact, it seemed he was crying more loudly than when she'd handed him to Elam.

"I heard you married," Pa said. His voice was gentle, questioning, almost fearful.

"You can thank our good neighbor for helping me remain an honest woman while putting a roof over my head."

"That's what I came to do. I mean to thank him. And Keara, child, you have my deepest apologies. I'll make it right to the both of you. I promise you that." As if his words would pave his way, he pushed from the stone buttress and walked along the flagstone path toward her.

She would have met him halfway. She almost took another step toward him. But then she thought of Susanna, who had taken to calling down the stairs when she needed help. Not that she called often, but what if she did with Brute McBride within earshot? The woman was greatly burdened with fear, with secrets that she held too closely to her heart. Keara could not betray her.

Keara had once known her father to be a man of integrity, but now? When he was in his cups he became a different person. He could swear from here to kingdom come that he had changed his ways, but he must prove himself. She could not risk revealing Susanna's presence to a man who allowed whiskey to loosen his tongue. Even if that man were Pa. Even if he needed his daughter now.

With a tug of pain that tore at her, Keara raised her hands at him. "Don't take this so lightly, Pa. You've uprooted all we've ever worked for. You've destroyed too much. I've managed to save the animals from the farm, and because of Elam's great sacrifice, he has a right to them."

Her father's eyes closed in misery as his shoulders slumped.

"Elam has refused them," she said, her voice softer. She couldn't break him completely. She would hold him off, but despite all he'd done, she loved her father. "He has told me that when you settle in a place of your own, you may have your livestock."

The eyes opened again, and she was relieved by the renewal of hope in them.

"Elam Jensen would know, more than any man, how it feels to lose the love of his heart," Pa said.

The words bit into her. "And I know, as well as any woman, how it feels to be a pawn at the mercy of a man." She turned from him and raced back up the steps and into the house.

* * * * *

Thanks to Cash's cries, Elam could hear little of the conversation outside the front door of his house, but he saw the storm in Keara's expression when she pounded inside and thrust the door shut behind her with too much force. He saw the big frame of Brute McBride as the man climbed onto his horse and rode back the way he had come—though with less spirit and much less speed.

Keara reached for Cash, and Elam saw her tears mingle with those of his son's as she whispered calming words to him.

"You sent him away?" Elam couldn't believe it. "Keara—"

"We can't risk it," she said. "Bringing the children back home can't be helped, but we'll need to keep them away from others until we know Susanna's out of danger. My father is man enough to find his own job and make his own way."

"But he's been freed?"

Keara shushed Cash and pressed her lips to his forehead as the baby calmed. "He has."

"I knew it would happen. Your father is not a killer."

"But until the judge can prove to me that Pa is not a gambler or a loud-mouthed drunk, it won't be safe for Susanna to have him in this house."

"He has no home to go to."

"Neither did I, and through no fault of my own. The farrier in Eureka Springs, Herman Daugherty, has been asking Pa to work for him for the past two years. He knows how good Pa is. As soon as Pa gets to town you can bet that's where he'll be."

There was a rustle near the stairwell. They both glanced up to see Susanna leaning heavily against the banister at the top of the stairs. Her face was still flushed with fever, her eyes bright, her long black hair tousled around her shoulders.

"I can't keep disrupting this family," she said, her voice weak.

"What you cannot do is take a chance on falling down those stairs." Elam rushed up the steps to Susanna's side. He took her by her unhurt shoulder to help her, while Keara returned to the kitchen counter with Cash on her hip.

Elam led Susanna back to Britte's bedroom. "I know you're the doctor with the medical school education, but Keara isn't fighting fever and a battered body, and she's got a good foundation of common sense. You need to trust her and listen to her advice."

Susanna followed Elam's orders without argument, obviously realizing, as she stumbled into the room, that she had misjudged her strength.

"I'm glad you're bringing the children home," Susanna said as Elam helped her back into the bed. She laid her head back on the recently changed pillowcase and looked up at him.

The deep blue of her eyes and the shading of sunlight through the windows played tricks with his mind, and once again he saw Gloria's face, heard her voice.

He shook himself and stood back.

A quick knock at the doorway, and Keara hustled into the room, bearing a bowl of cold water, a towel, and a glass.

"Elam, Kellen is here to see to the livestock. I need time alone with Susanna." She placed the glass and bowl on the dresser and dipped the towel in the water.

Elam made his escape.

Eleven

Keara had released most of her anger by the time Elam left the house on the buckboard with Cash to collect Britte and Rolfe. Her poor father had endured a measure of her temper, but Elam had borne a bit himself, as would Susanna if Keara didn't take some deep breaths and focus on treating her patient.

"Elam's sweet new wife has a definite bite," Susanna said.

Keara frowned as she listened to the solid thump of wood on wood of the wagon when Elam rode off. It sounded as if he was going the opposite direction of David and Penelope's farm, but she shrugged it off. Too much to attend to right here in this room.

She unbuttoned Susanna's dressing gown and began to cover her chest with the cold, wet cloth. "I don't remember ever claiming to be sweet."

Susanna gasped as the cloth settled over her skin, but she didn't complain. She nodded toward the glass on the dresser. "More of your brew?"

"Cold this time. You need to cool down."

"I'm not the only one."

Keara ignored that. "Your temperature is back up, and I saw you wince when Elam accidentally touched your shoulder on the stairs. Is it becoming infected, do you think?"

Susanna closed her eyes. "Too soon to tell."

"Then perhaps the children should stay with their cousins for the rest of the week."

The eyes opened. "No."

Keara was tired of arguing. A word of thanks might be appreciated now and again. She shrugged and reached for the glass of cold tea.

"I hear a lot more from this bed than you think I do," Susanna said.

Keara didn't ask. She wasn't sure she wanted to know.

Susanna jerked her head toward the open window. "You didn't try to keep your voice down when you were chasing your father away or when you were arguing with Elam. I think I have most of the pieces in place."

Keara removed the towel and dunked it into the cold water again. "I don't see why you're concerned about my father."

"In other words, mind my own business?" Susanna gave a brief smile. "If not for my presence here, perhaps you and he could have breached a divide between you. For my safety, you sent him away."

Keara remained silent as she washed her patient's face and held the glass for her to take sips of tea. When she turned to place the cup on the dresser, Susanna took her arm and squeezed gently.

"You're a surprise."

Keara met the woman's gaze. They took each other's measure for several long seconds.

"I needed refuge." Susanna closed her eyes and bit her lip.

"And you have it. Who is chasing you across country?"

Susanna looked away as her shapely lips drew together into a tight, resistant bow.

Keara studied the finely honed lines of her patient's high cheek-bones, the darkness of her brows and lashes, the high color of her neck and face. "We drop everything to help you, and yet you won't tell us what kind of trouble you're in, why you were shot?"

"I'm afraid my husband's killer may have shot me."

Keara held her breath. "And who would that be?"

Susanna shook her head. "I shouldn't be talking about this. The more ignorant you are of what's happening, the safer you'll be."

"You truly believe that? Trouble has arrived on our doorstep, and yet we don't know when to duck, or who to duck from."

"I'm the trouble. It would be best if I weren't here at all."

"Sure, and it would be best if you hadn't been shot, if time could turn back and Nathaniel were still alive, as well, but this is not heaven we're living in yet, and we have to take things as they come. You're here, Susanna, and you'll be here for a while yet."

Susanna looked up at her. "First of all, I do not plan to be here any longer than I have to. I can heal elsewhere, and I have the means to find lodging away from family. I can hide where people will not know to search. Second of all, don't speak to me of a place that doesn't exist."

"You don't believe in heaven?"

Susanna shook her head. "If it does exist, I won't be going there, and don't try to convince me otherwise. Nathaniel learned quickly that it wasn't a good subject of conversation for me."

"Heaven wasn't for Gloria at first, either." Keara gestured for Susanna to take the rest of the tea, and she did so without argument. As Keara placed the glass on the dresser and reached for a fresh towel, she glanced over her shoulder to find Susanna watching her again.

"Nathaniel has been gone a month, and the shock of it seems to have grown in my heart, not diminished," Susanna said.

"Well, if you don't want to join him soon, I'd suggest you conserve your strength. You're not even recovered from your fever yet, and we don't know how that bump on the head is affecting you."

Susanna blinked up at her, and Keara realized she still seemed to be wearing invisible battle armor. She didn't need to be taking out her frustrations on a helpless patient.

"I know you must be reeling," she told Susanna as she sank to the side of the bed and laid a hand on her arm. "Of course you are. If Nathaniel was murdered, the horror of that must tear at your insides."

"It does, and I've had…no one to talk to about it." Susanna swallowed back apparent tears.

Keara took a deep breath and thought about what Jael would do in her place. Jael was so good with people.

"Why don't you tell me a little about Nathaniel," Keara suggested. That was what she'd encouraged Elam and the children to do over this past winter. They'd shared memories of their lost wife and mother.

"Gloria must have told you I was taken to live with my aunt June at an early age," Susanna said. "If I hadn't been, Nathaniel and I would never have met."

"Then it's a good thing you did go to live with her. I know Gloria envied you." Keara got up and stepped to the open window and relished the coolness of the spring breeze. From the windows, she could hear the horses in the corral, the chickens outside the coop, the cattle in a nearby field. Sound seemed to carry, reflecting against the rock wall that separated the yard from the orchard. No wonder

Susanna had been able to hear the arguments with Pa and Elam.

"Though I kept in touch with my sister after my marriage to Nathaniel," Susanna said, "I didn't write detailed accounts of my experiences with him. Our brothers knew hunting and fishing and how to round up a herd of half-wild hogs, but the girls learned how to sew, keep house, cook, cure meat, all the farm chores that kept us close to home. Gloria wanted the kind of life I was given. I did not. We weren't given a choice."

"She was happy here with Elam."

"And I was happy in Blackmoor, treating patients and living a quiet life."

"Yet you set out across country after Nathaniel's death."

"What would you have done in my place?" Susanna asked. "Waited for his killer to shoot you as well?"

"Why was he—"

"Nathaniel took me around the world and taught me how to survive on my own," Susanna said in a rush, obviously to prevent more questions and allow her secrets to remain unspoken. "Under Nathaniel's tutelage, I learned to outshoot pretty much any man in Blackmoor. That's why I thought I would be safe coming west by myself."

"Yet you were followed."

Susanna nodded. "I didn't use common sense when I chose to ride Duchess. I should have realized she would be a red flag."

"Second-guessing yourself isn't helpful now. We have to figure out what to do about this dilemma."

"I'll heal quickly."

"It's obvious you're trying to push yourself too hard. You could have a setback."

"I have to get out of here."

"You can't do anything on your own right now. While you're healing, our neighbors and family living in the hollow need to be prepared for any trouble that may have followed you from Pennsylvania. Telling them is the prudent thing to do."

"No."

"Folks in this hollow are good people, and they're trustworthy. You need their help."

Susanna raised a hand to silence her. "You should be glad to be rid of me."

Keara felt her temper begin to simmer once more. This was one stubborn woman. "I may not be a doctor with a degree, but I can't believe you'd expect me to shove you out of the house the way someone might shoot a lame horse. You've refused to see a doctor in town."

"I'm not convinced any of the doctors in Eureka Springs know their jobs. Otherwise, why would they have staked their reputations on plain old water from local springs?" She fixed her stare on Keara. "Water helps with a lot of things, but cancer? Women's ailments? Blindness?" She shook her head. "Craziness."

Keara decided not to add her own advertisement for the healing springs of this land. She dabbed at Susanna's neck and face once more. Her skin was still hot, her eyes over-bright from fever. She wasn't thinking clearly. Now was not the time to argue with her.

"I realize I've been a bit of a challenge for you," Susanna said, "but I misjudged you on your wedding night, and I wish to rectify that."

Keara decided to humor her patient the way she used to humor Pa when he'd had too much to drink. "How do you plan to do that?"

Susanna tugged on Keara's sleeve. "The first thing we must do is get you out of this homespun rag you call a dress and find you more appealing clothes. I do know how to sew, and I do it well. I'm sure you know how to thread a needle."

Despite her determination to remain unmoved by this woman's words, Keara felt her jaw tense. "I'm not interested in showing off—"

"You're married, and you have a husband to please. After we repair a wardrobe for you, then we will repair your hair—something you don't seem capable of managing while you spend all your time caring for me and the baby and doing chores."

"My clothes are fine."

"There's nothing I love more than a good challenge," Susanna said. "You're a tiny thing, but you've got spirit."

Keara's face felt tight. "I'm not a young filly to be judged for having all my teeth and well-curved haunches."

Susanna closed her eyes again, but she laughed, and the golden sound of her laughter warmed Keara despite her irritation. Maybe it was because Susanna sounded like her sister. Susanna could simply be reacting to the fever, but at least she still had strength enough to talk and laugh and make plans. Maybe she was strong enough to fight her way out of this.

* * * * *

Elam held Cash in his arms instead of setting him on the bumpy board at his side. The roads to Eureka Springs were often misused and rough, and he didn't want his son bouncing off the wagon before they could catch up with their quarry.

"Lord, guide my words and my steps. Give me wisdom."

He breached the rise that would take him into a deeper hollow along White River. With a quick glance over his shoulder, Elam couldn't see Keara watching him, but she might glance out a window and wonder why he was headed in the direction of Eureka Springs instead of David and Pen's. The way Brute had been riding, it appeared he was in no hurry. All Elam could hope for was that his old neighbor had bypassed the farm he'd gambled away.

Keara hadn't mentioned whether or not Brute was drinking. Elam prayed the bad patch had passed and Brute was his old self again, because if he picked a fight with the man who took his farm, he might not live long.

It took only a few more minutes before Elam found what he was looking for. Recent tracks led toward the cemetery near the little settlement of Beaver, where the McBrides had attended church when the family was together. The train crossed the river here on the bridge called the Narrows.

Mrs. McBride was buried in the church cemetery beneath a young oak tree. Elam saw Lass tied nearby and found Brute kneeling before an uncut headstone.

Brute hadn't once darkened the doors of a church after his wife's death.

For the first time since Gloria's death, Elam found himself having difficulty feeling compassion for Brute. How could he identify with a man who disregarded his faithful daughter and left her to fend for herself?

Of course, if a man could turn against the God who made and kept him, then why not disregard his daughter as well?

Still, Elam believed with his whole heart that Brute would have provided for his daughter if not for his jail sentence. How could Brute have predicted he would be blamed for protecting himself in a fight he hadn't started?

Elam pulled the wagon to a halt a distance from the graveyard. Had Keara known her father would be released from jail two days after losing the farm, would she have been so frantic to find a home for herself? Would she have married?

Elam didn't know the answer to that, but as he studied Brute's bowed head, still heavy with grief, unfamiliar emotions warred in his heart.

He didn't know what to expect from Susanna's arrival, but he knew, despite all, the wedding on Monday was right. It was supposed to happen. Faith in God's providence helped him understand that nothing happened that God could not bless. That blessing could be hidden or obvious. This time many of the blessings were obvious. Many of them Elam understood and appreciated. Many of them, he looked forward to discovering.

A butterfly landed on Cash's nose, and Cash laughed out loud. Brute looked up. He made a quick swipe at his eyes. He stood as Elam climbed from the wagon with Cash.

"I wanted to thank you for visiting me in jail," Brute said, hat in his hands.

"I knew you were at the house, but I figured you'd come inside."

Brute grimaced. "Didn't realize my girl had taken things so hard. I'll never be able to thank you for"—he spread his hands—"all you've done."

"Maybe you will."

Brute's thick, dark eyebrows shot up in surprise. "You have something in mind?"

"I guess you know my ranch has grown by several animals the past months. We've nearly doubled our number of new little ones this spring, not counting yours."

"Keara told me about your generous offer, but I won't have a place to keep anything for a long time."

"You might if you work things right."

"Not sure how. I'm on my way into town to find a job as a farrier. The trade is always in demand, what with the town so popular with visitors and sick folk looking for a cure."

"I might need a farrier before long as well," Elam said. "You're good at it. You taught Keara well."

Brute sighed. "Ah, Keara."

"She had her own reasons for turning you away, and they aren't what you think. I believe she's pretty much over her anger with you for letting that scoundrel beat you out of the farm."

Brute's eyes darkened. "Cheated, you know."

"Figured as much. Going to do anything about that?"

"Not unless I can prove it."

"Good. If you can, call on me. I'm family now."

Brute fiddled with his hat and looked away. "Takes quite a man to shoulder another man's responsibility."

"It doesn't take much of a man to realize the worth of the woman I married."

Brute looked up. Elam couldn't tell if it was hope he saw in his father-in-law's eyes, or wonder.

"She's quite a gal," Brute said softly.

Elam nodded.

"She doesn't hold a grudge for long."

"Why don't you go see Herman," Elam suggested. "You'll be a quality addition to his workforce for now, but don't make it permanent. Soon I'll need someone who can be more than a farrier."

Brute straightened. "I hear you got company."

Elam didn't allow his surprise to show. "Now, who would start a rumor like that?"

"Strange goings-on the night of your wedding, people thinkin' they saw Gloria in town that day…and that mare you're keepin', your sister and brother-in-law hanging around the house most of yesterday." He shook his head. "Never saw a horse like that before, except in books."

"Books?"

"You know, pictures and magazines. Keara always gets them when she has a chance to get to town with money in her pocket. She knows I like horses, so she's brought me books about them."

"You…know what kind of horse is with Freda Mae?"

"Could be Friesian, though it's not likely. Just looks that way to me."

Elam frowned. "Friesian. Didn't know there were any like that in these parts."

"Rare horse."

"She's not mine. I'm…keeping her for a friend."

"You got rich friends?"

Elam shrugged. "Rich people come to the Springs all the time."

Brute eyed him for a moment. "Others come to the Springs too, I hear."

Elam braced himself for more comments on their visitor.

"A fella hears a lot when he's sitting in a jail cell and the sheriff and deputies sorta trust him. I heard about the wedding from Kellen. Came to town with an engraved invitation just for me. Said he knew I probably wouldn't be able to get out for it, but I might want to keep it for a memory."

"Did you?"

"It's one of the few things I did keep."

"Where are you staying now?"

"Sheriff Nolan let me spend last night in my old bed in the cell. Figure I'll find a place soon as I land a job. If I get the farrier job, Herman has a fine shed that's warm and dry."

"Do you figure on farming again?"

"Soon as I get my farm back, I'll make a start."

"I'll help. Someday your boys may come back home."

Brute waved the comment away. "They're fine. Out working themselves to death in the California heat. Orange groves, walnut trees." He gazed around the horizon and his attention settled on Elam again. "Heard another piece of information, this one from the sheriff himself."

"You and the sheriff become friends while you were sitting in that jail?"

Brute gave a brief grin. "He's a good guy. He mentioned there's a US marshal following a killer all the way here from Pennsylvania."

"A marshal, huh?"

"That's what he said."

"Know much more about this fella?"

"The sheriff said he went rogue."

"The marshal came after a rogue?"

Brute shook his head. "The marshal *is* the rogue. Not with the force these days."

"Did you catch a name?"

"Nope, but he swore Nathaniel Luther was murdered by his own wife."

It took all Elam could do to keep breathing as Brute studied him. "My late wife didn't come from a family of killers."

Brute shook his head. "Never met the woman, of course, but no sister of Gloria's would kill her own husband. Not sure what this marshal's trying to prove, but just thought you'd be interested in some town news. As I said, strange goings-on."

"Thank you."

"A few other things I've heard kind of surprised me," Brute said. "Been a few more tourists in town than usual, men, mostly. Not taking advantage of the springs or baths, not here for any reason anyone can figure except to gather together outside the saloon on Mud Street. Been one fight already, and you know who was involved? Young Timothy Skerit, who was with his father to bear witness and get me out of jail."

Elam recalled his wedding night when he'd overheard Raylene mention a man named Skerit. "Troublemaker?"

"Not Skerit. Good boy. It's one reason the sheriff's het up about the new gang of men. Not sure what to make of it."

Elam didn't know either, but he couldn't imagine what it might have to do with his present problem. He had to collect his children.

"You know, Brute, for a man who knows so much about horses, you never built a horse ranch of your own. I always wondered why not, seeing how many horses are in demand in a town the size of Eureka Springs."

Brute grimaced. "A man with a wife who can't care for herself or her family has to do what he knows best to survive. Following dreams is a luxury. I know farming. I'm not much on the business side of things, and you have to know folks in the business."

"I'm in the business. It's growing, and I can't expect Keara to keep helping me with the ranch when she has her hands full in the house. She learned all she knows from you."Brute's gaze softened. "Thank you."

As he mounted Lass and tipped his hat to Elam, he looked like a man with hope for the first time in two years.

Elam left with a sense of urgency. He had to make sure his children were safe and that word didn't spread about Susanna's presence in their home.

Twelve

Keara was weeding the garden when she heard the wagon coming down the road. Britte's chatter echoed against the treetops after her exciting two days with her cousins. Elam's laughter blended well with his daughter's voice, and Keara smiled.

How good it would be to have the children back home. She dusted her hands against her skirt and thought, too late, about the dress Susanna had suggested she wear. But why change into another dress when this one would work just fine for the chores that would need doing later? And why listen to a woman half out of her mind with fever?

Fashion seemed to change almost as often as Keara could get to town—for those wealthy visitors who kept up with fashion. Out here in the country, nobody kept up with the latest dress styles. She remembered the time Jael and Penelope noted with great joy that the bustle that looked like a horse's backside had passed on through Eureka Springs and out the other side. But that was the exception.

Still, as Keara rushed around the side of the house, she wiped her face with her sleeve and tried to tidy her hair. She glanced down at the dirt that blended well with the brown skirt—which had no kind of bustle or corset beneath it and never would.

Britte and Rolfe tumbled from the wagon at the sight of her and raced to see who would reach her first. Britte beat her brother by a horse length and flew into Keara's arms.

"We missed you so much!"

Rolfe charged after her, nearly knocking Keara over with the second whammy. "And we have so much to tell you! Peter's cat had kittens while we were there and we got to watch, and the pigs got into the garden and Auntie Pen couldn't stop them before they got the carrots, and so she said the first pig she caught would be breakfast, and—"

"My turn," Britte said. "I got to help with the twin calves when they were born, and we got to feed them by bottle, and—"

"Auntie Pen said you had a cow with twins once and you had to share milk from another cow, and—"

Keara burst into laughter as Elam carried Cash over to join them. Britte grabbed her papa's hand and Keara's hand and placed them together. "Auntie Pen says we need to make sure you and Papa get to spend a lot of time together, Auntie Keara."

"And Peter says you shouldn't be sleeping with Britte," Rolfe said. "You should be—"

"We have a surprise for you," Elam told the kids before they could say more.

Both children fell silent, eyes wide, while Keara struggled to keep the sudden heat from her face. She released Elam's hand, though he seemed to let her go with reluctance.

"We have company." The laughter gradually eased from Elam's face. "Britte, she's staying in your room right now, and she's sick, so you and Rolfe will have to bunk together for a few days."

Britte and Rolfe grew still at last.

"Who is she, Papa?" Rolfe asked.

Elam looked at Keara, who reached for a squirming, fussing Cash.

"She's your aunt from back East," Elam said. "You've never met her because she's lived so far away."

"Which one?" Britte asked. "Ma said she has a lot of sisters. There's Auntie Matilda and Auntie Gretchen and—"

"Auntie Susanna was your ma's baby sister," Elam said.

"The doctor?" Britte's eyes grew wide.

"That's right, and she looks a lot like your ma," Keara said.

"Can we see her now?" Rolfe asked, looking toward the house.

Keara glanced at Elam, and his dark brown eyes reflected her own concern.

"Her fever's dropped some the past hour," Keara told him. She nodded to the children. "I know she's been hoping to meet you." And with the lowered temperature, perhaps she would be more lucid.

As if catching the air of gravity in their father and Keara, Britte and Rolfe walked side by side in silence up the stairs. Elam took Cash into his arms again as Keara knocked on the door and checked to make sure Susanna was alert and presentable.

She was lying with her hands folded over her chest, face still flushed, but not as much as before. She nodded to Keara. "Bring them in."

She glanced toward the door eagerly, almost hungrily, and her gaze lit on Britte, the first into the room. Her lips parted, and she caught her breath quietly.

"Oh, Britte, I've heard so much about you. How you look like..." Susanna glanced at Keara, as if for direction.

"She looks like her mother," Keara said. "Isn't she beautiful?"

Susanna's already bright eyes glistened with additional moisture as she turned her attention to Rolfe. "And you are the image of your father."

Britte stepped closer. "Auntie Keara said you look like Ma, but you don't."

Susanna blinked. "I don't?"

Britte shook her head. So did Rolfe.

Something appeared to ease in Susanna's expression. She, too, had obviously been concerned that seeing her would bring back to the children the heartbreak of their loss.

She aimed a charming grin at Elam and reached up to place her hand on Cash's head. "Every fiber of a mother's appearance is etched in her children's hearts. We had nothing to fear."

"You're sick?" Rolfe asked, glancing at the medical and herbal supplies on the dresser.

"Yes, and your auntie Keara is helping me get well."

"And speaking of that," Elam said, "it's time we left you alone so you can get well more quickly."

Rolfe stepped to the side of Susanna's bed and gently touched her hand. "You'll get well. I know you will. Auntie Keara can doctor anybody."

As the children and Elam left the room, a fresh breeze blew through the open window, and Susanna shivered.

Concerned by the moisture in her eyes, Keara reached down and touched her forehead. "Are you feeling worse?"

"Rolfe says I'll be well soon." Susanna quickly dashed a stray droplet from her face, staring at the closed door as if she could still see the little boy.

Keara poured another cold glass of tea from the pitcher. "I'll check your temperature, then you can drink this."

Susanna closed her eyes. "Interesting, isn't it, how our emotions have more sway when we're feeling physically weak. I was just trying to imagine what my children may have looked like had I given birth."

Keara reached for the thermometer. "There will be time."

Susanna held her hand up. "Did my sister tell you how old I was when Nathaniel and I married?"

"Eighteen."

"It's been ten years. You don't think I'd have had children by now?"

Keara held the thermometer in her hand but didn't attempt to put it in Susanna's mouth. "I dreamt of becoming a mother since I was ten years old, but I realized when I was a teenager that I would probably never marry. I had too many responsibilities, and I didn't have time to meet beaus."

"And yet here you are, with a husband and three children." There was a hint of resentment in Susanna's expression, and in her voice.

Again, Keara reminded herself to be gentle with her patient. But she was growing tired of the woman's tendency to set her up and then undercut her with a few sharp words. She left the room for a break, tired of arguing, tired of worrying, tired of her own quickly changing emotions.

* * * * *

Elam left Britte and Rolfe in charge of Cash so he could unhitch the wagon and turn Elijah into the corral. Freda Mae rushed to nuzzle the big draft horse's nose, while Duchess neighed at the house, as she'd done often since arriving with her mistress on Monday.

Recalling his conversation with Brute, Elam studied the regal mare. Though this ranch was far from the beaten path to town, and a stand of trees and a rise between the farm and the water totally concealed the presence of the house and barn, neighbors still visited on occasion, and there was traffic along White River every day. Strangers occasionally put to shore to explore, and once or twice someone had wandered through the woods the quarter mile to the house.

One never knew what to expect from the river.

Brute had been quick to notice Duchess when he rode up to the house; others were sure to do the same.

With reluctance, Elam whistled to Duchess, and the great black mare responded instantly to his command. She'd been well-trained, as Susanna had informed him more than once when she was alert enough to converse. Nathaniel himself had been the mare's trainer.

When she reached Elam, he smoothed his fingers over her velvet lips and turned to walk toward the barn. She followed closely, having learned to expect a handful of oats and molasses. He'd thought no one would consider Raylene Harper's claim about seeing Duchess on Monday night, but he no longer felt comfortable leaving the unique mare in full view of anyone who wandered near.

Richard Brown had obviously seen Susanna on Duchess in town on Monday, and as Brute said, word got around. Whoever shot Susanna would undoubtedly recognize her mount.

Duchess would hate being confined to a stall in the barn, but Elam knew he'd left her outside for far too long. He shouldn't have turned her out with Freda Mae.

Though Susanna had sworn she'd not ridden the main streets of

Eureka Springs, she had ridden along Dairy Hollow. Anyone could have seen her. What if her attacker had followed her from town?

Once Elam had Duchess settled comfortably munching in her stall, he gave Elijah and Freda Mae their own servings and brushed Elijah down.

He glanced toward the house again. Since Gloria's death, he'd begun to dream in color—the blue of her eyes, the flush of her cheeks, the iridescent lights of her black hair. All winter, she'd haunted him in his sleep, sometimes with her smiling face, sometimes with horrible visions of her final days of life. He still recalled vividly the night early this spring when she'd visited him one final time. This time in the dream, when she turned to leave him as she always did, he'd reached for her, held her, unwilling to let her go.

There in his arms, her face had distorted, melted, until only her skull stared back at him, as if she'd just come to him from the grave that very night. He'd jerked awake, drenched with sweat, and tossed off the quilt. He hadn't slept the rest of the night. After that, however, he'd recalled no more dreams, not of Gloria, not of anyone. Until now.

Since Susanna's arrival, Elam had begun to sleep, once more, with his dead wife. During his waking hours, he'd kept busy, comforted by Keara's presence in his home, but these past two nights, with Susanna fighting for her life down the hallway, he couldn't stop thinking about Gloria. And dreaming.

If only a man didn't need sleep to stay alive.

* * * * *

After checking Susanna's temperature and finding it down by almost a degree, Keara placed more cold cloths on her patient's face and chest, gave her more tea. She hesitated at the side of the bed then turned to leave. What was there to say? She was so tired of arguing with the headstrong woman after two nights of fitful sleep.

"Wait."

Keara stopped at the door, gave herself a moment to put on a pleasant face, and turned back, but instead of looking at Susanna, she allowed her attention to be drawn to something outside the window.

"I can be a handful," Susanna said.

Keara nodded as a dark splotch on the horizon became horses, nearly half a mile away as the crow flew—though farther for the horses, as the dips and forests interfered with any kind of straight path. Two horses with riders. Looked like they might be following the same general direction as the river.

"Yes, I know," Susanna continued when Keara said nothing. "Nathaniel told me that often enough. Runs in the family, I suppose. Gloria had…her ways."

At the sound of her friend's name, Keara looked at Susanna. "She did, yes. Especially early on, after she and Elam moved to this ranch."

"I'm sure she didn't fit in."

Keara couldn't resist a smile as she recalled her best friend's outspokenness, her rebellion against what she called the "commonplace" lives of people in the valley.

"When did Elam have this house built for her?" Susanna asked. "I imagine that's when she settled a little."

"Elam didn't have it built, he and the neighbors built it. She worked as hard as anyone."

"She was never afraid to work for what she wanted."

"They built this house five years ago, after Gloria had all but given up her dream of having a fine home like the ones in Eureka Springs."

"That's about the time the tone of her letters changed."

"She changed," Keara said. "Her tongue grew less sharp, and she learned to place the needs of others ahead of her own."

"She hated farm life when we were growing up."

"She loved Elam, and her priorities changed." Keara remembered when it began.

"That was quite a change," Susanna said.

"Gloria painted most of the house herself. She chose the colors. Every time I walked or rode up to the house, I was reminded of Gloria by the colors she chose."

Susanna chuckled. "I saw the colors and the gingerbread trim just before I fell off Duchess Monday night. I'd like to have seen Gloria with paint in her hair."

"God made the change in her." Keara glanced again out the open window. The riders were in no hurry, it seemed, but they'd drawn close enough for her to see that one sat slumped low in the saddle. "We've got a lot of devoted Christians in these parts, and it took a few years, but she was impressed by the kindness of her neighbors—"

"And, most likely, their patience with her. Our father always did say Gloria was the most headstrong child he'd raised. Gloria wanted to go to Aunt June's when I did, and she threw a fit when she had to stay on the farm. She always wanted to live a life of refinement, with a proper home and well-educated children."

"She wanted more for her children than what she believed they could have here, but she came to realize that a relationship with God was more important than a fine home for her family," Keara said.

Susanna frowned at her. "Did you have anything to do with that?"

"No, not me. I think her good marriage to Elam drew her to God."

"And it took." There was a sound of wonder in Susanna's voice.

"You know your sister was serving those who had been stricken with smallpox when she was taken."

Susanna closed her eyes. "I've done that myself. I've put myself in harm's way for patients, but I didn't have children."

"You mean you would have stopped being a doctor if you'd had children? After all that training?"

"And risk the lives of my own flesh and blood?"

Keara stepped to the window, and her disquiet grew when the flap on the jacket on the rider on the right showed a shaped object that glinted in the sunlight. A badge?

"She had a home and family," Susanna continued. "Children who needed her, a wonderful husband who loved her enough to build her the house of her dreams. A colorful, elegant Victorian, of all things."

"In the end, the house never mattered," Keara said. "Not really." Outside, the breeze kicked up, and dust from the road rose like smoke around the riders—both men.

Something wasn't right. This felt off. Keara looked at Susanna, who had taken the cloths and rearranged them, cool side to her skin.

"We have visitors."

Susanna looked up at her. "Your father again?"

"Looks like the law, but not anyone I know."

Susanna tensed, tried to sit up, groaned. "Where's Duchess? Get her into the barn."

Keara eased her back down. "I will. I think Elam's out with the horses."

"Go. Now. Hide her. Close the window and pull the curtains. Close the door. Please, Keara, hurry!"

Thirteen

The familiar thud of horse hooves on grass drew Elam's attention to the track past the orchard wall. He saw two men, one slumped in his saddle, with handcuffs clanking softly. The taller man, sitting straight, wore a brown, broad-brimmed hat and a long, tanned-hide coat with a US marshal badge prominently displayed on his chest. Dust covered both men.

This was not a social call. This was an officer of the law and his prisoner. A glance at the prisoner's left thigh told Elam the man had been wounded midway between knee and groin, possibly with a bullet or knife, and a stained rag of sorts had been tied around it to stop the bleeding.

Elam's first thought was for Keara. Word had spread about her abilities in these parts. She'd had the occasional visitor when she lived on her family farm, because it was a long ride to Eureka Springs when a patient was sick or in a lot of pain.

His second thought was of Susanna, and then Duchess, and his conversation with Brute. Was it only coincidence that Brute had warned him about Susanna's pursuer? Or maybe not a coincidence at all, but a nudge from God.

He dusted off his hands and stepped through the open barn door. He usually left it open, but this time he turned and closed it behind him as if this were habit. He eyed the prisoner. Young man, looked to be in his early twenties, face as gray as a graveyard tombstone.

Next, he eyed the man's captor. As they drew closer, Elam stood a little straighter. He knew what the badge represented, but he could almost hear Brute's voice in his ear, reminding him of a rogue marshal.

A US marshal was required to be tough, spend long hours in the saddle, and hold to a high moral standard. Those few Elam had met would fit that definition. For all he knew, this one did as well. Right now, though, strangers of any stripe made him wary.

"Afternoon." Elam nodded to the man with the badge.

The marshal nodded and eased from his horse as if he'd been riding a distance. "Elam Jensen?"

Elam's wariness felt like a knot getting tighter in his chest. "That's right."

"US Marshal Driscoll Frey. Got a wounded prisoner." He gestured to the rider slumped in the saddle. "Heard from along the river apiece that you have a doctor here." The man had a voice that sounded as if he'd choked on too much dust over the years. He had a straight, silver-eyed gaze that seemed to look past Elam's eyes and into the thoughts behind them.

That gaze spooked Elam, and he couldn't decide if it was the need to hide Susanna's presence or the inflection of the man's words.

Whatever it was, Elam held the gaze without wavering. "You heard wrong about my wife. She isn't a doctor, merely good with herbs and teas, roots, and plenty of prayer. She's pulled a few bad teeth in her life, as did her mother before her, but little more." He jerked his head toward the prisoner in the saddle. "You'll find what he needs in Eureka Springs. Lots of doctors there."

The marshal turned to look at the younger man, and for the first time Elam noticed that the marshal's hair was long, tied back with a piece of rawhide, and red as bonfire embers glowing in the dark.

"Too bad for my prisoner we're not headed that direction," the marshal said. "We don't have time for a dunk or a drink of the healing waters."

"Only five miles east of here, not a hard ride. Medical doctors there, with real medicines and utensils."

The marshal shook his head. "Man accused of murder in three states? Not one to allow near a populated city."

"And yet you'd risk my wife and family?" Elam swallowed, trying to judge how far he could push this. "Already stood trial, has he?"

"About to."

"Then he's still an innocent man."

The marshal held Elam in the steel of his stare.

Elam returned it. "I've never met a US marshal given to vigilante justice."

"You know a lot of us?"

"I've met a few, yes."

The prisoner raised his head for the first time. He looked at Elam, eyes imploring.

The screen door of the house slapped shut, and Elam's jaw clenched when he saw Keara stepping from the porch, hand shading her eyes from the glare of the sun. Something in the way she moved—something only those who knew her well would notice—betrayed tension.

She met his gaze then quickly looked away, ignoring the caution she must have read in his eyes.

"I thought I heard horses out here." She gave a broad, visitor-welcoming grin that showed nearly every one of her small, white teeth. "Care to rest a spell? Refreshment?" She glanced at the prisoner, then at the bloody wrap around his thigh, and her grin died. "You folks need help?"

The marshal raised his red eyebrows, gave Elam a narrow look, then removed his hat and nodded to Keara. "Ma'am, I'd be obliged."

"What did that to your leg, stranger?" Keara stepped toward the prisoner as if it were a natural thing for her. And it was. Keara feared no one.

The young man gave her a quick glance then looked at Frey. "Lead."

His horse shied, and Keara calmed him then reached up and gently unwrapped the rag from the thigh, ignoring the handcuffs. "Deep?"

"Can't tell if it hit bone," the prisoner said.

Keara turned back to the marshal. "You know there are doctors who handle these kinds of things in Eureka—"

Frey held his hand up. "I've been over this with your husband. I'm taking this man to Missouri for what will most likely be an execution. Be nice for him to be in good shape for the show, but that's not my concern."

Elam could see Keara's mouth twitch at the crude declaration.

"We're shorthanded in law enforcement lately," Frey continued, "what with the growing population. I just came by out of good will—"

"Bring him into the house," Keara said, turning away. "I've already got water on to boil, I'll see to him in the kitchen."

Elam was the only one who saw the darkening of her eyes and the grim set of her mouth. He thought again of Susanna, of the bloodstains on the front porch steps that had been washed nearly clean by the elbow grease from Jael and Keara. Why couldn't he shake the idea that this visit brought trouble with it?

* * * * *

Keara stepped hard on the stains in the porch wood with her dust-covered shoes, hoping the faint outlines would be covered by the loose powder of her tracks. Britte and Rolfe were playing in the front room with Cash, and Keara gathered them together.

"Britte, I need you and Rolfe to take Cash out to the far side of the orchard to play. Keep a close watch for snakes, of course, but I don't want you to come back in until I come get you. Can you do that for me?"

Instead of the questions she could always expect from Britte, and usually Rolfe as well, this time they must have felt her tension. Britte picked up Cash, and then she and Rolfe went quietly to the back door.

Britte turned and gave Keara a wide grin. "Auntie Pen said there would be times like this. Don't worry, we'll stay far from the house."

Rolfe nodded. "Just like Auntie Pen said to."

For once, Keara blessed her sister-in-law for her interfering ways as she rushed upstairs to Susanna's sickroom. Susanna sat nearly upright, clutching the blankets across her chest as if they would protect her. It was exactly the way she'd been when Keara left the room.

"What's he look like?" she whispered.

"Which one? There was a prisoner in handcuffs, who didn't look old enough to shave, but I—"

Susanna gasped. "So there was a lawman?"

"Badge of a US marshal."

"What does he look like?"

"Tall. Long hair tied back, gruff, rude to his prisoner, talking about his execution." She refrained from speaking her thoughts more completely.

"Was his hair red?"

Keara tried to remember. She hadn't noticed. All she'd seen was the fear in the young prisoner's eyes. "I believe he had reddish-orange eyebrows."

The color in Susanna's face drained away. "I have to hide."

"We'll keep him away from you." Keara dropped to her knees beside the bed. "Do you think he's the man who shot you?" she whispered, listening for the sound of the door and for footsteps downstairs. Nothing yet. She couldn't look out the window and see from this angle, and even if she could, she didn't want to draw the marshal's attention upstairs.

Susanna took a deep, quivering breath. She studied Keara's face as the lowing of cattle and the neigh of a horse reached them through the closed window. "If this is who I think it is," Susanna said at last, "he's followed me from Blackmoor to shoot me."

The words hit Keara with a jolt of shock, though with Susanna she'd thought she'd learned not to be surprised. "Why?"

Susanna closed her eyes. "I'm so sorry I got you all involved."

"Nonsense. You came here for help, and that's only right."

"I hadn't realized he was so close behind me. I never dreamed I'd be followed here."

"Why is a US marshal after you?"

Susanna began to tremble. "We'll talk about it, just not now. You need to do whatever he says so you won't raise any suspicion."

Keara reached up to feel her patient's forehead. Her temperature was down.

Another horse neighed out in the corral. Susanna looked at Keara. "Tell me Duchess isn't in sight."

"She isn't, but the marshal expects me to remove a bullet from his prisoner's leg. You've got to tell me what to do." Keara explained what she could about the prisoner's wound.

There was a sound from downstairs.

"Use the hemostats," Susanna whispered. "Whiskey, just like you did on me."

"You were unconscious when I removed your bullet. I don't know if I can—"

"I don't have anything else for you to use."

Keara closed her eyes and prayed then took two deep breaths, reached into the top drawer for the utensil she'd used to remove Susanna's bullet, and turned back to Susanna.

"If you've ever considered prayer, now would be a good time to try it."

Susanna nodded and laid her head back against the pillow, her skin as pale as it had been the first night she arrived.

* * * * *

Elam had never been as proud of Keara as when he watched her move around the kitchen, looking calm and purposeful. He'd received a new keg of whiskey from Carl Lindstrom as a wedding gift—along with a great deal of razzing about his new bride. He fetched the keg from the top cupboard to apply not only to the wound, but also to pour down the prisoner's throat to stave off some of the pain.

The marshal had dusted off his clothing outside on the porch, removed his hat, and sat on the sofa at the far end of the room when invited.

Elam studied the young prisoner as Keara worked around him. He was slender, with light brown hair, blue eyes, kind of a baby face. His forehead was dotted with droplets of sweat, and his jaw was clenched in an obvious attempt to not give away his fear or pain.

"I don't believe I've seen you in these parts before," Keara said to him. "You from around here?"

"Don't get to Eureka Springs much. Come from Clifty."

"Nobody mentioned your name," she said gently.

"Tim." He leaned forward then winced and stiffened. "Timothy Skerit. My father is Thomas."

Keara's movements stilled. "Well, sorry we had to meet like this, Timothy," she said. "I'll do all I can not to hurt you, but you know we've got to pull the lead from your leg."

He nodded.

She looked up at Elam. "I could use a cup of that whiskey, and then would you please bring a pitcher of water?"

When Elam returned from the springhouse with the water, Timothy was choking, with tears running down his face as Keara held a cup to his lips.

"I know it tastes bad, but it will help," she said.

Elam took over for her. "Sassafras and whiskey?"

She nodded and grinned up at him then went to work preparing utensils, homemade ointment, and boiled towels for bandaging.

The marshal continued to sit at the far end of the long great room, taking it all in. Keara had apparently given him a glass of sassafras tea, and he sipped at it while keeping a close eye on his prisoner.

Elam caught sight of his children playing out in the orchard, and he knew without asking that Keara had sent them from the house. Bless her for her wisdom.

Ordinarily, Elam would have already invited their visitors to have dinner with them and spend the night. Though it wasn't too late in the afternoon for the men to ride to Seligman, Missouri, someone with a gunshot wound would need rest. Even the marshal looked weary. Elam, however, couldn't possibly offer them lodging. He needed them to get on down the road in a hurry.

"Not much of an imbiber?" Elam handed Timothy a cup of water fresh from the spring.

Timothy shook his head, thanked Elam, and gulped the water as if to get the taste of the alcohol off his tongue.

Elam reassessed his judgment of the young man's age. He was younger than Delmar, possibly younger than Raylene Harper, who had seen him in Eureka Springs on Monday. He had the calluses and muscles of a hardworking farmer, and he didn't look old enough to have been to three states on a killing spree. Elam couldn't help wondering about the fight Brute had mentioned. Maybe Raylene would have more information about him.

"Where are your parents?" Elam asked the kid softly.

"Probably home, wondering where I am by now." Timothy glanced toward the marshal then back at Elam. "Everyone in Clifty knows Thomas and Miriam Skerit, and half the town's probably already out looking for me. If I don't come back through here, would you get word to them?" Fear shook the boy's voice.

"I will. We've got to get you treated." Elam mixed more whiskey with tea and honey and handed it to the boy. "Drink a little more to help with the pain."

The sofa squeaked, and Elam turned to see the marshal straightening, stretching, gazing out the window toward the orchard to the left of the house.

"Those your kids?"

"They are." Elam tensed as the man studied Britte, Rolfe, and Cash, and now he wished he'd left them with David and Penelope for the rest of the week—or until Susanna had healed and was able to travel.

The marshal turned and caught Elam's gaze. "Got any other family here?"

"Water's boiling, Elam," Keara said as she took the empty cup from Timothy's hand. "Would you help me?"

"I'd be glad to help," Frey said.

"Thank you, Marshal," Keara said, as if he'd just offered to do her a great favor. She dipped the hemostats into the boiling water. "You have experience working with gunshot wounds?"

"I've seen a few."

"Elam and I have worked together on a few injuries in the past. He can practically read my mind."

"Get a lot of patients out this way?" Frey asked.

"Yep, we do." Elam cleared the dining room table. "Just not a lot of humans. Most of our patients are horses."

"I'm not a horse," Timothy's words slurred.

"Don't worry," Elam said as he helped the kid from his chair. "We know better. We don't usually numb our horses with our best whiskey." He helped Timothy lie down on the sturdy dining room table, where just a couple of nights ago the ladies had argued over the best way to remove blood from Keara's wedding dress. "I know it's a hard bed, but it's got the best light."

"I've slept on the ground a lot of times." The young man's eyes had grown blurry, a good sign he'd have a hangover later.

Elam turned around to find that Frey had stepped closer, arms crossed over his chest, as if he were sitting in the front row before a stage.

"I'll just be here if you need me," Frey said.

"We don't usually perform in front of an audience, Marshal." Elam couldn't quite keep the sharpness from his voice. "Unless it's a couple of stock horses."

"Actually, we may need the help." Keara smiled up at the marshal. Not once had she even glanced in the direction of the stairs, though Elam knew she must be terrified for Susanna. Of the two of them, Elam was well aware she was better at acting.

"Sweetheart, do you need more towels?" Elam asked her.

If his words of endearment startled her, she didn't show it. "Thank you, honey, I may need them. I have no idea what to expect when I go digging…" She stopped herself and glanced at the patient, whose eyes had closed and who had a dribble of drool trickling down the edge of his mouth.

"I'd be glad to help fetch and carry," Frey said.

Elam eyed the man. Did he think a grown man would have trouble carrying a simple bundle of towels all by himself? Or did he want a guided tour of their house?

"I appreciate the offer, but since you've had all that experience removing bullets," Elam said, "then we'll need you to assist down here."

Frey nodded at the hemostats. "Glad you're so prepared, Mrs. Jensen. Where'd you get those tools?"

"Why, Marshal, these can be ordered from any mercantile in town. We have to be prepared for anything, this far out."

Elam listened to his wife's calm voice as he rushed up the stairs, and he offered up a silent, heartfelt prayer of thanks for her presence in this house. In his life. And then he begged God to keep her hands and voice steady in the moments ahead.

Fourteen

Keara stared at the oozing wound in the center of Timothy's left thigh and kept her expression calm as she listened for Elam's returning footsteps. Why was he taking so long? She needed him down here to distract the marshal, keep him from hovering so close. Frey was going to realize any second that she barely knew how to hold this awkward, scissor-like contraption the right way, though it looked well-used.

"Marshal, would you mind scrubbing your hands over at the basin? I'm going to need help keeping him still."

He nodded and did as he was asked without argument. US Marshal Frey was a big man, almost as big as Elam, probably a little older, in his midthirties, skin leathered and heavily freckled. He obviously spent a lot of time in the sun. Keara had been startled by the bright red of his hair when he took his hat off upon entering the house.

How many US marshals had hair this long, this color? Susanna believed this was the man who had shot her. Keara couldn't help wondering what he was up to and what Timothy Skerit had to do with it, but of course, she couldn't ask questions and give the marshal an opportunity to start asking more questions of his own. He'd asked enough already.

Keara doused a towel with whiskey and cleaned Timothy's wound as deeply as she could, controlling her own reaction when he groaned with pain. She saw no sign of lead anywhere near the surface. When Frey handed her more towels and stepped across the table from her, she willed her hands not to tremble. She'd removed bullets before. Susanna had been her first human.

She'd pulled plenty of teeth, however, and they were harder to pull than a bullet that wasn't rooted into the bone.

Blood didn't bother Keara. She was never the squeamish sort. But causing pain? That bothered her a lot. She reminded herself that if she didn't get the lead from Timothy's leg, he would be in much more pain later.

"I don't suppose you've had any strangers through here lately," Frey asked.

Keara stopped trickling whiskey on Timothy's skin and looked up at the marshal. "We had a whole farm full of friends and strangers and family here on Monday night after Elam and I got married. Are you married, Marshal?"

He frowned, shook his head.

"That's a shame. Every woman in the world would be happier with a strong man to come home to her at night." She nipped at her tongue, sure that Jael and Pen would laugh until their sides ached if they heard her using "feminine wiles" in this manner. "I guess you wouldn't get home much though. I think I read US marshals travel a lot."

"They do."

"Well, let me warn you," she said, hoping the smile she pasted on her face wasn't crooked, "if you ever decide to marry, just go to the justice of the peace and get it done without any fancy wedding or hullabaloo. A chivaree may be fun for everyone else, but it's not the kind of party a bride and groom want on their wedding night."

"Was there a brawl out on the front porch that night? I noticed what looked like well-scrubbed blood stains on the steps."

She didn't hesitate. "Only brawl that night was between human flesh and those steps," Keara said. "Bloodied my own mother's wedding dress—the one I wore for the wedding? I was sure glad to have the ladies here then, much as I complain about the chivaree. They got the stain out with nary a blemish. It would've broken my heart if I'd ruined that dress. Someday I hope Britte will wear it for her wedding."

Keara hadn't talked this fast since the day she hiked to this place to convince Elam to marry her. She felt breathless, and when she heard Elam's footsteps coming down the stairwell, she went weak. But she couldn't let down her guard.

She reached forward and touched Timothy on the cheek. He swallowed and muttered incoherently. Good. Maybe this wouldn't be so bad after all.

"Where do you live, Marshal?" Keara asked.

"Philadelphia."

"My goodness, you are a long way from home."

"We go where we're told."

Elam set the towels down on the corner of the table and stepped around to put his arm over Keara's shoulders, like any happy newly-wed husband.

She looked up at him and felt the deep tremors in her belly begin to still as she allowed the assurance in his dark brown eyes, and the touch of his arm, to flow through her.

"You know, Mrs. Jensen," the marshal said, "for someone without a medical degree, you're handling this situation well."

"I haven't gotten the bullet out yet," she reminded him.

And so she began. With Elam holding Timothy's legs down and Frey holding the strong shoulders, Keara prayed as she cleared away blood and plunged and explored, glad for the sunlight shining through the kitchen window. She couldn't very well ask to retrieve Kellen's battery light that she used the night she removed Susanna's bullet.

Timothy muttered in his semi-consciousness. "You got the wrong guy." His eyes opened and he looked up into Frey's face. "Why are you doing this? Why'd you take me from home?"

"This is for your own good, son."

"Arresting me?"

Frey looked up at Elam. "More whiskey?"

"He's already going to have a nasty hangover from what he's had."

"He barely drank half a glass."

"It doesn't appear he ever tasted the stuff before today. Can't have him getting sick." Elam's words had become clipped once more, and Keara could feel his temper rising again. She cast him a warning glance. A strong sense of justice had always run through him. Elam obviously believed Timothy was being blamed for crimes he didn't commit.

"I can send a jar of tea and whiskey with you, Marshal," Keara said. "And more tea to brew if need be. But if he starts to bleed, you can't give him much of the tea, because it'll make the blood flow more freely. You can use the whiskey to clean the wound."

Frey nodded. "Thank you."

"If you were going to shoot a man in the chase," Elam said under his breath, "the least you could have done was get him to a regular doctor."

"I did not shoot this man," Frey snapped. "There was no chase.

Maybe you should stop jumping to conclusions and get the facts before you start laying the blame at my feet."

"Then who shot him?"

Frey took a deep breath, let it out, and slanted a glance at his prisoner. "Why don't you ask him?"

"My li'l brother," Timothy muttered. "Not hish...not his fault. We were huntin' rabbits. He tripped...gun went off."

"I hope his little brother didn't see you slap the handcuffs on him and haul him—"

"Where in Missouri are you taking him?" Keara asked, shooting a hard look at Elam.

Frey sighed. "You sure do ask a lot of questions."

Keara forced a fresh smile. "You don't know much about women, do you, Marshal Frey? We can be a curious bunch." She gave Elam a quick frown. "Not polite to argue with the law, honey." And certainly not smart.

Timothy's eyes closed about the same time Keara saw the black lump of lead in his flesh. She glanced up at Elam, said a silent prayer for help, and reached for the hemostats.

Perspiration dripped down her neck as she paused and took a deep breath. "Marshal, why don't you give us a little rundown, distract our patient while I work?" she suggested quietly.

Frey nodded, and so while he himself was distracted, explaining his reasons for not stopping in Eureka Springs—the gang of outlaws Timothy ran with were heard to be in town...Timothy's little brother believed the marshal was taking Timothy to have his gunshot wound treated...the little brother had been assured he hadn't killed his older brother—Keara managed to reach into the wound with the hemostats and pull out the bullet with no more than a grunt from her patient.

She held the red-coated slug into the light. It looked like a .22 bullet, not the same size as the one she'd taken from Susanna's shoulder. It seemed young Timothy and the marshal told the truth about that. It made her feel better.

She placed the slug on a bloody towel and looked up at Elam.

He nodded. "That's my wife." The anger had left his voice, and in its place she heard admiration that warmed her all the way to her bloodstained fingertips.

"Marshal Frey, the bullet wasn't as deep as I'd expected," Keara said. "It just took a little turn after it hit flesh. You might not want to ride farther than Seligman tonight. They have a very nice inn there."

The marshal studied the wound and the bullet. "I think that's a good idea. Don't worry, I have to get him to Cassville to stand trial in two days, but there'll be doctors there."

Relieved that the marshal hadn't asked to lodge at their house, Keara set about treating the wound and packing it with whiskey-soaked gauze.

"His pants are ruined," Elam said, pointing to the bloodstained material that had been clipped away by Keara's scissors. "I believe I have a pair that will fit him."

At Frey's nod, Elam went back up the stairs.

Timothy began to snore, his mouth open, the smell of whiskey strong on his breath.

Frey chuckled. "He'll be out for a while if we don't do something. Got any coffee? He'll need to be alert enough to ride."

"I'll brew a pot as soon as I'm finished here."

"I know how to brew coffee, Mrs. Jensen." The marshal's voice was surprisingly quiet, almost gentle. "Tell me where things are and I'll do that."

She blinked at him. She didn't much like the man pawing through her kitchen cabinets, so she told him exactly where the coffeepot was. She watched as he worked to make sure he didn't do any snooping. After emptying Susanna's saddlebags of the few supplies she'd brought with her, Keara had placed them in the back pantry. Too close to the kitchen for comfort right now.

"I have ham and dried fruit out in the springhouse," she told the marshal as she wrapped Timothy's wound with a fresh cloth and tightened it just enough so the leg wouldn't start bleeding again. "If you'd like a meal before you go—"

"I'll take some along for the both of us. It'll break the monotony of biscuits and hardtack. Thank you."

Elam came back down the stairs with a pair of work pants that looked too long for Timothy, but they could be rolled up. As Keara busied herself preparing food and jars of whiskey and tea, Elam and Frey changed the patient's clothes.

"Looks like you've got your hands full, Marshal," Elam said. "I think I'll saddle up and ride with you a ways, make sure Timothy's going to travel well."

Frey looked surprised. He held Elam's gaze for a moment. "You intend to see me safely out of your territory?"

"I aim to see you safely around fallen trees on the trail, past sinkholes that could break a horse's leg if you're not careful."

Frey hesitated a moment more before he nodded. "Well then, you'd be welcome to ride with us."

After Elam stepped out to see to the horses, Frey helped Keara pack the foodstuffs in a saddlebag, cooling the coffee with cold spring water and bracing his prisoner up to sip it.

"You really think he's killed people in three states?" Keara asked.

"It doesn't matter what I think, ma'am."

"But you said—"

"The day you and your husband got married, did any of your visitors ride a black horse to your party?"

Keara halted halfway through wrapping a loaf of freshly baked bread. "Now who's the curious one?"

"That'd be me." He smiled. The marshal had a charming smile, probably had a good way with the ladies. "Black horse? Did you see a woman riding a big black horse on Monday?"

"Well, yes, I suppose there were a few, though it was dark by the time the party began. The transportation companies in Eureka Springs like to use white horses and mules, so the black ones aren't in high demand. A lot of reds, roans, draft horses..." She finished wrapping the bread.

Frey picked up the handcuffs he'd removed from Timothy's arms and recuffed the boy's hands in front. "When I bring up the subject of Elam Jensen anywhere in these parts, all I hear about is the big wedding on Monday, about how you are good at doctoring people. Folks say neither of you would ever harbor a criminal."

Keara dropped the wrapped loaf on the counter. "A criminal!"

Frey helped Timothy swallow a little more coffee, patted him lightly on the face a couple of times in an attempt to rouse him, then looked back at Keara. "As you reminded your husband, I'm the law, Mrs. Jensen. Most times, folks know it's best to cooperate with a US marshal."

"Well, of course we do, but I don't understand. What on earth are you talking about?"

He leaned forward and held her gaze, and she felt a chill. She could imagine how his quarry might feel when he'd set the sights of his gun on them. But she returned that gaze with the same steady poise she'd used on Monday when it seemed the whole of Eureka Springs was studying her every move. She thought of the children and their safety. Their future. She thought of Susanna.

Keara would do whatever it took to protect those she loved.

Timothy snored.

Keara grimaced at the young man. "I think you may need a wagon to haul him."

The marshal studied his charge. "He'll be better off riding while he's loosened up and feeling no pain. Set him in a saddle and he'll hold on. I think I'll go help your husband with the horses." He reached for his hat and walked out the door with a nod to Keara.

* * * * *

Elam led Moondance from the barn barebacked and unbridled. He went back in for the blanket, saddle, and bridle. He scooped a double helping of oats into the stall trough for Duchess, to keep her mouth occupied so she wouldn't whinny at the wrong time. He then filled the feed trough outside with oats for the other horses. He and Frey had removed the bridles so the horses could more easily eat and drink without the bits in their mouths.

Elam closed the door and bolted it behind him just in time—Frey stepped out onto the porch, settling his dark, dusty brown hat onto his head. Elam prayed that Duchess wouldn't raise her head from her feed trough and call out to Susanna, as she'd done a couple of times from the barn.

Frey looked grim as he studied the steps—obviously the bloodstains that had spilled from Susanna's shoulder. He straightened and looked at Elam then shook his head and made his way across the yard.

"You folks seem like good people." He opened the gate, glanced back at the house, and shut the gate. "Your wife's in there watching over her patient like he was her own, and she's probably got herself convinced I'm the devil, carting an innocent kid off to his death."

"He is just a kid."

"He's older than some of the relatives of Jesse James when they made their first kills, but this whole trip out West is just an effort to combine two chores." Frey shifted his hat on his head, and as he did so, his gray eyes seemed to glint like gunmetal in the rays of sun that hit them. He braced his boot on the lower board in the fence, looked at Elam, then back out into the corral.

"As I mentioned earlier, Tim Skerit's been flitting around the edges of that outlaw gang that's hanging around Eureka Springs these days."

"I didn't know there was an outlaw gang in town," Elam said. "Sheriff Nolan usually keeps an eye out for such types." But they could be the ones Brute had mentioned.

"They've not done anything against the law in your town yet, but they have in others. They'll be rounded up before they wake up in the morning, and most of them will be tried and convicted of robbery and murder. You'd best stay clear of the Springs tonight."

"So it's a fact? He's running with a gang?" Elam didn't believe it for a moment. Something about this man irritated him like gravel in his shoe.

Frey stepped over to his chestnut gelding and scratched his ears as the horse chomped on the oats. "It's a fact. What isn't a fact is that Skerit's been seen taking part in any of their misdeeds."

Elam glanced up at that.

The marshal nodded, giving Elam a tight grin. "This trip's a warning. I owed his pa a favor from ten years ago, and since I happened to be in the area, I stopped by their place for a visit. This is payback."

Elam settled the blanket over Moondance's back then reached for the saddle he'd braced on the fence rail. "You're going to let the kid go?"

"Not until he's actually seen a jail cell in Missouri." Frey fixed Elam with a glare. "None of this to the kid, you understand? You start hanging back, talking to him alone on the ride to Seligman, and you're not riding with us. This is a lesson he's got to learn early, or he'll end up like his friends."

As Elam slid the bit into Moondance's mouth and settled the straps over the supple ears, he gave the marshal a second look and found Frey watching him.

"Misjudged me, did you?"

Elam held the man's gaze. "Could be."

"I didn't ride all the way here from Pennsylvania just to escort an old friend's son to an execution."

Elam waited.

Frey glanced toward the house, straightened his leg from the fence, and stretched. "I came here on the trail of a murderess, and I tracked her to within a few miles of here."

"Murderess? You tracked a woman?"

"Dr. Susanna Luther."

Elam narrowed his eyes at the marshal, not doubting for a moment that this was the rogue Brute had mentioned. And yet, he had the sense to add a touch of surprise to his instinctive anger. "That's not possible."

"Now, I've heard you're a decent man, Jensen, and a decent man isn't willing to believe ill of any of his late wife's kin, but I have too much proof that backs me up. I have no way of knowing if Dr. Luther reached you here, but she tried to kill me in cold blood just this side of the Springs. Hid in wait for me. She shot at me, I shot back. Couldn't see if I got her, but that big black horse of hers took off like a field afire, and she clung to it like she'd been nailed on."

Elam wanted to curse the man for his lies, but he'd played poker a few times in his life—taught by Brute McBride himself—and he knew how to keep the tell from his face. He wasn't as good at it as his new wife, but he'd learned a thing or two. The trick, in Brute's words, was to pretend to be someone else, holding a different hand. Elam pretended to be Timothy Skerit's father back on the farm, too worried about his son to be interested in the marshal's other activities.

"You're risking that young boy's life in there to see if we're harboring your fugitive?" Elam asked.

Frey shook his head. "I know where to stop if he spikes a fever, and I know how to dress a wound. All he's going to suffer from this is fear and pain, and that's what I want. Then he'll realize that's what's in store for him if he mingles with the wrong people." Frey leaned closer to Elam. "Outlaws aren't fashionable or flashy. They stink from being on the run, they stink of greed for the working man's earnings, and they all need to be rounded up and kept away from the innocents of this world. Like you and your new wife."

"I don't believe for a minute Susanna Luther could kill another human being. She's a doctor, pledged to save lives, not take them."

"So was her husband, but it didn't stop him from offering hospitality to outlaws."

The front door opened, and Frey stiffened and turned. Keara stepped out first, her shoulder under Timothy's arm to help him through the threshold.

"Time to saddle up and get on down the road before his leg gets too stiff to mount the horse," Frey said. He held Elam with a straight look. "Those little kids of yours? That pretty new wife? You're their protector. You can't let a killer get between you and them."

"I haven't." Elam checked the cinch on the saddle then walked over to help Frey with the other horses, trying to read the man, and failing. Did he really think he was after a killer, or was he just that good a liar?

With another look in the marshal's eyes, Elam shook his head and walked to Keara. He lowered his head and kissed her on the cheek then whispered, "Get word to Tim's folks."

She reached up and wrapped her arms around his neck. "Don't turn your back on him." Her breath was soft and warm against his cheek then she released him. "Be home in time for supper?"

Elam nodded and tipped his hat. "I'll just see them past the bad spots in the road."

He straightened and mounted Moondance. Keara's instincts matched his. He could trust her to take care of things here.

Fifteen

The sound of horses' hooves echoed from the side of the barn, and dust became gritty on Keara's skin as she watched Elam ride away with the marshal and his prisoner. Timothy swayed in the saddle a bit, but he stayed astride, as the marshal had said he would.

She turned and walked back to the house, trying to clear her mind of the confusion that had whipped up inside her as the day progressed. The man who had first seemed harsh and judgmental toward his prisoner had revealed a different side soon after he entered the front door of their home. It was as if stepping inside a beautiful painted lady like this house with the gingerbread trim had reminded him he was among civilized people.

He seemed so sincere that most people would've been fooled. Elam didn't trust him, and she was glad.

Once the men had gone outside to prepare the horses, Keara had left Timothy to snore a few moments on the sofa and slipped to the window to watch Elam and the marshal in deep discussion out by the fence. Judging by Elam's expression, she gathered he was playing a close hand. Could Susanna be the subject of discussion?

"Never rode..." Timothy's voice had cracked, and he took a breath and tried again as Keara hurried back to his side.

She pressed her hand to his back and helped him straighten.

"Never rode with any outlaws."

"I know. Was this shooting really an accident?" Keara asked.

He nodded, looked at her for a moment, and then his eyelids shuttered down again.

She helped him drink more coffee and pressed a cold cloth to his face. "You'll need to drink a lot of water to keep from having a bad hangover tomorrow." She'd waited until he told her he was ready and then helped him out the front door.

And now, Elam wouldn't be able to tell her what he'd discussed with the marshal until he returned.

Supper. He'd be home in time for supper.

Keara called to Britte and Rolfe. The children came tumbling through the back door, Britte struggling with Cash, eyes wide.

"Who did Pa ride away with?" she asked, lowering Cash to the floor until he settled onto his rump. "Who were those men?"

Before Keara could reply, there was a whisper of noise on the stairwell, and she looked up to see Susanna, hair in tangles, sweat dripping down her face, obviously in pain.

"Keara?"

"You should be in bed." Keara rushed up the steps, gesturing to Britte for help. "What were you thinking? What if he'd still been here in the house?"

"I opened the window, heard them leave." Susanna rested most of her weight on Keara. Britte rushed to her aunt's other side and helped Keara get her into the sickroom.

When Susanna settled back onto the bed, she groaned aloud and grasped her left shoulder. "It hurts."

Keara felt her forehead. The fever was still down.

"Britte," Keara said, "I want you to run back downstairs and bring me the pot of tea I left on the counter to cool." It was willow bark and sassafras. Susanna had shown no problem with excess bleeding, and the willow bark would help with the pain. "Also bring the rest of the glass of whiskey on the dining table and water straight from the spring."

As soon as Britte left the room, Susanna grasped Keara's hand with unexpected strength. "I heard him ask you about Duchess."

"It's a good thing Elam had put her in the barn."

"You covered for me."

"Of course I did. You think we're going to turn you over to the man who shot you?"

Susanna's grip weakened. She looked away. "I shot first."

"I didn't see any bullet holes in the marshal. Gloria was always bragging to me about what a good shot you are. I figure if you intended to kill him, he wouldn't have been in our house today."

Susanna's gaze returned to Keara. Her jawline relaxed. "You and Elam could be in a lot of trouble for harboring a fugitive."

"You think he might have killed Nathaniel."

Susanna's eyelids fluttered, her breath still quick and shallow. "I suspect so."

"We'll take care of some of that pain and let you rest."

Susanna glanced out the window, frowning. "It's been such a confusing couple of days. I've not been in my right mind most of the time."

"I'm not sure you are now."

"There are things happening that I don't completely understand."

"Let us help you with them."

"You have the children to consider."

"You're their aunt."

Susanna kept her hand in Keara's, her blue eyes still filled with pain. "I don't suppose you were able to hear what the marshal told Elam when they were saddling the horses."

"I never learned to read lips, but I could read Elam's face well enough."

"And?"

Keara shrugged. She gently sat on the side of the bed. "US Marshal Driscoll Frey disturbed Elam."

"He disturbs me too. You should listen to what his poor young prisoner told you."

"I did," Keara said. "You can be sure the marshal won't find out about you through Elam or me or Jael or Kellen."

Susanna laid her head back and released Keara's hand at last. "I've been trouble to you ever since I arrived, and all you'd have had to do was point him up the stairs and it would have been over. I'd have been out of your life."

Keara placed a hand on Susanna's unhurt shoulder. "Would Gloria have ever betrayed you?"

"Never."

"And neither will we."

Susanna's eyes filled with tears that joined the perspiration on her face. She lowered her lids and nodded. "As soon as Elam returns, I'll tell you both all I know. I'm afraid it won't be enough to answer all the questions that have tracked me from Blackmoor. I don't know the answers. In fact, I don't know much of anything right now, and I wish I did."

"I need to get word to the Skerits. I'll bring your pistol in case there's trouble."

"You're riding all the way to Clifty?" Susanna exclaimed.

"No, I'm riding to Kellen and Jael's. One of them can ride to the telegraph office in Eureka Springs and get word to Clifty. Timothy said everyone in Clifty knows them. You'll have whiskey to sip if the pain gets too bad, but I should be back in thirty minutes at most. I'll ride Buster bareback."

Susanna nodded. "Bring me my gun, but I won't drink the whiskey until you've returned. I don't want to handle a pistol if I'm loopy. Not with the children around."

Keara laid a hand on Susanna's arm. "Thank you. I won't be gone long."

* * * * *

About halfway through Butler Hollow, still a ways from Seligman, Missouri, Elam was catching dust as he trailed the marshal and his charge alongside the railroad tracks. His thoughts were back home. He needed answers he would not get from Frey.

Murder and cross-country chases were far out of the realm of Elam's experience. He simply didn't know what to think. Frey was a double-sided man—dark and threatening on the one side, and yet on the other side he could charm gentle company. Elam didn't trust either side. That much he did know.

He caught the sound of a whistle in the distance and gave a gentle tug on his reins. "Hear that?" he called ahead to Frey and his still-wobbly prisoner. "There's a train coming." He patted his stallion's strong neck and dismounted. "Moondance hears that sound a lot and he's used to it. How about yours?"

The marshal nodded. Timothy looked at them blankly, but

he'd been pretty blank for most of the trip. Definitely not a whis-key drinker.

Frey rolled his eyes, slid from his mount, and looped the reins around a sturdy tree limb. He pulled the rope from his saddle and wrapped it around the neck of Timothy's horse. "Hop down, Skerit. Can't be delivering my prisoner any more damaged than he is right now or I'll be accused of brutality."

The kid groaned as he leaned to dismount, and Elam rushed forward to help catch him. Frey took the full weight with no prob-lem and set his prisoner onto his feet. He tied the horse to the trunk of a sturdy tree and nudged Timothy clear then reached into his saddlebags and pulled out the jar of tea Keara had sent. He checked the wound, nodded at the lack of bleeding, and handed Timothy the jar as the train rumbled in their direction around a curve and through the trees.

The kid's horse screamed and pawed at the tree trunk. Frey's horse and Moondance remained unmoved except to look at the inexperienced gelding with dark-eyed disdain. The sound and weight of the huge cars rumbled against the hillsides and made the earth move beneath their feet.

Elam had guided them past a cluster of downed trees that had been blown over by their roots when a twister hit earlier in the spring. He'd shown them where the sinkholes were, how to circle the trees without falling through the ground. What he hadn't managed to do was figure out the marshal's real intentions toward the kid.

When the final rumbles of the train had passed, Elam nodded to the marshal. "I think you have everything pretty well under con-trol. I'm going to get back home to my family."

Timothy cast him a nervous glance, and for a moment, Elam hesitated.

"There's an inn at Seligman, only a couple more miles up the road," Elam said. "Last I heard, there was a doctor nearby. Reasonable rates, and staying there could keep you from stumbling over a rough road to Cassville tonight."

Frey nodded. "It's been a long day. I think we'll stop. Take care of that little family of yours. Don't forget what I told you."

Something in his gaze and voice warned Elam that he might have company again in the next couple of days, as soon as Frey had delivered his hostage to Cassville.

* * * * *

Keara returned home less than thirty minutes from the time she'd left, secure in the knowledge that Jael would have word to the Skerits within the hour about their son's dilemma.

She checked on Susanna then took the gun from the room and left Susanna with the whiskey and her niece and nephews, hoping maybe they could help distract her from her pain.

Keara had seen the expression of longing more than once when Susanna caught sight or sound of the children or heard mention of them.

There'd been very little time to cook since Monday, but the partiers had left enough beef, pork, and various side dishes and desserts to last the family a week. Now that Susanna's temperature seemed to be lingering near normal, Keara felt the urge to do something besides make tea and poultices in the kitchen.

After cutting stale bread into squares, she spread them into a buttered pan and prepared the spiced egg and milk, raisin, and nut blend to pour over it. She put it in the oven to bake then pulled out the big cast iron skillet to fry the freshly butchered chicken Penelope had sent home with Elam and the children earlier today.

The bread pudding was just ready to come out of the oven, its vanilla-cinnamon aroma filling the house, when Keara turned to find Susanna sitting on a step halfway down the staircase. Her black hair had been combed, and she'd changed into Gloria's dressing gown the color of a field of new wheat. The sight of her in the gown was startling.

"I couldn't stay in bed." Susanna's voice was stronger than it had been earlier, her eyes clear. "The children are better medicine than whiskey. You'll find the glass as you left it. Britte combed my hair for me and brought me some of her mother's clothes."

"You look better." Keara glanced up the stairwell past Susanna. "The children?"

Susanna had a smile that showed straight, white teeth and revealed the immediate affection she had developed for her niece and nephews. "All three of them fell asleep while I was telling them about my travels with Nathaniel."

"I'd like to hear about your travels too, but I'm not sure you're ready to be up and around. I've noticed you tend to push yourself a little hard. Seems to be a family trait."

"It is. You'd have made a good doctor. You're bossy enough."

Once again, with the light just right and Gloria's gown fitting her sister so perfectly and the warm tone in Susanna's robust voice, Keara felt as if time had shifted back a year. Then Susanna tried to stand. She swayed and grasped the railing, and the image of strength dissolved.

Again, Keara found herself rushing up the steps to steady her. "Why don't you come downstairs for a spell and lay on the sofa? I'll get a quilt."

Susanna grimaced. "After all my study and all my travels with Nathaniel, it took getting shot myself to realize how helpless my patients sometimes feel. I don't like it."

"It's never convenient to be sick or injured—not for hardworking, industrious people like you," Keara said, "but you know better than I that if you don't take it easy, things will become even less convenient."

"And yet I've found that the sooner a person gets back to work, the faster that person will heal. Within reason, of course."

Keara guided Susanna across the room to the sofa and pulled the curtains, just in case someone should ride past the house…just in case the marshal should ride back with Elam.

"You treated a lot of people with gunshot wounds?" she asked Susanna.

"It was Nathaniel's habit to treat anyone who walked through our office door, and ask no questions. I found it interesting that those men who were notorious outlaws tended to pay more. I told Nathaniel they were buying his silence, and he would be sorry for it someday."

When Keara returned with a quilt and a pillow, she rested her hand on Susanna's forehead. "How does the goose egg feel?"

"Sore."

"Shoulder?"

"Like there's a razor blade digging into it."

"I'm going to raise your head and shoulders and slide this pillow under them," Keara said. This proved to be more difficult than she expected, since Susanna was lying with her wounded left shoulder outward. Once she was situated, her breathing grew shallow.

"Hurting worse now?"

Susanna nodded.

"I'll change your poultice and get you more tea."

"Add whiskey," Susanna murmured.

By the time Keara had Susanna's pain under control, Britte came downstairs with Cash, her face imprinted with sleep. Without complaint, she went to the little table and changed her baby brother.

"Didn't get much sleep at your cousins'?" Keara asked.

Britte gave her a mischievous smile. "Katie and I sneaked out to the barn after everybody went to bed."

"Did you sleep there?"

Britte nodded. "I'd never slept in a barn before. The baby pigs were noisy. One of them nestled under my chin and went to sleep, but it pooped on my blanket and we had to clean it. We weren't supposed to let the piglets sleep with us."

"Sometimes I used to sleep in the barn with the babies if they were struggling." Keara spooned lard into the skillet and watched it melt as she coated pieces of chicken with flour and seasonings. The children loved fried chicken. It was Elam's favorite.

She glanced out the window, wondering how much longer he would be. He said he'd be home in time for supper.

"You could stand a change of clothes." Susanna's voice from the sofa was slightly slurred, but she sounded as if the pain had eased. "Make him glad he came home. You've got horsehair on your backside from riding bareback. Put your hair up. Your face could use a little color."

Keara smiled at Susanna and shook her head. "I've got food to cook, and if Elam doesn't return soon, I'll have stock to see to."

"He'll return soon."

Keara tasted the bread pudding to make sure she'd sweetened it enough. It was perfect. That was what would please Elam. He hadn't married her for the color of clothing she wore or the way her hair looked.

And yet, he was a man...

She'd noticed enough over the years to realize a man did appreciate a pretty woman who kept herself up. Elam had often remarked on Gloria's beauty, and Gloria took pains to wear dresses that would appeal to him. Keara knew this because she'd gone shopping with Gloria to the dry goods store to purchase material for new dresses.

Gloria had told Keara that Elam never failed to notice and appreciate a new dress, and he never denied Gloria the cost of a new outfit. Elam Jensen's generosity was legendary, and no one had appreciated it more than his wife.

When the lard sizzled with a droplet of water, Keara placed the chicken pieces into the hot grease and wondered what Elam's reaction would be if she were to take Susanna's advice and start paying more attention to her reflection in the mirror.

While Britte played with Cash, Keara looked down at her stained work dress then looked at the clock. She went to the west-facing window and checked the wagon track Elam and the others had taken. The sun would be setting in another couple of hours. If all went well, he'd surely be back before it got too dark to see.

She went upstairs and changed into a pretty periwinkle-blue dress Gloria had made for her two years ago. She'd always loved the dress, but the lines followed her figure a little closely, and the neck showed a little too much of her chest—nothing indecent, of course, but enough to make her look…different when she looked in the mirror. A bolder woman—almost a stranger—stared back at her. She suspected that had been Gloria's intention when giving her the dress.

The scent of frying chicken hurried her movements, and she feared waking Rolfe, but she took the time to comb her hair and pull it away from her face with a ribbon. She did look like a different woman.

Would Elam see that woman?

The direction of her thoughts disturbed her so that she nearly changed back into the work dress, but there was no time. The chicken would burn. A burned dinner wouldn't put a man in a good mood, no matter how good the dress looked on her.

She pulled on an apron—something she seldom felt the need to do—before she rushed downstairs in time to turn the chicken, feeling foolish to even consider such silliness. Of course Elam wouldn't notice her dress. He wouldn't notice her. He'd taken her in because he was an honorable man who did the right thing, and she'd best continue to keep that in mind.

She went to the cellar for a jar of green beans she and Gloria had canned with ham bones last year. She prepared them for heating then mixed up a batch of cornbread batter, flavored with the molasses she always used. Tonight, dinner was going to be good.

All the time she worked, she listened for the sound of hoofbeats outside, casting nervous glances toward Susanna as she slept on the sofa, and smiling as Britte and Cash played in the corner of the kitchen. Cash's giggles and cries of delight didn't seem to disturb

Susanna. In fact, there was a slight smile on her face too, as if she enjoyed the sound of a child's laughter even in sleep.

How sad that Susanna and Nathaniel had never had children.

That thought led to another. If Keara hadn't begged Elam to rescue her from homelessness, then in time it might have turned out that Susanna would have been raising her niece and nephews, whom she obviously loved. Susanna was the type of woman Elam preferred—tall and bold and black haired, refined and graceful, like her sister had been.

As Keara was taking the chicken from the skillet, Britte picked up Cash and lugged him over to Keara. "Auntie Keara, what should we call you now?"

Keara turned off the burner and placed the chicken in the oven to keep it warm. "What do you mean, honey?"

"You're not really our aunt, but Ma always told us to call you that. But now you're our ma."

"I'm the same to you I've always been, don't you think?"

A movement behind Keara drew her attention to the stairs, and she saw Rolfe creeping down to sit at eye level with her. Both children watched her, waiting. This was obviously a subject they'd discussed.

"Did someone tell you that you had to call me by a different name?" Keara asked.

Rolfe nodded. "Hutch and Leland both said we have to call you Ma now."

"How would Hutch and Leland feel if they were you? You still have your ma. She's in heaven, but she's always going to be your ma." Keara brushed the hair from Britte's face and reached through the railing to squeeze Rolfe's arm. "I'm going to love you two and Cash as if you were my own, but your ma could have taught you things I can't teach you, like culture and refinement that will help you in life. She was special, and we all need to remember that, not just replace her as if she'd never been."

"What's culture and refinerment?" Rolfe asked.

"Refinement," Britte said. "It's a way of knowing how to live in town and be fancy."

Keara chuckled. "Your mother was smart about a lot of things besides work on a ranch. Culture helps you socialize with others of polite society, and travel like your auntie Susanna and uncle Nathaniel did. Your aunt has a good education. She's a sophisticated lady who could dine comfortably with kings and queens and presidents. She's a doctor who knows so much more than I do about caring for patients. She can afford nicer things for herself than I ever could."

"But why would we want to move to town?" Britte asked.

"I don't want to be a doctor," Rolfe said.

Keara sighed. "The point is having the chance if you change your mind later, but I guess none of this has to do with whether you call me Auntie Keara or Mother or Ma, does it?"

"Well, you're not a wicked stepmother," Rolfe said. "We can't call you that."

Keara laughed. "I should never have read you those stories, should I?"

Rolfe shook his head and scooted closer to the railing until his face was within inches of hers. "You're a good mother."

When Keara was a little girl, she used to dream of having a wonderful husband and lots of children. She'd even dreamed about what she'd want her children to call her. "How about Mama?"

Britte and Rolfe looked at each other, then Britte scrunched her face, obviously thinking about it. "Brian and David Jr. call Auntie Pen that."

"Your first ma will always be Ma," Keara said, "and we will always love her. But I'm your second ma."

"Ma-ma," Britte said, testing it. "I like it. But I might slip and still call you Auntie Keara."

"That's fine, honey." Keara kissed her darling new stepdaughter's forehead and then reached over the railing and lifted Rolfe into her arms. "I'm going to love you two and Cash no matter what you call me."

"Oh, uh, Mama...?" This voice, tinged with wry amusement, came from the sofa, and Keara looked over her shoulder to find that Susanna was awake and watching them. How long had she been listening? "I think you look beautiful in that dress, but you should take off the apron. I think I heard the sound of horse hooves in the distance."

Keara placed Rolfe on his feet and rushed to help Susanna from the sofa. "Kids, we need to get Auntie Susanna back up to Britte's room, and I want you to stay with her up there."

"But why?" Rolfe asked.

"Just help me up the stairs, sweetheart," Susanna said, "and I'll tell you all about it." She nodded to Keara. "Probably Elam. We can only hope." She was slightly wobbly, and her breath smelled of whiskey, but her color was better for now.

Keara did as she was told, removing the apron and straightening her dress.

Susanna nodded with approval. "You could still use a little more color in your cheeks and a different hairstyle, but your face is clean. Go on out. The kids will take good care of me."

Despite what Susanna said, Keara waited until the children had Susanna out of sight upstairs, and the door closed firmly behind them.

Sixteen

The sun was still bright when Elam rode Moondance through the tunnel of trees at the edge of his ranch. If he listened hard enough, he could imagine he heard the rushing gurgle of Sweet Water Creek as it ran into White River up ahead. He could see the peak of the house and smoke drifting from the kitchen chimney as he neared the pasture clearing.

Most times, Elam considered himself a good judge of character, but today he doubted that ability. US Marshal Driscoll Frey had thrown him, and that was disturbing. Usually, if he was able to read a person, he could predict future actions. Timothy was easy to read. He was a farm boy who only wanted to get home.

Frey, however, was a different story. Would he even release the kid? What part of his talk today was lying and what was truth? Elam knew he was lying about Susanna being a killer, but how far had he taken those lies?

Elam patted Moondance's sweaty neck and gave him his lead, knowing the stallion would head straight for the barn, where he would expect a good combing and an extra portion of oats and molasses.

When he reached the top of the ridge and started down toward the house, a woman in a blue dress stepped off the porch and across the yard, shading her eyes from the late evening sun. Keara.

As if sensing his master's eagerness to get home, Moondance broke into a trot and then eased into a ground-covering canter. The closer Elam drew to the house, the more he liked what he saw.

Keara carried a dress well. Her pale gold hair was tied back from her face, revealing the high cheekbones, pointed chin, and enchanting golden-brown eyes. This woman—his friend, his occasional farmhand, who roughhoused with the kids and had been known to snort like a foal—could also be a lady. He'd discovered that on their wedding day, but he'd expected her to revert to her old self after the festivities were over.

He'd never seen her in that dress before, and he'd never seen so much of her skin. Beautiful, creamy-looking skin without a flaw.

He couldn't stop looking at her, and as he rode into the barnyard, he slowed so the dust wouldn't cover her and then stopped in front of her. The creamy skin turned rosy.

"Ready for supper?" she asked.

He grinned. Keara was always practical. "Did you get word to Timothy's folks?"

"Jael was saddling up when I left their house. The Skerits are likely on their way to Cassville by now."

"Good job. I wish I'd had time to explain."

"I understood well enough."

He slid from the saddle. "I can smell the fried chicken from here."

"And bread pudding, green beans, cornbread."

His smile widened. "All my favorites." He turned and looked down into her face, which held a blush as well as her body held a dress.

"I figured Susanna could use a solid meal now that her fever's gone." Keara reached for Moondance's reins and started to lead him toward the barn. "Get washed up and I'll get this saddle off—"

He took the reins from her hand. "Not in that dress, you won't. Let me do the outside chores today so you can stay pretty for a little while, okay?"

She blinked up at him as if flustered.

"Susanna's better?" he asked. "That was fast."

"I don't trust it to last, of course. There's always a setback when a person refuses to rest." Keara followed him into the barn with her hand on Moondance's sweaty rump. "She's weak, but she's showing signs of impatience already. It could get her in trouble if she's not careful."

"Which goes to show you have more doctor sense than a sick doctor. We'll have to watch her closely."

"I have been."

He looked over his shoulder at Keara. "Gloria did that kind of thing, you know. She was always impatient with her own illnesses."

"She sure was. I could never get her to slow down when she had a goal to reach, and she always had a goal to reach." Keara hesitated. "I don't mean to be disrespectful of the dead."

"It's not disrespectful to recognize the truth." He uncinched the straps of the saddle and glanced at Keara as he bared Moondance's back. She was staring into the deepening shadows of the barn, her eyes darkened, her small teeth worrying her lower lip as if the memories of Gloria continued to haunt her.

Keara lifted the lid from the bin of oats and reached inside, obviously unaware that she was likely to get molasses on her sleeve.

Elam just shook his head and removed Moondance's bridle as Keara ladled the oats into the trough.

"Did you get any more answers from Susanna while I was gone?" He ran a curry comb over Moondance's haunches.

"She was waiting for you to return so she could tell us all she knows."

"Good. At least she finally trusts us. Maybe we can help."

"She always trusted you. I was the problem."

"Obviously, you've proven yourself to her since Monday."

Keara grabbed a brush and started to work on Moondance's haunches. Elam took the brush away from her and gently eased her aside. He allowed his hands to rest on her arms as he looked down into her face and enjoyed the curve of her chin, the surprise in her eyes, and the slight dimple on her cheek when her face flushed once more.

"Sometimes, all a lovely lady needs to do is stand there and look lovely," he told her. "You're not a servant on this ranch, Keara, you're the lady of the house. Don't feel you must always be busy serving others."

"But what could it hurt if it helps get you to the dinner table faster?"

Elam chuckled and turned back to the horse. "I'll work quickly."

"You and the marshal were in some pretty deep talk before you left. How far did you go with him and his prisoner?"

"Far enough to keep a horse from breaking a leg near the caves or bolting when the train came through Butler Hollow."

"You could have simply warned him before they left."

"I'm still trying to figure the man out. I wanted to observe him a little longer, see how he interacted with Timothy."

"What did you find out?"

"He didn't mistreat him while I was with them."

"I didn't see any other marks besides the bullet wound," Keara said.

"Frey insisted his prisoner isn't headed for the gallows, that this trip to Cassville is just a warning. I'm not sure I believe him." Elam explained what the marshal had told him about being a friend of Timothy's father and wishing to keep Timothy from riding with the gang.

"I may not know any outlaws," Keara said, "but I'd bet my horse that Timothy Skerit isn't riding with any outlaw gang. He told me he wasn't, and I believe him."

"You actually got a coherent word out of him?"

"Enough that I could understand that much. So you think the marshal intends to hurt Timothy, even after assuring you he wouldn't?"

"I don't trust anything he says."

"He seems convinced Susanna's here."

"He knows we're related." Elam tamped the dust and hair from the curry comb against the railing. He glanced at Keara. "Simple logic led him here. That's why I think he'll be back around. We need to find out all we can about him from Susanna tonight. Is she thinking more clearly now?"

"I believe so, but that bump on the head still bothers me. Those can be tricky."

"You've read up on the trephining procedure she told you about?" He placed the curry comb and brush in their cabinet and reached into Duchess's stall to caress her soft nose.

"Yes, but it's been a couple of days. Let's pray that isn't necessary."

"While we're at it, we should pray that Frey is telling the truth about his destination. If he's going to Cassville, he shouldn't be back this way until at least Friday."

"We should take no chances with Susanna. I'll keep her in the house."

Elam narrowed his eyes into the same darkness Keara had been watching in the far reaches of the barn. "I say we take no chances with you or the children either. He told me Susanna shot at him, admitted he shot back. He tried to convince me she's dangerous."

"She told me herself that she shot at him," Keara said. "But she'd have killed him if she'd meant to."

"I guess we'll hear all about it tonight, won't we?"

Keara straightened Moondance's bridle on its post. She adjusted the saddle and spread the horse blanket out to air.

"Time for you to get out of the barn before you mess up that pretty dress," Elam told her.

He caught the edge of her smile as she turned away, and something urged him to venture a little more. "My mother always said that it's the wearer that makes the dress pretty."

She didn't stop, but he heard a whisper of a chuckle as she left the barn. He turned back to his work and wondered how Keara's very presence here could make the worries of the day less burdensome. And he wondered how long she'd had that effect on him without his even knowing it.

* * * * *

That evening, Keara carried Susanna's supper up to her, just a small plate with a few bites of each dish she'd prepared.

Susanna went for the bread pudding first.

Keara smiled. "Your sister used to do the same thing. Dessert first. I'd ask you to join us downstairs at the table, but I don't think you should tackle the stairs again until you're stronger."

"Plus you're afraid that snoopy marshal may have trailed Elam back to the house." Susanna took two bites of the pudding. "Delicious. Gloria never made anything like this. Your recipe?"

"Yes. About the snoopy marshal—"

"He's a strange one." Susanna put her fork down, and a cloud seemed to dim her sunny blue eyes.

"Eat your dinner and I'll bring Elam up with me later. The three of us may be able to put our heads together and figure out what to do."

"More bread pudding?" Susanna asked.

Keara grinned. "Of course."

Susanna poked at the chicken with her fork. "Gloria's recipe?"

Keara nodded. "It was a family favorite."

"Our mother always was a good cook. She passed her skills down to Gloria." She looked up at Keara. "I observed you with the children when you didn't know I was watching and listening."

"You were eavesdropping."

"I was in no eave, I was lying on the sofa, simply listening with my eyes closed. I've had to do that a lot since I lost Nathaniel." She paused. "It's hard to sleep when you're on the run, listening with your eyes closed. Actually, both of us were watching our backs before he was killed." She swallowed. "We didn't watch closely enough."

"Don't ruin your appetite. You're not alone now, Susanna. We'll talk about this later. I'll bring you more bread pudding." Keara turned to leave.

"Keara," Susanna said, and waited until Keara had turned back. "You're a kind person." Her voice had softened further, as had her eyes. "I can imagine no woman I'd trust more with my niece and nephews."

The admission surprised Keara. She moved closer to the bed. "I can't teach them the things Gloria would have wanted them to know."

"Dining with kings and queens and presidents?" Susanna said dryly. "As if that's so important. Those people are just people like you and me. Most of them take themselves too seriously, and they call that culture or refinement. I call it silliness."

That statement surprised Keara into laughter.

"Just so you know," Susanna continued, "physicians do not make a great income, so don't encourage the children to follow in their auntie's footsteps for that reason."

"I don't believe you entered the profession for the love of money," Keara said.

Susanna shook her head then winced as if the movement jarred her shoulder. "Most doctors struggle to make a living, and women in the profession are few because they aren't taken seriously. The reason Nathaniel and I did well was we weren't picky about who we treated, and Nathaniel's portion of family wealth was enough to support us the rest of our lives, and several more lives, besides. When his father died last year, we received his portion. Combined with my own inheritance from my aunt June, I am now left with enough extra income to support a small independent state, but what good will that do me if I'm dead?"

"So why did you choose to become a doctor?" Keara asked.

"I could say it was because it was the first time I had the courage to flout Aunt June's rules, but that was only part of the reason."

"You didn't really want to become a doctor?"

"Oh yes. I was always interested in medicine, but my parents sent me to live with Aunt June so I would have the advantages of proper society and an education that my other siblings never had. What that really meant was that they wanted me to marry well and become a part of the social elite. But that was Gloria's dream, not mine."

"Was your aunt angry that you chose medicine?"

Susanna nibbled on a corner of the small square of cornbread. She chewed it as if tasting it thoroughly then swallowed. "No. My parents were upset, but June surprised me. I lived with her all those years, afraid to offend, and when I finally did something I was sure would infuriate her, I think I earned her respect. When I met Nathaniel in medical school my whole family was pleased. Nathaniel, of course, earned his father's ire for his choice of profession, but not enough to disinherit him."

"Your aunt sounds like you."

Susanna stuck her fork into the remaining bread pudding. "You think so? I always thought Gloria would have become most like June. Maybe that's why our mother didn't send Gloria to live with June. Gloria already had plenty of backbone. June and I became dear friends until her death two years ago."

"Why don't I bring that pudding now," Keara suggested. "I made plenty."

Susanna smiled up at her. She was a different person from the frightened and suspicious woman Keara and Elam discovered on their front porch Monday night. She motioned Keara out the door. "I think that whiskey you gave me this afternoon is loosening my tongue. I'll take that pudding after the children have gone to bed. And then you and Elam and I can have a talk."

Seventeen

Elam leaned against the door verge of Rolfe's bedroom, arms crossed over his chest. The three children were bunking here for the night.

Britte had spread her pallet beside the crib in case Cash should awaken. It was one of the multiple things her auntie Pen had told her to do. How had the children managed to have any fun at all with Penelope filling their heads full of matchmaking tips?

He couldn't help wondering what else Penelope had said to the children to "help his marriage along."

He couldn't stop watching Keara now, with the children, as she told them about a princess and a knight. There were no wicked stepmothers mentioned in this story. In fact, she had no book. She was either making this story up or had memorized it.

She had Britte and Rolfe totally engrossed, and the softness of her voice lulled Cash to sleep. Elam realized she had him engrossed, as well, with her tender behavior toward his children.

He'd come far these past few months of the new century. After Gloria's death, he'd spent a long time trying to deny his anger with God. At Christmas, he'd finally given in to it, mostly with silence, but he'd raged at God a few times when he was out in the pasture checking on the cattle. Moondance had borne silent witness to those rages.

Only once had God used human intervention to defend Himself.

Keara's intervention. It was New Year's Day, sunny and mild, with the sound of birdsong competing with the rush of White River.

Elam had even raged at that. What right did the world have to sunshine in January when Gloria would never see this sunshine again? When her children would never see her again?

"She was only a loan."

The voice had startled him mid-rant. It was feminine. Timid. He turned to find Keara standing several yards away with a basket of cracklin' cornbread and ham. For the first time he could remember, he was too surprised to speak.

"God placed her on loan to us for as long as He felt she should stay." Keara stepped closer, holding out the basket to Elam. "Who are we to complain, when she was His to loan to us in the first place?"

He took the basket. The food was still warm from the oven. He'd missed the New Year's meal with his family because he couldn't face Gloria's empty chair. And for the first time, with Keara standing there watching him with sad eyes, God whispered in his ear that not only had Britte, Rolfe, and Cash lost their mother, but because of Elam's actions, stalking off into the field every time he was angry with God, they'd lost part of their father as well.

If not for Keara, they'd have no one.

"A loan, you say."

Tears filled Keara's eyes. She nodded. "That's how I've had to look at it, or I'd be lost in my grief. I have to tell myself she is living in the presence of true Light, not just our piddling old sunlight."

Because of Keara, the children had been given Christmas gifts and homemade candy and had heard the Christmas story read from the Bible while all Elam could feel was bitterness.

"Nothing's for sure on this earth," she said as she turned and gazed around the winter pasture then reached up and scratched Moondance's ears. "God never promised us an easy time of it here. In fact, He promised troubles. We just weren't ready for this one."

Her words, spoken at just the right time for Elam, began to change his heart over the following weeks. And it was still changing. He'd never have imagined how much.

By the time Keara finished her story to the children, Rolfe was snoring softly. She turned to look up at Elam with a smile. "Knights and princesses. Fit for both boys and girls."

"I noticed Rolfe fell asleep during the kissing scene."

Keara stepped over Britte on the pallet and joined him at the doorway. "I promised Susanna more dessert, and it's warming in the oven. Why don't we see if we can finally clear up all the mystery?"

Elam picked up the flickering oil lamp and closed the door on the sleeping children. He turned to follow in Keara's wake, enjoying the scent of fresh air, spice, and tea leaves that was her own, which mingled with the heavy scent of the lamp oil.

"Did you make up that story?" he asked.

She nodded without turning. "A long time ago, I used to make up stories to keep the boys quiet while my mother rested. They always wanted stories of knights and conquest, but I wanted to pretend I was a princess who lived in a castle. So I combined everything together."

He smiled, shaking his head. "You tame horses and little boys, and you can cook and doctor humans and animals back to health."

"I don't think I ever did tame my little brothers."

"Of course you did. They're mature young men who have set out to take on the world."

"I'm just glad the world hasn't sent them back with their tails between their legs."

He caught up with her and touched her shoulder, holding the lantern high as he enjoyed the flicker of golden lights and enhancing shadows that played over her face when she looked up at him. "Is there anything you can't do?"

His own boldness surprised him. He never would have spoken to her so personally like this before their wedding.

Or perhaps he would have been just as bold, but he would have meant his words in a different way. As a friend to a friend. Now he couldn't even look at her past the frame of Monday's wedding.

She returned his gaze for a long moment, as if she also enjoyed the lines of his face and the words that came from his lips. Then color deepened on her cheeks, and her chin dimpled as she grinned.

"Well, I've never been much good at fashion or flirting." She chuckled and turned to walk ahead of him down the stairs. "I've only worn a corset once, and that was on my wedding day, and I don't plan to do that again. It's no wonder women of fashion always seem to faint so easily." She raised her hand to her cheek with a mock gasp. "And of course for me to even mention the word corset to a man—even my own husband—is simply outrageous. It's a wonder the Age of Victoria hasn't killed us all."

He laughed as he followed her down to light her way. That was another one of her talents. She could make him smile when he'd decided there was nothing to smile about. And she could speak her mind when she felt comfortable with a person. That was one thing she had in common with Gloria.

How could two women be such opposites in appearance, yet both draw his attention with such underlying power?

* * * * *

Keara preceded Elam back up the stairs, surprised she hadn't dropped the dish of bread pudding. The way he'd been watching her tonight—the way he'd watched her ever since he'd arrived back home from his ride with the marshal and Timothy Skerit—made her clumsier than she'd been the day of the wedding. Until tonight, his every touch had brought heat to her skin. Tonight, however, he didn't have to touch her to make her skin feel warm.

To make all of her feel warm.

She opened Britte's bedroom door and stepped in ahead of Elam, holding the unbroken dish of warm bread pudding in her hands. The sight of her patient cooled all the heat.

Susanna looked pale, with dark circles under her eyes. Her hair appeared more stringy and matted than it had just an hour ago—as if she'd been trying to find a comfortable position to sleep, with little success. The lines around her eyes and mouth were tight.

"Your fever back?" Keara touched her fingertips to Susanna's forehead.

"No, I'm just hurting."

Keara reached for the whiskey-laced willow bark tea Elam had carried up for her. "Drink this before you eat the pudding so it'll start working on you faster." She sat on the side of the bed, easing down gently so she wouldn't disturb Susanna's shoulder.

The blue eyes, so like Gloria's, remained dull. "You're going to get me drunk again today? Wasn't once enough?"

"You're still hurting."

"You want me to tell you everything, don't you?" She was obviously trying to be funny, but she didn't sound strong enough to carry it off.

"If that's what it takes." Keara held the cup to her patient's lips.

Susanna took the cup in her good hand and thanked Keara then sipped. She wrinkled her nose. "I hate whiskey."

"But you love how it relieves your pain."

Susanna nodded and took a bigger sip, eyeing the bread pudding. "I feel like a helpless child."

Elam reached for the only chair in the room, set it next to the bed, and sat down on it. "Then you should be glad you're here, where you're safe."

Susanna glanced toward the closed and curtained window. "I don't know if any of us are safe. For your sake and the children's, I should have never come here. I should have thought of someone besides myself."

"US Marshal Frey told me he'd followed you," Elam said.

She nodded. "I don't remember seeing anyone follow me. My other siblings and my parents still live in Pennsylvania, and I would expect that if the authorities tried to find me, they'd go to my family."

"He must be a good tracker," Keara said.

"I'm not so sure good tracking skills were what brought him here," Elam said.

"So you're saying he knew my destination when he set out from Blackmoor?" Susanna asked.

"Possibly." Elam nodded. "Did you tell anyone where you were coming?"

"If I did, I don't remember doing it."

"What do you mean?" Keara asked.

Susanna took another few sips of the tea, but it didn't seem to ease the tension. Instead, the lines grew deeper in her face. "There are blank spaces in my memory, probably from the concussion. As

I've become more lucid, I've become more aware of those blanks. I was thinking clearly enough to make it here after I was shot, but other things have been hazy. I think when I fell from Duchess on the porch steps, that's when I hit my head."

Keara realized why Susanna had been so frightened. That fear was contagious.

The speed with which Susanna drank the tea told Keara the extent of her pain. She took the final swallow and then lay back on her pillows, eyes closing, face relaxing.

Keara took half a spoonful of the pudding and held it to Susanna's lips. "How about something to kill the taste of that nasty whiskey?"

Susanna willingly opened her mouth, like a child, looking up at them.

Keara spooned a small bite into her mouth and watched with satisfaction as the enjoyment became obvious on Susanna's face.

"If I live through this, you'll have to give me your recipe."

"You'll live through this."

"Help us get you safely through it, Susanna," Elam said. "I know this is hard, but what happened in Blackmoor? We need to know what you do remember."

Susanna reached for the spoon and took another bite, savored it for a moment, then placed the spoon back in the dish. "Nathaniel was the instigator, I'm afraid."

"I have trouble believing that," Elam said.

"Oh, believe it. He went digging where he wasn't welcome. Had he chosen politics as his family wished him to in the beginning he likely would have…" Her voice wobbled. "He would have died sooner than he did." She swallowed. "I blame Nathaniel's family for his death. His father even threatened to disinherit him at one time—encouraged by his older brother, Sikes—for choosing medicine as his career."

"His brother was that hostile toward him?" Elam asked.

"No, not hostile, he just always thinks he's right. He takes after his late father."

"Didn't I meet Nathaniel's family when Gloria and I got married?" Elam asked.

"Of course." Susanna's voice took on a chill. "Neither Nathaniel's father nor his brother ever missed the chance to be in the public eye. Though they opposed Nathaniel's career choice, they certainly weren't opposed to exploiting his natural popularity for political reasons."

Elam nodded. "It seemed half the state of Pennsylvania was at our wedding."

"Nathaniel and I had married only three months earlier, and Mother asked us to invite all our friends to your wedding. Nathaniel had a lot of friends." She glanced at the flicker of the lantern flame. "He was generous with his money, and that tends to bring the crowds. We discovered later that it was my father-in-law who manipulated Mother into turning your wedding into a political campaign, Elam. I'm sorry about that."

"Gloria loved it," he said.

"Of course she would have. I did not."

"What does a wedding a decade ago have to do with US Marshal Frey?" Keara asked.

"Something happened recently that forced Nathaniel to reconsider his decision not to enter politics," Susanna said. She glanced at Elam and then reached for another spoonful of bread pudding. "This is so delicious. Are these chopped black walnuts?"

"Yes. Susanna," Keara said gently, "you're stalling. Can't you remember?"

Despite the prodding, Susanna indulged herself in a final bite of the pudding. She glanced once more at Elam then at Keara.

"Unfortunately, though Nathaniel was much more open-minded than the rest of his family, he did have a little too much of the Luther mindset. He encouraged my pursuit of medicine, but when it came to his new activities in the political arena, he was a bit too close-mouthed for my liking."

"Was he involved in something top secret?" Keara asked.

Susanna grimaced. "Sikes knew better than to place his loquacious younger brother in such a sensitive position. All I knew these past few months was that Nathaniel grew quiet, even sullen at home. It wasn't like him at all. When I questioned him he would snap at me."

"You're right. From my memories of Nathaniel, he was soft-spoken, always ready with a joke or humorous story," Elam said.

"That's why I watched him more closely," Susanna said. "I even followed him into town a couple of times. The second time I did that, I caught him arguing with a big man with long red hair. It was the same man who shot me on Monday."

"Frey?"

"Who else has long red hair like that? Two days after seeing the man with Nathaniel, I returned home with a wagon full of supplies and found our office door standing open." She swallowed again and paused as the pain of memory shadowed her eyes. "I found Nathaniel in his study, lying in front of his rifle cabinet, with a shotgun on the floor beside him." Tears formed at the corners of her eyes and trickled down her face. "He bled to death from a shot to the neck."

Keara took her hand and squeezed. "What awful things you've

been through. What kind of monster would do such a thing and then follow his victim's wife to shoot her as well?"

The sound of a bell reached them from downstairs, startling Keara.

Susanna squeezed her hand more tightly. Her eyes widened with fright. "What was that?"

"Someone's at the front door," Elam said. "I'll go see who it is. Keara, you stay here with Susanna. We have more to discuss."

Susanna wouldn't release Keara after Elam walked from the room. "Could that be Frey?"

"I doubt it, but if it is, Elam will handle him. Maybe I should bring you another cup of tea."

Susanna took a shaky breath. "No, I'll be fine. Thinking about Nathaniel's death always does this to me."

"How you must have loved him."

Susanna gradually released her hold on Keara's hand. "Oh, I did. Had I known how our marriage would end, I'd still have married that man a dozen times over any other."

Keara remained by Susanna's side and waited in silence as she listened to the sound of Elam's footsteps down the stairs.

Eighteen

Elam lit another lantern and carried it through the house to the front door, where he found Jael standing on the front porch.

He opened the door and stood back. "Why didn't you just come in like you always do?"

She gave him a sassy grin as she stepped inside, her riding boots echoing on the wooden floor. "Because you're married again, and I wouldn't want to come barging in on—"

"What are you doing out this late?" He noted she had a fine coating of dust on her clothes, and several long strands of her brown hair had fallen from their fastener.

"I'm on my way home. I thought I'd stop and let you and Keara know that I hired one of the Johnson boys to ride to Clifty with a message about Timothy Skerit. The boy was already heading out when I left their house, so I'm sure the Skerits know by now. Did you know there's only a part-time telegraph operator in Clifty? How's Susanna doing?"

He drew her to the sofa and kept his voice down just in case all the commotion hadn't already awakened the children. Quickly, he filled his sister in on everything that had transpired that day.

She whistled softly when he finished. "So you still don't know what that fake marshal's planning to do with the Skerit boy? Because

I'm telling you, Elam, something's all wrong. I stopped by the sheriff's office just to drop a bug in his ear—you remember Sheriff Nolan and I courted for a few months before I met Kellen—anyway, he wasn't happy to hear about the arrest. Folks think highly of the Skerits around these parts."

Elam nodded. "I'm concerned White River Hollow may be in for trouble, and you should keep the kids close to home. I think you and Kellen need to be prepared for anything."

"After Susanna got shot, you think we aren't? Now, just let me tell David and Pen. It's been killing me to keep quiet about all this—"

"Tell them. I want you to tell every family member along the hollow to keep their ears open for trouble. Don't mention Susanna yet, though, except to David and Pen. One stray word to the wrong person could lead to trouble."

"I'll be glad for the day when that woman is out of danger."

Elam thanked her and gave her a hug then saw her to the door. He'd be glad when they were all out of danger.

As he listened to the sound of hoofbeats racing away along the road—his sister always rode like she was running from a pack of hungry wolves—he stopped in the kitchen to mix another cup of Keara's brew for Susanna with an extra splash of his wedding present from the men. She could use a couple more swallows to help her calm down.

At this rate, if they kept pouring alcohol down her throat like they'd been doing, her liver would be as pickled as Brute McBride's.

Before he turned away from the stove to return to the sickroom upstairs, he opened the cooling oven door and pinched a bite of drying bread pudding. It had just the right blend of sweetness and spice—sort of like one golden-eyed Irish lady he knew.

He was smiling when he entered the sickroom. The women looked up at him expectantly.

"It was Jael," he said. "She got word to Timothy's family about his arrest. She and Kellen will spread word to the rest of the family along the hollow to be on the lookout for trouble. Don't worry, Susanna." He handed her the cup of Keara's brew. "Your name is staying out of it for the time being."

He returned to his chair as Susanna took a deep swallow of the tea. "Now, why don't we pick up where we left off? We need to have an idea what Frey's up to, and what we could be up against."

Susanna handed the cup to Keara and dabbed at her lips. "I hesitate to reveal a secret about Gloria that you may not have known, Elam."

"Gloria and I had no secrets."

"You knew of our ancestry?"

"Of course. You and your siblings are American, with a little mix of many nationalities, including Italian and Cherokee."

"You knew we were part Cherokee?"

"Yes. Cash had a Cherokee wet nurse over the winter. Her family was on their way to the Oklahoma Territory. We shared several stories over those long, dark winter months, and I found myself wondering if they might have been distantly related to Gloria."

"She never told me that," Keara said softly.

"Old history," Susanna said. "She probably didn't think to mention it. At one time, it wasn't safe to reveal too much when the wrong person may be listening. Not that you would be the wrong person, but old habits don't die easily. When Gloria and I were growing up, our Cherokee cousins lived on our land."

"In Pennsylvania?" Keara asked. "All Cherokee weren't forced to move to the Oklahoma Territory in the march of '38?"

"Most were, and the government continued to move them out of the East for the next forty years. My family protected our own."

As if by instinct, Keara pressed the backs of her fingers against Susanna's forehead then nodded with satisfaction. "Good for them. I've heard too many horror stories of that death march. How were your ancestors able to hide them for so long?"

"When my great-grandfather moved to Pennsylvania from Northern Italy in 1834," Susanna said, "he was a wealthy man. It cost a lot to buy land and settle it, but he knew how to handle money. He married a Cherokee woman whose family lived on the adjoining land, and they taught him what crops to grow on the soil, how to rotate those crops, how to use the native plants for medicines."

"And yet you turned up your nose at my teas and treatments?" Keara asked.

Susanna gave her a grin. "Did I ever refuse them?"

"You complained a lot."

"How was I to know you were truly knowledgeable about the proper preparation and use of the local herbs? I could have taught you, but I was a little under the weather."

"So the American government wasn't able to force your relatives to leave their homes?" Keara asked.

"No. It cost my great-grandfather everything he had left, but he purchased the land where his in-laws lived and kept them there. My grandfather followed his father's lead. Our Cherokee relatives were saved from the forced move because of my great-grandfather, and because they lived so far out in the hills that they were able to conceal themselves. Some of my other ancestors also married into the Cherokee tribe who lived there. Even though they wouldn't be forced to move now, many of my relatives moved west in the past couple of years to take private ownership in the division of Cherokee reservation land executed by the Dawes Commission."

"After this much time, there must be hundreds of descendents," Elam said.

"Many of them intermarried and blended in with the immigrants from other countries, but they were able to prove their lineage."

"I thought Cherokee didn't believe in ownership of the land," Keara said.

"They don't, but the white man does, and because of that he can take advantage of my Cherokee relatives. They've already lost so much."

"I remember hearing a few years ago that the Dawes Commission was not able to convince the Cherokee to cooperate," Elam said.

"Of course, so the commission delegates went back to Washington and requested more clout from the federal government." Susanna shrugged then winced at the movement. "The final division of Cherokee reservation land was doled out to individual families last year, and the reservation land that wasn't given to private Cherokee citizens was returned to federal hands for development."

"But didn't private land ownership also give the Indians American citizenship?" Elam asked.

"I don't think my Cherokee relatives see that as fair," Susanna said. "But much is unfair in this life, isn't it?"

"What's to stop the government from claiming eminent domain if they want more of the privately owned land?" Keara asked.

"The treaties were written in a way that would prevent that. They varied for each tribe, but the lands allotted to the Indians could not be taken away for a minimum of twenty-one years."

"I still don't understand what this has to do with Nathaniel's decision to enter politics," Keara said.

"Nathaniel's brother Sikes is an operative in the Dawes Commission," Susanna said. "Earlier this year, he let slip to Nathaniel about a small but powerful faction of our government that's making noise about oil discovered on parcels of that privately owned land."

"Oil?" Keara asked.

"It's a commodity in the Oklahoma Territory that's becoming more valuable by the day," Susanna said. "These government men are after that oil, and they're frustrated that Dawes may have handed over a great deal of wealth to people they consider to be below themselves on the social ladder. Nathaniel was worried about what might happen."

"But the land division was legal," Elam said.

"Greedy people can stoop pretty low when it comes to that kind of wealth," Susanna said.

"What was Nathaniel afraid would happen?" Elam asked.

"Genocide. Or at least decimation."

"Because of oil? And the American government would do such a thing?"

"Not again. There was too much public outcry against the Trail of Tears. Nathaniel was afraid that the next attempt would be more subversive, even more lethal, by a small number of agents."

"In what way?" Elam asked.

"That's what Nathaniel was trying to find out."

"But you've no idea if there was an attack of any kind being planned?" Keara asked.

"None, but I don't believe my husband would have been so willing to enter the political arena with his brother this year if he wasn't convinced of the danger."

"What did he intend to do about it?"

"Investigate until he found the truth and then stop it by any means possible. Nathaniel would have given his life doing anything he could to stop such a massacre."

Silence filled the room so profoundly that they could hear the clock ticking from downstairs and Duchess whinny from inside the barn.

"And he did," Elam said softly.

Susanna's face reddened, and tears filled her eyes. "It seems someone must have thought he knew more than he did."

"Did he tell you anything?" Keara asked.

"Only what I've told you. I'm afraid Nathaniel was too outspoken with too many people, except for me and for his family. I think he felt he was protecting me from the cold harshness he was encountering, and he didn't want Sikes to know what he was doing, because Sikes dismissed the faction as a small group of riffraff. I suspect Nathaniel said the wrong thing to the wrong person."

Susanna closed her eyes and breathed a weary sigh. "Personally, I don't know why Sikes even wanted Nathaniel working with him, except to keep him closer so he could prevent his little brother's outspokenness from interfering with family politics, especially after my father-in-law passed away last year."

"You don't think Sikes is part of this faction," Elam said.

Susanna brushed the tears from her face. "No matter how I may feel about my husband's self-righteous, controlling brother, I know

Sikes would never do anything to harm Nathaniel. And he's not a killer. The Luther family has nearly limitless wealth. There's no reason for Sikes to be so greedy."

"Too many folks can never get enough," Elam said.

"No, you don't understand," Susanna told him. "The Luthers feel it is their God-given duty to take political power to protect the country from people like these land mongers. Sikes truly believes in his sworn duties to protect all. He's a die-hard Roosevelt supporter, and I know he would willingly die for his country, just as his brother did. For all his faults, his heart is true."

"Then if we need an ally with political clout, your brother-in-law is the one we need to contact," Elam said.

Susanna scowled. "I'd just as soon leave him out of this if possible."

"It may not be possible," Elam said. "But we'll see. I'm not sure I believe Marshal Frey's claim that his main intent was to come out here to intercept you, a dangerous killer. It doesn't make sense."

"Unless he thinks I know something I don't."

"So you do believe he was sent by this group?" Keara asked.

Susanna nodded. "Why else would he come after me?"

"But there's more than that," Elam said. "Even if Nathaniel had told you what these men were about, who would listen to you once your reputation was destroyed? If this faction could convince others that you did, indeed, kill your husband, then no one would listen if you sounded the warning about their true intent. He told me you and Nathaniel fought a few weeks before Nathaniel was shot."

Susanna's eyes flashed and she tried to sit up. Then she winced and eased back to her pillows. "Preposterous! All married couples squabble. It doesn't mean they're going to shoot each other."

"Of course not," Keara agreed.

"Nathaniel was gone for weeks at a time," Susanna continued, "leaving me alone to take care of the practice. He was even talking about actually moving to the Oklahoma Territory and setting up a watch to prevent anything from happening to the Cherokee."

"Why?" Keara asked.

"That was my question, so of course we fought. It was a silly idea. What were we supposed to do if we weren't even informed about what actions this group might take?"

"But with his warning, the army at Fort Sill could have been on their guard," Elam said.

"Against what? We didn't know. All I know now is that I'm in danger, as are you, and quite possibly every person of every Indian tribe who lives in the Oklahoma Territory, maybe even more."

"Why did you shoot at the marshal?" Elam asked.

"It was a warning shot only. He surprised me, got around me and was waiting at the other side of a cliff bank when I rounded it."

"Interesting that he told me you were the one lying in wait for him," Elam said. "That's how these people twist the truth around to suit their needs."

"He had his rifle up and drawn," Susanna said. "I had no choice, but I've never killed another human being, and I couldn't kill him. I hit a ledge of stone beside his head, and it broke off and fouled his aim."

"What are we going to do now?" Keara asked. "The man must know you're here at the house or he wouldn't have come here."

"He may have guessed," Elam said, "but he couldn't know for sure."

Susanna spread her hands. "Then I'll have to be gone when he returns."

"You're in no shape to travel," Keara said.

"I'll do what I must. My brothers and Nathaniel have taught me well. I know how to handle that pistol of mine, and I can survive in the wild as well as any man." Susanna looked at Elam. "Surely you've noticed that Duchess is a rare breed. She can nearly read my mind."

"She's an amazing animal, but Susanna, you're a doctor. You know you can barely walk, much less ride yet."

"Even if you were able," Keara said, "Duchess would stand out in any crowd. You said yourself that she drew attention to you when you wanted to remain incognito."

"I recently learned that a rogue US marshal was headed this direction," Elam said. "I'm sure it's Frey. He happened to mention to me that Timothy Skerit has been fraternizing with a gang of men who have begun to gather in Eureka Springs."

"But we don't believe that," Keara said. "He told me he wasn't running with any gang. I believe him."

"And I heard from another source that Timothy had a falling out with that gang," Elam said. "Susanna, if Frey is a rogue, then he might well be hunting you, but I don't think you're his only focus."

"What is?"

"You've been riding in the direction of the Oklahoma Territory. Since Nathaniel was attempting to protect the Cherokee, Frey may indeed think you know more than you do."

"You think he could be part of the splinter group that wants the Cherokee land?"

"It makes sense," Elam said.

"Elam, what about the gang of men in Eureka Springs?" Keara asked. "They must be gathering for a reason."

Elam spread his hands. "There's so much we don't know. Susanna, is Duchess of the Friesian breed?"

Susanna caught her breath softly. "You recognized it. I knew clipping her beautiful feathering, mane, and tail wouldn't be enough to hide her breed."

"I only suspected. My father-in-law knew." He glanced at Keara. "I had to talk to your father. I couldn't allow him to ride away without knowing if he had a place to go. I followed him before I went to get the children today."

Keara's eyes softened. "You heard all this from Pa?"

"Yes, and he heard it from the sheriff. If he got a job with Herman Dougherty, we may be able to use his help to distract Frey from you, Susanna. You can't travel, but Duchess can."

"What are you saying?"

"We've had a dry spell this past week, and there's a lot of dust on the road to Eureka Springs. Jael was covered in dust when she stopped by here. Duchess's tracks would have been blotted out by all our company Monday night, but now they would stand out. Anyone who's skilled at tracking can tell the difference between the size and shape of Duchess's hooves and the hooves of another horse. Even a draft horse would have wheel marks alongside or over its tracks, and this man must know the tracks Duchess leaves. I could ride Duchess into town and leave her with Brute."

"How do we know we can trust Pa?" Keara asked. "He's loose of lips when he's in his cups."

"I believe I saw a change in him today," Elam told her. "I'll have a talk with him first, though. You can be sure of that, Keara. He loves his daughter, and he won't put her in danger if he knows what's afoot."

"The gang of men you mentioned," Susanna said. "Could they be Frey's own little army?"

"Frey may not be connected to them in any way," Elam said. "Someone higher in the pecking order may have sent him on his mission, but we won't take chances. I'll ride Duchess to Herman's stables, keep to the back roads and shadows."

"Are you also going to wear a dress?" Susanna taunted. She glanced toward the curtained window. "That marshal could be watching this house right now."

"He can't see a rider in the dark."

"If anyone were to recognize her breed in town," Susanna said, "I could lose her. Horse thieves abound, and she's worth a fortune. Last I heard there were only three Friesian stallions left in the world."

"Your life is worth more than money," Keara said. "If my father stays sober, nothing will happen to Duchess. I could ride her to Kellen and Jael's place, but there are too many talkative children there." She looked at Elam. "I should be the one to ride her to town. You should stay here and protect Susanna and the children, in case Frey does return here."

"No," Elam said.

"Absolutely not," Susanna said. "I know how to shoot. I hit where I aimed on Monday, remember?"

"You're wounded now," Keara said.

"You know how to handle a rifle yourself," Elam told his wife. "I didn't see or hear anyone following me back home, so if Frey does plan to come, he hasn't arrived yet."

"Then it's decided," Keara said. "Elam will ride Duchess to town, trade horses with my father, and then we will all try to rest."

Nineteen

A whisper of breeze flitted through the leaves, and tree frogs sang a serenade to Elam as he rode the wonderful Duchess along the trail through the dark forest. No wonder Susanna had been so reluctant to part with this beauty. Not only did she give a smoother ride than any horse he'd ever owned, she had sidestepped at least three low-hanging limbs that might have hit him. She instinctively protected her rider and kept a fast pace with her head held high. He would see to her protection.

When the road forked, Elam took the one that led north into Missouri, not Eureka Springs. Misdirection. He rode for about a mile into the hills, past the farmhouses of some men with whom he'd done business in the past. At Ray Harper's ranch, he turned east and rode through knee-high grass until he came to Gravel Creek. He rode Duchess down the center of the water, back toward the city. If Frey did track Duchess with the notion that Susanna was riding her, he might track her to Ray's place, but no one could track her back to Eureka Springs through the creek.

Once he passed the train station and entered the town of Eureka Springs, he slowed the horse but left the creek. He remained in the shadows. Someone might well try to steal a horse as rare as Duchess. He didn't want word to spread that she'd been seen in town.

When Elam reached the farrier's stables, he stopped Duchess in the shadows and dismounted as quietly as possible. As suspected, he had no trouble finding his father-in-law.

Brute was camped out in one of the stalls, sitting beside a lantern, humming softly to himself as he whittled on a piece of wood. He wasn't drinking as far as Elam could tell. Instead, as he whittled he studied a book by the light of the lantern. It looked like a book on woodcarving.

"You don't have a place to live?" Elam asked quietly by way of greeting.

Brute looked up, and a smile eased across his handsome features. He certainly seemed like the old Brute McBride, the good neighbor Elam had known for so many years. The big man set his book and his carving aside.

He stood to his feet and walked toward Elam. "I'll have a place by the end of next week. Meanwhile, I take my meals here, and this bed is almost as comfortable as the one I had in jail." He gestured to a cot at the end of the stall, and then his gaze trailed to the dark shadows where Elam had left Duchess. "What's that I heard stomping around like an elephant back there?"

"I thought we might do some temporary horse trading," Elam said.

Brute frowned and stepped out into the night, away from the glow of the fire. He gave a low whistle. "You can't be serious. What are you doing with a prize like this in town?"

"I need help." Elam glanced toward the street, where few lights glowed except for the squares of windows in the humble homes along Mud Street. Only a few blocks down was the saloon where he'd been told the gang of outlaws had been congregating. "Has there been an arrest anywhere near the saloon today?"

"Nothing's happened since the scuffle with young Timothy Skerit, and he doesn't hang out with those newcomers anymore." Brute rejoined Elam inside.

"I'd be shocked to see him tonight."

"Why?"

"He's in custody."

"Why would the sheriff do that?"

"He didn't. That rogue marshal you told me about? He brought the kid by our place this afternoon. I'll tell you all about it, but first, does Herman have you working long hours?"

"He says I'll have as much work as I can take."

"I doubt he knows how fast you can shoe a horse. Keara and I need your help if you can spare the time, but we also need your silence."

Brute watched him a moment then looked again toward Duchess. "This have anything to do with the friend of yours who owns that horse?"

Elam glanced around them. This part of the stable was no more than a covered corral with a few stalls. Anyone within hearing range might be interested in this conversation.

He stepped closer to his father-in-law. "Before I tell you, Brute, I need to know I can trust you with someone's life, that you won't... forget yourself and let important information slip."

"If you're asking about my drinking, rot-gut coffee is the strongest I've had since I was thrown into that jail cell, and it's the best thing Sheriff Nolan could've done for me. He helped me through the shakes and a couple of days he fed me like a baby. A fella doesn't find friends better than that. I won't be loosening my tongue."

Elam sat down on the cot to tell his father-in-law a tale of intrigue and to beg his help for information that could save Susanna's life… and maybe the lives of many more in the Oklahoma Territory.

When he finished telling Brute about Susanna's story and his impressions of Marshal Frey, he asked, "Can you keep Duchess hidden?"

Brute gave a deep sigh. "I might've lost one or two friends with my shenanigans the past couple of years, lad, but I still know a few true folks who've known me a long time. You just keep that daughter of mine safe. She'll see your sister-in-law back to health. I've always thought it would be fun to be a man of mystery. A spy. Maybe I should get a book on spying instead of whittling on that chunk of wood."

Yes, Brute McBride was back in stride, and Elam grinned despite the seriousness of their conversation. "You should know, Brute, that the only reason Keara turned you away today was because she feared for Susanna."

Brute stared into Elam's eyes for a long moment as the movement of the horses in the stable brushed through the darkness with the sound of peace.

At last, Susanna's father released a long, slow breath. "Son, you don't know what that means to this rowdy ol' father's heart."

"I'm a father too, you know."

"That you are." Brute slapped his knees. "Now, back to the subject at hand. I would like to know what Skerit's reaction was when he found out Frey has his son. I'm hoping he went after the boy."

"And possibly half the community of Clifty went after him as well."

"The sheriff can telegraph Cassville and check on Timothy. He'll take my word for it."

Elam smiled. He could imagine Sheriff Nolan's relief when the Skerits had stepped forward to testify for Brute. In his right mind, Elam's father-in-law was known and loved by all, the sheriff included.

"And you may see increased activity amongst the newcomers you told me were hanging around the saloon," Elam said. "I believe there must be some kind of connection between that rogue marshal and the segment of rogue government, and if my hunch is right, there could also be a connection between those newcomers and the marshal."

"Timothy Skerit tell you that?"

"He didn't have a chance to tell me anything. He did tell Keara he wasn't an outlaw."

Brute chuckled. "As if anybody would believe he was. I think the marshal suspects the kid knows something, and the only reason he'd know something concerning the marshal is if he was hanging out with those so-called outlaws and overheard them talking."

"Makes a lot of sense, but what do they have going on?"

Brute shrugged. "I haven't seen any of them around today. Seems after the scuffle with Tim they decided to move their meeting place. They must think he tipped off the sheriff."

"Have you seen them in town at all?"

"Sure have."

"Keep watch and let me know about anything unusual."

"You'll know it nearly as soon as I do," Brute said. "And so will Sheriff Nolan."

"Jael and Kellen will be spreading the word along the hollow to prepare for trouble."

"Just don't include that rascal who's squatting on my land. He's not a good neighbor."

"When we're finished with this, we'll see what can be done to get your place back."

Brute placed a strong hand on Elam's shoulder as he stood up. "No, son. You have your hands full right now. I wanted my daughter safe, and she is. I can think of no finer man for her to wed. Now you get home and see to her. I've got your back, and I cast a wide shadow."

Elam led Duchess into the stable and placed her saddle and bridle in the storeroom where Brute directed him then prepared Brute's mare, Lass, for travel.

"Think I'll get some shut-eye," Brute said as he handed his beloved horse over to Elam. "I have some work to do before sunup. I'll see you soon." He slapped Lass in the rump.

As Elam rode toward home along Mud Street, which circled East Mountain, square windows of light hovered over his left shoulder like a glowing wall, where bathhouses and springhouses and markets and hotels had been flung up in just a few years' time.

He couldn't help wondering who might be hiding in the shadows, watching him leave.

* * * * *

Keara turned the key in the lock of the front door then walked to each window and peered out at the night. It could be past midnight before Elam returned, but she would be waiting here for him. Meanwhile, she could take some precautions with door locks and her hunting rifle, which she'd set beside the front sofa.

Folks along this section of White River seldom had need to bolt their doors at night, but when Elam had built this house, he'd fitted these with sturdy locks. Keara remembered Gloria teasing him about it, and she remembered the kiss he'd given his wife to silence the teasing.

To be kissed like that, Keara might resort to a little teasing herself. She grinned at her own thoughts then sighed. No time to dwell on something that wouldn't happen.

She continued her study of the windows and doors. The windows couldn't keep a determined man out of the house, but any sound of breaking glass would alert her. She didn't believe the marshal would show up tonight. Elam read people well, and he would not have left her here alone with an injured woman and his three children if he'd thought there would be any danger tonight—despite the fact that he knew Keara could pick off a mess of squirrels from a tree at the far ridge and have them cleaned and cooked for supper. Still, she did not intend to be caught unprepared.

She took a cup of warm tea and another dish of bread pudding up the stairs to Susanna, where she'd left a lantern glowing on the dresser.

Susanna was awake when Keara entered the sickroom, which had begun to smell exactly like what it was.

"How are you feeling?" Keara asked.

"I'm not hurting too badly now."

"Let's keep it that way." Keara settled into her usual perch on the side of the bed and placed the dish in Susanna's hand, enjoying the way her patient's eyes lit up at the sight of the pudding. "Tomorrow, if you're still feeling better, I'll run you a bath and wash that hair."

"Are you saying I smell?" Susanna teased as she set the dish on the bed beside her and raised the spoon.

"You smell like willow bark and sassafras tea with a hint of bread pudding." The true test of a lady was that she made her guests feel at ease at all times—not remarking on appearance or other... unpleasant effects of illness.

"No whiskey?" Susanna asked, nodding toward the cup.

"This should do you fine. I've added some chamomile and mint, with a little valerian root. It should help you sleep through the night. You know," Keara said as Susanna took a bite of pudding, "as much as we've argued over proper medical treatments, you've not suggested anything from your bag to ease your pain."

"I didn't have anything that would work. I did have some laudanum, but I used that on my way here when I happened on a couple of people who were in dire pain."

"You stopped to treat patients on the way?"

Susanna took another bite of pudding. "I'm a doctor."

"That you are, obviously." What an admirable trait in a woman who was running for her very freedom, possibly her life. Keara studied Susanna's face. "Though you have black hair, your eyes are as blue as a summer sky, like Gloria's were. She never told me she was part Cherokee. I never would have guessed."

"I'm also a descendant of Italians from the north of Italy, remember, and they were fair-haired with light eyes. My mother came from Switzerland. And you?"

"With a name like Keara McBride, what do you think?"

"Yes, I believe I picked up on a bit of the Irish accent when your father spoke to you today, and I've noticed a touch of the Ire in you a time or two."

"I tend to speak my mind when needed," Keara said with a grin. She'd surprised herself with her forwardness with a woman of such knowledge and experience. But for the most part, Susanna had been a patient in need. The kind of patient who needed boldness.

"I saw some powders and a vial of liquid with strange markings on them in your bags," Keara said. "Is there nothing there that could help you with the fever or pain?"

"No, I'm ashamed to say. The vial of liquid is for toothache, something Nathaniel and I found in India when we traveled overseas. The powders are for other ailments, also from overseas. I was in such a hurry to leave, I just grabbed what was closest and tossed them and some utensils into my saddlebags. I have double the utensils I need, very little of the medicines."

"Why were you in such a hurry? Had you heard that Frey was after you?"

Susanna took the final bite of her pudding and handed the dish and spoon to Keara. "Thank you. That was perfect. I'll take my medicine now."

Keara handed her the teacup.

"My head's been clearing, and I've remembered more." Susanna took a sip of the tea. "About a week before Nathaniel was killed, he told me that if anything happened to him, I was not to remain in town. He wanted me out of Pennsylvania. It wasn't until after he was shot that I realized how dangerous it had been for him to enter the political arena."

"That's why you left in such a hurry?"

"That's why I closed the office. I didn't leave until I discovered I was about to be arrested by the local sheriff for the murder of my husband, even though he considered it an accident at first."

Keara was outraged for Susanna's sake. How could such malevolence exist? "How did you know he had changed his mind?"

"I have a lot of friends in Blackmoor." Susanna closed her eyes. "Nathaniel and I also had enemies in high places because we treated anyone who came through our door, outlaws and law-abiding citizens alike. Our sheriff didn't appreciate that much. After Nathaniel's funeral, the wife of one of his deputies—who believes I saved her life through two difficult deliveries—warned me the sheriff was seeking out witnesses who would testify against me."

"They would have to be liars, of course."

Susanna gave Keara a grateful smile. "No wonder my sister loved you so."

Keara allowed those words to settle like a balm over her heart. It was more than enough thanks for her efforts to aid such a strong-willed patient. "Do you think the sheriff might have been a part of the political faction that hates the Cherokee people?"

Susanna leaned forward and put the teacup to her lips again. "I think he's a bit of a bully who likes to use his power, but I don't think he's the kind of man to be concerned about what takes place beyond his reach."

"So there were two sources of wickedness, not just one," Keara said. "Not only were evil politicians out to take more Cherokee land, but the sheriff of Blackmoor used his power to intimidate you."

"You'd make a good statesman. Good insight into the vastness of human corruption," Susanna said. "You know, I'm beginning to like the taste of this brew."

"Sweetened with honey from bees who like to visit the orchard every spring. Are you feeling sleepy already? I can leave you in peace."

Susanna shook her head. "I'm sure it will help eventually, but would you stay and talk to me for a few moments? I feel as if my mind is beginning to focus again. I want to find out for sure."

"Okay, then, why don't we talk about how far-reaching this political splinter group could be?" Keara asked.

Susanna finished the tea in a big gulp and handed it to Keara then lay back with a sigh of relief. "Thank you." The skin beneath her eyes attested to her weariness, to long days of travel by horseback and long nights of sleeping on the hard ground, of the constant fear of being arrested or killed. Grief still held her in its hold. And now, the lingering pain of a gunshot wound.

"I'm afraid to guess, Keara," she said at last. "It's something I've thought about until I'm sickened by my feeling of helplessness. There is so much beyond my control because I don't know the extent of the danger, or the people involved."

"There are a lot of things beyond our control, but I believe nothing is beyond God's control." Keara placed the cup on the dresser and lowered the lantern light. "Could it be that you were brought here just for this purpose?" she asked softly.

"I wasn't brought here, I came here of my own accord to escape unjust lawmen, and possibly, in the back of my mind, I had thought to ride into the Oklahoma territory and warn my kinsmen to beware."

"The Cherokee live only past the Arkansas border, maybe two or three days of hard riding. Much less by train. Could God be using you to help save them from annihilation? They won't have the protection they would have if Oklahoma were a state."

"How could I be used to serve a god I don't even believe in?"

"I might be wrong, but if I read my Bible correctly, I don't think He needs you to believe in Him in order to work through you."

Susanna turned her head as if to get a better look at Keara's face. "You talk so much about God. You and Elam are strong, independent people. Why do you feel you must have God to direct your lives?"

"You're a strong and independent person, but look at you now. You need us. You need help. None of us is completely independent."

Susanna looked away. "I don't think I'm up for a debate about the reality of God tonight."

"If Marshal Frey is a part of this political faction out to destroy the Cherokee, and if the sheriff of your town isn't connected to them, then wickedness has already begun to undermine itself. I believe God will prevail."

"I don't understand."

"One wicked man frightened you into escaping here to us, and that sudden flight may have kept another wicked man from killing you. By coming here and warning us, you may have done the most you could possibly do to save hundreds of people. Maybe thousands."

"How?"

"Elam won't give up until he's done everything he knows to do to stop the marshal—and he has a lot of good friends and family. My pa, when he's in his right mind and not sloppy drunk on his whiskey, is a force to be reckoned with. Together, they can be fearsome foes because of the number of loyal friends they have in this area."

"We haven't seen the ending to this drama yet. We may all die and the wickedness may grow." Susanna's voice had grown weary, and her despair touched Keara.

"Anything could happen," Keara said, gently touching Susanna's arm. "But it doesn't seem so dark to me. The only way we could have discovered this danger was through you, someone whose motives are strong and pure. It simply feels to me as if God has a hand in this, and when He does, it's a righteous cause, and one that will not be stopped."

Susanna blinked slowly, as if the tea was beginning to affect her the littlest bit. "I believe you're a force to be reckoned with yourself, Keara Jensen. It's no wonder Elam looks at you the way he does."

"He looks at me as a friend."

"You would make a stalwart friend." Susanna studied Keara for a long moment. The window rattled. The wind had begun to pick up outside, and Keara glanced into the darkness, wondering about Elam.

Twenty

A branch slapped Elam in the forehead and he ducked as Lass carried him beneath still more low limbs. This ride home wasn't nearly so smooth as the ride to town, even though he'd tried to remain on the road for the most part.

Barely a mile from home, however, he'd heard voices and seen shadows ahead of him. He was glad Lass didn't have Duchess's tendency to whinny at the sight of other horses or people.

Another branch raked at his arm, but he ignored it as the two riders ahead of him left the road and entered the woods in the direction of the river. He knew that the cattle trail through those woods led to the McBride farm. Were Rod Snyder and a friend returning from a trip to the saloon in town?

Elam scowled. Had Snyder cheated someone else out of their home tonight?

He halted Lass and slid from her back. Despite her ugly tendency to lower her head and try to brush her rider from her back beneath the trees, she was a good riding horse. Unfortunately, she was about as noisy as a rooting hog.

He tied her loosely to a tree and continued following the men through the woods on foot. If they reached the McBride place and kept going, he would turn back. But if one of those men was Rod

Snyder, Elam wanted all the information he could get on the man. He intended to find a way to get Brute's home back to him.

Though the moon was nearly full, the shadow of the woods made it hard to remain quietly on the trail, but it also slowed the horses in front of him. He was able to catch up enough to overhear a few words here and there. Nothing made much sense.

"…tired of waiting around. Why can't we get on with this…"

"…fortune involved. We can't afford to be impatient…"

A branch cracked beneath Elam's foot. He froze, but the men ahead of him kept going and kept talking. He reached a clearing where the moon lit the trail, and he rushed forward, chancing discovery, in order to hear more.

"…wife to get home to. Can't understand why he chose Eureka Springs, in the middle of nowhere."

"Don't forget the best source is there. And visitors come and go there all the time. We're less likely to be noticed in a tourist town."

Elam reentered the shadows and had to slow, but he was close enough to hear the men more clearly. What kind of source were they talking about? The only thing that was sourced in Eureka Springs was the water, wasn't it?

"I only hope someone beat up Carl Lindstrom for inviting that Skerit kid in the first place. He could've blown this thing to kingdom come."

"Well, he didn't, so calm down. We're earning our keep."

A dog barked in the distance, and Elam hesitated.

"Good thing Lindstrom knows folks around these parts," one of the men said, his voice more difficult to hear as he moved away.

A dog. Elam couldn't risk following farther and letting the

animal catch his scent, though he wanted to know more about Carl Lindstrom's activities. He needed to get home to his family.

But the mention of Lindstrom's name bothered him a lot. The man's younger sister, Cynthia, might know something about her brother's activities. The woman's tongue was vicious and her influence on young Raylene Harper troublesome. Perhaps she'd said something to Raylene. Or possibly Delmar. He had danced with Cynthia on Monday night.

Elam would have to catch Jael and Kellen in the morning before they set out to spread word to the neighbors. He had more to share. Perhaps Delmar could have a talk with Raylene.

* * * * *

Susanna continued to nod off, but she seemed reluctant to let Keara leave. She reminded Keara a little of Rolfe after his mother died. He'd been afraid of the dark for months.

"I was not raised in a religious family," Susanna said, "but you say my sister became a believer?"

"I thought you didn't want to debate the existence of God."

"I only want to hear more about my sister. As I mentioned to you, I did notice a change in her letters a few years ago. She grew up. Accepted her fate." Susanna raised her eyebrows at Keara. "Not that marriage to Elam would be a horrible fate. Indeed not."

"She was always bright and funny," Keara said, "with a quick retort to any comment. I enjoyed her company, even though I sometimes sensed a brittle bitterness in her. She resented the fact that you were taken to your aunt and she was not. She felt you were stolen from her."

"Sometimes we exchanged some hard words with each other in our letters."

"But then she changed," Keara said. "Elam came from a family of strong Christians, and I think they were concerned when he married someone who didn't share his faith."

Susanna's eyes narrowed. "Did they feel she wasn't good enough for him?"

"Not at all. They simply knew how important it is for people of faith to share that faith with their spouses, because living by faith is such a different way of life. There can be a lot of conflict in a marriage when one spouse doesn't understand."

Susanna appeared somewhat mollified. "Well. I think Elam is the kind of man who sees the potential in people."

"Everyone in the hollow saw that he was madly in love with Gloria from the moment he brought her home from Pennsylvania, and that love affected her. She never lost her sense of fun, but she grew gentler."

"Motherhood could have done that."

"I wasn't a mother, but she and Elam had an impact on my life as well. I finally saw what I was meant to be. My parents had grown up believing that there was a God, and they attended church, but I think our jaunts to church were more for social connection than for connection with God. When I saw the change that took place in Gloria, I discovered that I wanted the same faith she had discovered—an abiding faith that God is in control and will guide us if we ask."

Susanna nodded, her blue eyes losing some of their luster as drowsiness continued to affect her. "You have a strength about you...your Irish family must have encountered a bit of trouble with prejudice."

Keara recognized Susanna's need for another change of

subject. "Lots of Irish and Scots here. My ancestry isn't why some disapprove."

"Folks were uncomfortable because you and Elam married so quickly?"

Keara shrugged. "Some ignorant folk still think a woman who makes teas and potions for healing is a witch, not a lady. I don't always behave the way they believe ladies should behave. I'm from the backwoods, never got out much, and I worked with Elam in the corral." Keara shook her head. She didn't know why she was telling these things to a person who might hold some of the same things against her.

"We're not so different underneath," Susanna said, as if she could read Keara's mind. "I understand that you've taught Gloria's children well over the winter months. You have a good grasp of the essentials."

"I read. I love numbers. I went to school as long as I could, but with only two brothers to help with chores and all the planting and harvesting to be done, I was needed at home. It's the normal life on a farm, though I guess you remember some of that yourself."

"That I do, but I had plenty of siblings to share the work."

"And I didn't. When Ma was paralyzed there was no time for anything else."

"Were you the only one who could see to her needs?"

"I was the only girl."

"I can understand a woman being desperate for the help of her only daughter, but my friend, I think your mother may have been afraid to lose her caretaker to a husband and family."

Keara felt herself stiffen. She'd loved her mother dearly. No one had a right to speak of her like this. "I stayed and cared for my mother of my own accord. I wasn't right for marriage anyway. I wasn't built for childbearing."

Susanna's lips parted. "Oh really? And just who told you that?"

"My mother delivered many a baby along the hollow. My hips are slender. I once overheard her remarking to Clydene Brown that she feared I might have trouble giving birth. She'd seen two women die in childbirth, and she was afraid for me."

Apparently, the tea had taken yet more of the edge off Susanna's pain, because she laughed so loudly Keara feared it would wake the children.

"You obviously lacked only one thing necessary to have children of your own," Susanna said, "and that was time. You will be able to bear children as well as any other woman whose babies I've delivered."

"But my mother—"

"Obviously taught you well about herbs and teas, but she was not a doctor. Just because you're slender from working hard and feeding others all your life instead of yourself does not mean you aren't built for childbearing. I read letters from Gloria about how her friend worked her fingers to the bone for her family, and was never allowed out of the house to meet other people her age."

Keara felt heat rising in her. "I loved my family, and they loved me."

"So much you weren't allowed out for social gatherings?"

"You don't know what it's like to be the only female in a home with a paralyzed mother and two rowdy boys. Pa worked so hard—"

Susanna placed her hand over Keara's. "And your heart was so tender you couldn't force yourself to let them struggle. That's why the other ladies your age—who are not ladies, in my opinion, if they hold someone such as yourself in such low regard—might seem to look down their noses at you. They barely know you. And as for your mother, she may have needed you at one time, but she doesn't need you now. She, also, is obviously up in that heaven you believe in, chattering on with Gloria and comparing stories about you."

Before Keara could further explain why she'd stayed at home so often as a young woman, Susanna said, "I think it's time you learn a little more about the joys of true romance, and I'm just the one to teach you."

"Romance? But I don't—"

"You're every inch a beautiful woman, and you have what it takes to be a loving and nurturing mother to more than three children. Get your mother's voice out of your mind and get on with your life…and your marriage."

Keara turned her back on Susanna and paced to the window. She had forgotten how Gloria used to be able to rile her early on in their friendship.

"You know so much about us from your letters from Gloria," Keara said, keeping her voice gentle, "but we don't know much about you. Why don't you tell me about yourself?"

There was a long pause and then a soft chuckle. "Very well, I'll change the subject for the moment. I was well-educated by the standards of the day when I went to live with Aunt June in Philadelphia, but I, too, was a country girl from the backwoods of Pennsylvania. I know how it is to feel intimidated by societal rules."

"I'm sure you missed your home." Keara glanced over her shoulder at her patient.

"I was so homesick for the first few weeks I could barely sleep at night. I also found my aunt to be intimidating, with her culture and education. It took me a couple of years to become accustomed to that."

"I probably never would have."

"I believe you to be capable of doing anything you set your mind to." Susanna looked at Keara in silence for a moment as her eyes continued to reflect her desire for sleep. "I hope I haven't given you reason to feel intimidated."

Keara's gaze skittered from Susanna's face.

"I'm sorry," Susanna said. "I would never wish to do that to anyone. I noticed you're not intimidated by my brother-in-law."

"Elam?"

Susanna blinked sleepily, smiling. "I can teach you about romance."

"I thought you agreed to change the subject."

"I said for a moment. It's been a moment. There really is some romance in your marriage, after all you've tried to deny," Susanna teased.

"I've told you the circumstances."

"My brother-in-law is one very handsome man, with a pure heart. He's your rescuer. What woman wouldn't love him? It's certainly no sin."

Keara didn't reply, but she felt her cheeks grow warm. "More tea?"

"I'll be fine."

"Whiskey?" Keara teased, stepping to the bed and straightening the covers.

"I think I'm plenty sleepy already. You're still avoiding the conversation?"

"I think I gave you too much whiskey earlier."

Susanna chuckled again. "You gave me whiskey to ease my pain and loosen my tongue so I would tell you the truth. Therefore you must agree that what I'm telling you is merely the truth as I see it." She reached for Keara's arm with her good hand then gasped when she leaned too far. "Ouch. I'm a horrible patient."

"Yes, actually, you are," Keara said with a grin. "I can quite imagine why Marshal Frey would want to shoot you." She raised the bandage from Susanna's shoulder and peered beneath the poultice. She nodded with satisfaction. It didn't look infected, as they had first feared, but it would be best to take precautions against that possibility. "Tomorrow, I'd like to make a different poultice to speed the healing."

"Gathering more weeds, are you?"

"Trees, actually. I have fresh sassafras and witch hazel gathered to boil. You obviously enjoy the sassafras tea, and we have more wild honey to sweeten it. You just relax and let me do the doctoring for a little longer."

Keara took Susanna's temperature one final time and then rested her hand on the uninjured part of Susanna's head, as if in a blessing. "Get some sleep." She picked up the lantern and the empty cup. "Tomorrow you should begin to feel better, and after your bath we can wrap that shoulder and arm so you'll be less likely to cause yourself pain."

"Yes, doctor," came Susanna's sleepy reply as Keara closed the door behind her.

It was good that the children were sleeping in total innocence of the man who might be a danger to them. She hoped Susanna did sleep tonight. But Keara would not be able to close her eyes until she saw Elam walk through that front door, whole and strong.

She would pray for him as she watched through the front window for movement.

But for the moment, Keara could not prevent a grin. Something was happening here. Susanna was becoming a friend.

* * * * *

Hours later, Keara jerked awake on the sofa in the front room when she heard the sound of hoofbeats outside. She'd nodded off. How could she have done that?

She reached for the rifle beside her and stood up to peer through the closed curtains then put the rifle back down. It was Elam's outline in the moonlight, riding Lass into the corral.

She expected him to linger in the barn a few moments, but she unlocked the door for him. To her surprise, she heard the echo of his boots on the wooden porch before she could turn away from the door, so she opened it.

"Keara?" he called in the darkness.

"I'm here. Been waiting for you."

He stepped inside smelling like a fresh spring night and leather and horse. Keara loved those smells. "Why? Has there been trouble?"

"Nothing here. I just didn't want to take any chances. I see you rode Lass back. How'd it go with Pa?"

"He says he isn't touching any alcohol, and I believe him. I believe your father is back to his old self." To her surprise, Elam placed his hands on her shoulders and squeezed, as if he was happy to return to her.

His touch couldn't have been more potent had it been lightning. She swallowed and licked her lips, glad he couldn't see her expression in the darkness. She couldn't help thinking of Susanna's teasing about romance. "You're sure, of course, or you wouldn't have left Duchess with him."

"He knows all we do now, and he's in a position to ask questions and get answers."

"He'll take good care of Duchess."

Elam's hands tightened on her shoulders. "And he has been assured that I will take good care of his daughter."

Keara held his gaze in the filtered light, and as she had done many times, she wondered if he knew how his touch affected her. For a moment, she was tempted to stretch up on her toes and touch her lips to his, just to recall the shocking pleasure of the one kiss they'd shared.

And then Elam said, "I think you should sleep in my bed tonight."

Her breathing stopped, and for a moment she couldn't restart it.

He laughed softly and cupped his hand against her cheek. "You need rest, and Susanna seems to be out of danger, at least with the fever. I'll sleep down here on the sofa with the rifle, keeping watch, and tomorrow I'm hoping we'll receive the new mattress I ordered at the mercantile."

He smiled into her eyes then patted her on the shoulder and turned away. "Any new married couple would want a new bed, don't you think? No one's going to think it strange. Come, let's get you to bed."

Twenty-One

Thursday morning found Elam chopping wood out back of the house. When he and the neighbors had built the house, he'd gladly given in to Gloria's pleas for a real bathroom, with running water from a cistern, and also a flush toilet. They were the talk of the community.

He could still remember the teasing he'd endured from the men along the hollow that year when he'd devised that contraption. Now both his sisters had bathrooms, and his youngest brother, Delmar, planned to build his own house complete with bathroom. Other neighbors had asked for his help in constructing their own. No more running to the outhouse through the snow or rain for his neighbors. The men of White River Hollow knew how to treat their women.

Elam had found it well-nigh impossible to create the kind of water heater folks had in Eureka Springs, which used electricity, since they had no electricity so far from town. He had, however, managed to devise a wood stove to heat the water pumped into a large cauldron upstairs above the bathroom. One could stand beneath the trickling stream of warm water and have a satisfying wash. He just had to make sure the water didn't get too hot. It had happened a time or two, and he'd not take the chance again.

This morning his job was to chop enough wood to heat water for the huge iron tub in the bathroom. Keara wanted to give Susanna a bath.

He glanced toward the house, hoping to catch sight of Keara. Since the wedding, he'd had very little time to focus on the marriage part of their friendship—something, of course, that he had not intended to focus on in the beginning. How quickly things changed.

He'd been spending more time alone with his horses this week than he'd expected due to the emergency, so he didn't know how the days might have gone if not for Susanna's appearance. On his ride home last night he'd nearly talked himself into greeting Keara with more than that silly pat on the shoulders, though when she'd met him at the door, making it obvious she'd been waiting up for him, his boldness had failed him.

He missed the easy friendship they'd had for so long. That comfortable companionship had been harder to come by since the wedding vows were spoken, and he knew the moment that had happened—the kiss, the flare of wonder. The hope. And then came the crush of guilt at the betrayal in his heart of his wife's memory for just that moment.

Until then he'd been telling himself that he and Keara would, indeed, have a good partnership, as she had suggested.

He hurled the ax into a log and split it in two with one hit then set both halves up on the stump and split both of them.

This week had been one frantic moment after another. Before the wedding, he'd told himself he could wait until the dust settled to see how he and Keara would be with each other—whether things would be strained or whether they would carry on as before. A couple of times, they'd seem easier, but then back would come that tentativeness about pressing for more because he feared losing what they already had.

He tossed the four chunks of wood onto the pile then placed another log onto the splitting stump.

The dust he'd hoped would settle after the wedding didn't look like it'd be settling for a while, judging by Susanna's report.

Still, he couldn't totally blame Susanna's appearance for the occasional discomfort between him and Keara this week—partially, but not totally. He could avoid thinking about the subject, but if he was honest with himself, he would have to admit he hadn't been able to get that wedding kiss out of his mind. It seemed almost like a promise.

Of course, he'd known the comforts of marriage. Why hadn't he realized that a kiss like that—with a woman like that—would have ignited something inside him?

He could have put his foot down with his sisters and refused the wedding ceremony in Eureka Springs, but until Monday he had never before seen the woman who had come walking down that aisle toward him. There'd been no time to change his thinking before the words were said and their lips met.

For Keara's sake, whether she'd felt comfortable about it or not—and she obviously had not—she deserved that wedding. For once in her life she needed to feel as if she mattered more than the next necessary thing to be done.

What would Gloria have wanted?

Something Keara told Elam last week continued to echo in his mind. Gloria had wanted him to remarry, to be happy, to not be lonely, to have a partner in life. Hers had been that selfless kind of love, and if he turned it around, he'd have wanted the same for her.

He finished the next log and lifted it onto the woodpile. There would be plenty of hot water for all of them. His family would be clean in the coming days.

He returned to chopping and thinking. Sure, if he'd been the one to die, he would want his loved ones to grieve for him and miss him, but he couldn't have borne the thought of his darling Gloria and his children continuing in pain and sorrow forever. Not that he liked the thought of her with another man, loving him, sharing his bed, his life—but if it was the right kind of man, a good man, solid and strong and kind, he would want that for her.

Gloria had loved Keara as a sister.

The back door opened and out stepped the blond-haired woman of his thoughts in a pretty green calico work dress, her hair caught up in a loose knot, prepared to give a bath. Was it his imagination that she'd had fewer dust marks on her dresses, cleaner hands, tidier hair this week? And she hadn't worn her old work trousers one single time.

"You planning to bathe the whole neighborhood today, Elam Jensen?" The teasing lilt in her voice betrayed her mood this morning, and he couldn't help wondering if a good night's sleep in his bed—while he slept with the rifle on the sofa downstairs—might have helped her mood. She'd needed the sleep.

He gestured toward the wood. "I'll take a load up in a minute."

She stepped from the house and crossed to the pile. "I can carry it up. I've already got the fire going with the kindling. Wouldn't want it to go out."

He reached out and took her by the shoulders. "You've done enough carrying this week. How's Susanna's fever this morning?"

Keara looked up at him, her expression softening to something…

else. "Still normal. We may have this thing beat after all. She's got a constitution as strong as Freda Mae's."

"Let's hope her hooves don't grow as fast."

Keara chuckled, her golden-brown eyes lighting again with that humor he'd grown to depend on over the long winter.

"I'll have the wood upstairs in a minute," he said. "You take a rest. Have a cup of that sassafras tea you keep making for everyone else."

As she gave him a final grin and turned back toward the house, he found himself distracted by her small-but-strong form, the curve and movement of her—

"Hello the house!" came a call from beyond the orchard wall just before Keara reached the door. From here, he wasn't visible, but the voice was recognizable.

Keara stopped and turned. "It's Pa. I wonder what he's doing here this morning."

"He must have news for me, or he wouldn't have left work to ride all the way out." Elam leaned the ax against the woodpile.

Keara started back across the yard. "Well then, I'm sure you men will need to talk. I'll just take a log to keep the fire—"

Elam intercepted her with an arm around her shoulders this time. "You go greet your father. I said I would see to the fire, and that's what I'm going to do."

"I'm sure he came to see you."

"You need to make peace with your father. I'll talk to him after I carry the wood upstairs."

She blinked up at him. She didn't argue, but she didn't immediately withdraw. Like last night, it was as if his touch stilled her. He guided her toward the side of the house. "It'll be okay, Keara. Walk around to the front and greet him. His first concern is for you. He won't be angry with you."

When they were in sight of her father's solid form, she hesitated.

Elam tightened his arm around her. "You have forgiven him, haven't you?" he asked softly.

"I...believe I have," she said under cover of Brute's chatter to the horse. "I know I have no ill will toward him, but after these past two years I'm not sure what to expect from him, and the things I said to him on Wednesday—"

"You simply told him the truth, very forcefully. And he's still the same Brute McBride, he just has a little more humility than he once had. Not much of it," Elam said, smiling into her upturned face, "but it'll do."

He felt her shoulders square and heard her intake of breath. He gave her shoulders a final squeeze and eased her forward, out of his embrace. He watched her go, and he marveled at the change in her these past few days.

Or maybe he was the one who'd changed.

When he returned to the woodpile, he caught a movement in the upstairs window. Britte's room. He looked up, and for the briefest of moments, he saw his family, Britte and Rolfe...and Gloria, smiling down at him.

Not Gloria, of course. Susanna. But it was enough to give him pause as the curtains closed them away from his sight.

Gloria wouldn't have wanted him and the children to remain alone, but to replace her in their hearts before a year had passed? And to have awakened this morning with the recall of a dream of a woman with golden-brown eyes instead of blue?

* * * * *

Keara skirted the orchard wall, studying her father as he stood beside his mount, scratching the gelding's ears, unaware of her presence. He seemed to hesitate as he looked toward the front porch, as if afraid to approach and possibly receive the same welcome he'd received yesterday.

She closed her eyes as she recalled her words, and she hated herself for them. How could she have turned him away like that?

But how could she have known if she could trust him with Susanna's life? Maybe if she'd asked him, as Elam had, if he was still drinking...but would she have listened?

His continued hesitation told her that Elam was right. Brute McBride had been blessed with a new touch of humility.

He glanced up and caught sight of her at last, and he froze, his eyes widening. "Hello darlin'."

"Hello Pa."

He reached up and pulled his hat off his head, and the waves of thick black hair formed a frame around his face. "I don't reckon you'd care to have a word with your rogue father."

She took a step toward him, hesitated, then took another, and another until she was rushing toward him and her throat was swelling with tears she didn't want to shed, but they refused to be held back.

"Oh, Pa," she cried as she rushed into his open arms and felt him swing her up and around and heard his laughter in her ear and felt the soft brush of whiskers on her face.

"Pa, I'm sorry I—"

"Now, now, none of that." He lowered her to her feet and then kissed her forehead. "I'm the one to apologize."

"You did that last time you were here."

"And you let me know how much you've been through. I don't think there can be enough apologies for that. I'm here to try to make it up to you." His deep voice sounded solid, reassuring.

"You are?"

"That I am."

"What about your job?"

"I've talked to Herman. He knows what I'm doing. The sheriff and I've had ol' Pete at the telegraph office busier than a coon in a henhouse."

Keara stared at her pa, yet again amazed by his ability to make friends everywhere he went, even in jail. "You've got help from the sheriff?"

"Of course," he said, as if that were a silly question. "Sheriff got word back from Cassville that US Marshal Driscoll Frey never arrived with his prisoner."

Keara grasped her father's arm. "That man still has Timothy Skerit?"

"I don't know, darlin'. Elam told me Frey was planning to stay the night in Seligman, so they might not have even made it to Cassville yet, but you can bet Thomas Skerit has already lit out after his son. Telegraph's a wonderful thing. We may hear before the end of the day if the boy's been found and if he's safe."

"What else have you heard from the telegraph office?"

"We got quick word about Frey from the US Marshal's office out of Philadelphia, where he was headquartered until a few months ago."

"He really is rogue, isn't he?"

"Just like your ol' pa, only this'n's truly a nasty piece of work, not a loveable fella like me. The sheriff had Pete run down Marshal Albertson, who's been through Eureka Springs a few times and is friends with the mayor. Albertson hails from Philadelphia, and he remembers Frey, even filed a formal complaint about him when he saw too many of Frey's prisoners shot or beat half senseless for no good reason.

Keara gasped. "What if he's hurt Timothy?"

Pa shook his head. "Don't know. Albertson said the man has cold eyes. Of course, he couldn't say much else over the telegraph. It'd take too many words. I'd like to have a talk with him someday."

"There was something about him I didn't like, Pa. He was polite and all, but it was as if his politeness was a skin he could crawl out of anytime he wanted. He told Elam he was keeping Timothy out of the way of a big arrest as a favor to a friend."

Pa shook his head. "There wasn't any arrest, and a man like him wouldn't be a true friend to anybody. I've seen the like. Last time I saw one like Frey," Pa said, looking down at her, "was the night I was cheated out of the farm."

"Rod Snyder?"

"The cheatin' dog-eared—"

"You shouldn't've been betting."

"I know. I do. It won't happen again."

"You don't have anything left to bet." She paused. "You do still have Duchess, don't you?"

He gave her an innocent look. "Who's that?"

"Pa!"

He winked at her, eyes twinkling. Elam was right, her father had developed only a little humility.

"She's safely hidden back deep in Tilley Holler where few folks ever wander due to snakes and wildcats. I rode her there myself before sunup this morning, where the Tilleys are treating her like the royalty she is. They loaned me this gelding with a nasty temper." He gestured toward his borrowed mount.

"Elam said Timothy Skerit got into a skirmish with a gang of men. Have you seen those men today?"

Pa put his arm over Keara's shoulders and walked with her toward the front porch. "Not meetin' at the saloon anymore, but I know where they are meeting. Soon as I got back from taking Duchess to her deep holler keep and checked for news with the sheriff and had a long talk with Herman and other stalwart friends, I wandered the streets until I spotted a couple of the men I recognized. I followed them out of town. Guess where they went."

"I don't know, Pa. Did you get any sleep at all last night?"

"Slept like a baby from the time Elam left until I had to take Duchess away. Then after I followed those men to their new meetin' place, I had to get out here and warn you."

"About what?"

"Those men are meetin' at the farm."

"You mean our home?"

"That's right." His eyes darkened. "Couldn't get close enough to hear what the meetin' was about, but I reckon Timothy Skerit did, and that's why he got into that skirmish with them. They're up to no good, you can be sure of that. Too bad Timothy didn't see fit to tell the sheriff what he heard, but he and his pa were distracted when they saw me in the jail cell."

"You mean, that's why they were there and could testify for you?"

Pa nodded. "That's right. They wouldn't've known I was even

there if Timothy hadn't been brought in on charges of misconduct. As if that young man was a troublemaker."

"Elam followed a couple of men along the cow path from the road to our farm last night," Keara said. "But there's a dog there."

"I heard that same dog this morning. We may need to doctor up a few pieces of meat from the butcher's shop to quiet the hound."

Keara told her father what Elam had overheard from Snyder and his cohort last night. "Do you think the sheriff could call a couple of real US marshals in to stop these men?"

"From what? We don't have anything to show them." He stepped up onto the porch with her and patted her back. "But I mean to find out."

Keara wanted to cry with relief. Her pa was back.

Twenty-Two

Elam built just the right size stack of logs for a good draft in the stove then closed the door and adjusted the damper. That would be enough to heat the water in the cauldron and he would bring more wood upstairs after he talked to Brute.

He was dusting his hands, stepping from the hot water room, when he heard the feminine sound of a throat clearing behind him. He turned to see Susanna leaning against the opposite hallway wall, her hair mussed, her dress twisted awkwardly because of her shoulder.

He heard the sounds of Cash's squealing, Rolfe's laughter, and Britte's mother-hen voice downstairs.

"They're playing in the bathroom," Susanna told him. "I have to say, those little ones are three of the happiest children I've set eyes on. How did you get them through this mourning period with their gift of laughter still intact?"

He smiled as the sound of their voices continued up the stairwell. "Much prayer and help from friends and family."

"Especially Keara, I don't doubt."

"She risked her reputation so she could spend time with us over the winter months. She has a kind nature."

"And so do you. I think two kind people will be marvelous parents for a houseful of children."

Elam met Susanna's direct gaze and tried to read behind it. Was she being sarcastic or giving him her approval?

"You heard me," she said. "I arrived on your front step on your wedding night injured and defiant, and Keara and the rest of this family has nursed me and cared for me. I see nothing but goodness in that woman."

Those words eased a tightness inside him. It wasn't as if he needed her approval, but she was and always would be his children's aunt. "Then you see her as I do."

"I hope not."

He blinked at her.

"I realize you're still in mourning over Gloria, and that this was a rushed wedding, to say the least. Keara has told me a great deal now that I'm lucid and on the mend. I realize you're getting things backward, but I do hope you intend to court her as a suitor would court a young lady."

"Court?"

"As you courted Gloria on your business trips back East."

"But Keara and I are married."

Susanna straightened from the wall. "Elam, I know you've been out of the romance game for ten years, but would you please try to remember how gently you treated Gloria after you two first met? How you eased her into gentle friendship, made those first tentative steps toward romance, and then toward lasting love?"

"That was young love."

"And you don't think Keara deserves the same kind of love? Oh, sure, I realize she's a different woman, but she's not a second-rate woman. Please don't make her feel you settled for her as a consolation prize."

"Susanna, there's been no time—"

"A woman like her is worth the time. I see the way the two of you look at each other when each thinks the other isn't looking.

Don't forget I was trained to be a keen observer of people. It's often how I make my diagnoses."

He took a step backward. "Fancy yourself a bit of a matchmaker, do you?"

"Oh no. The match has already been made. My intention is to assure that my niece and nephews continue to live in a happy environment filled with love. In order to do that, their father must truly love their stepmother. She is a woman worth that love."

Elam suppressed a smile. "I met your aunt June a few times on my trips to Pennsylvania. She was a lady who spoke her mind. I can't help believing she rubbed off on you."

"I count that as a compliment, but she was my mother's sister, and Gloria tended to have nearly as much invincibility. Keara has the strength of will to stand up to even that kind of outspokenness, and to thrive on a friendship with another strong-willed woman. I count her as a true friend." Susanna reached for his arm. "Help me get down the stairs without falling, and I'll keep quiet about your need to be told how to romance your new bride."

He walked with her, taking care to move slowly. "I'm not sure Keara would appreciate any attempts at courting."

"Why is that?"

"She was the one who insisted on a platonic partnership."

"And you agreed to such an arrangement?"

"At the time I thought it best."

"Have you, then, changed your mind since?"

He hesitated.

"That's what I thought," she said as they reached the bottom of the stairs. "If you can't trust your own instincts—and I've found many a man who cannot do such a thing—why won't you trust mine? I don't think your new bride would be unreceptive to your charms."

"You think I should court her."

"Gently. As you were doing this morning out by the woodpile. I know you must remember a few things about it. I could see that she was charmed. Try it again, and again, until you get it right."

"I'll think about what you're saying." He glanced out the front window, where Keara and her pa stood in deep conversation. "Until I'm sure, I need to meet with a man about a plot to kill the Cherokee."

Susanna reached up and firmly pinched his chin between thumb and forefinger. "Consider me Keara's doting older sister. I have a great interest in her happiness. Don't disappoint me."

"Yes ma'am." He scooted away before she could read even more deeply into his thoughts. The woman was disconcerting, to say the least.

And yet…he couldn't help dwelling on her words as he stepped onto the porch to greet Brute.

* * * * *

Keara worked Susanna's long hair into a lather with bars of the scented soaps Jael and Pen had given her as a wedding gift. In an attempt to keep Susanna's wounded shoulder out of the water, she had Susanna lean her head over the rounded back edge of the tub and poured water from the tub over her hair and into a pan.

Keara had brewed a pot of strong tea and added whiskey to a cup to stave off Susanna's pain. It was a good thing Susanna didn't have a taste for alcohol, because if she did, she could become dependent on it in a hurry.

"I still hate that stuff," Susanna said. "But it works almost as well as laudanum."

"I'm glad."

"Once you get me out of here, it's your turn for a nice bath."

"I had one yesterday."

"Another one wouldn't hurt, as long as the fire's already going. Don't waste all this sweet scent on me. I'm sure Elam will love it."

Keara poured a pitcher of water over the soapy hair and watched the suds splash into the pan below. "I've told you, that isn't…the way it is with us."

"You're a twenty-six-year-old woman, and you can't see what's right in front of your eyes?"

"I can see you're going to talk until the water gets cold."

"There's still more heating up above our heads. Elam filled the stove full."

Frustrated, Keara finished rinsing Susanna's hair and reached for a towel. "I'll leave you in peace to soak for a while," she said as she wrapped the towel around Susanna's head and tucked the end of it so it wouldn't unfurl.

"I had a private conversation with your husband awhile ago," Susanna said as Keara reached for the door.

That stopped Keara short. She turned back to see Susanna grinning at her over the side of the tub.

"You undersell yourself so much, my friend," Susanna said.

"I don't undersell anything, I just know what I am and what I'm not."

"What are you?"

"I'm…well…I'm good with horses and children, I know how to care for the sick and tend a garden, milk cows, and goats."

"That's it? Then tell me what you aren't good at."

"This is silly. You need to finish your bath and I need to see to Cash."

"I asked you a question." Susanna's authoritative tone rose through the scented bathroom.

Keara took a breath, let it out, turned to peer through the gauzy curtain over the window. "We've already discussed this. I'm not a…I'm not Gloria. Nothing like her. You're her sister. You're like her in so many ways, you could have given the children a touch of sophistication had you been their new mother instead of me."

There, she'd said what she'd been thinking since Monday night, and she certainly didn't have to turn around and look at Susanna to imagine the surprise on her face in the silence that followed her words.

"I could raise her children the way she would have raised them and been a second Gloria to Elam Jensen?" Susanna asked.

Keara hesitated, nodded.

"Why would I want to be my sister's stand-in? I have no wish to remarry after ten years of marriage to Nathaniel." Susanna's voice began to rise. "Why, his brother Sikes looks a lot like Nathaniel. Do you think I would wish to be bound to that self-righteous clod simply because he resembles Nathaniel?"

"Of course not, but—"

"Then why do you believe Elam would wish to marry me? You're the friend who has seen his family through the winter. You're the woman he knows and loves, despite what you choose to believe."

"I was merely being practical."

"You were practical when you accepted Elam's proposal?"

Keara sighed. "He didn't propose. I did. I had to beg him to marry me." Why, oh why, was she spilling all this information?

"And he saw the good sense you made," Susanna said without hesitation. "Why are you now second-guessing yourself?"

"I didn't stop to think about the realities of marriage."

"You mean the intimacies?" Susanna grinned. "Nothing has changed since you proposed, but you are definitely lacking when it comes to romance."

Keara caught her breath and turned to glare at Susanna. "Do you have to be so cruel?"

"Honesty is important. You're the one who's being cruel. How can you think your husband would be such a cad as to look at another woman when he's married to you? Especially since he so obviously cares for you. Keara, you need to set things in order with that husband of yours before you both get off on the wrong foot and never get together again in this dance of love and marriage."

Keara frowned. Those words, the "dance of love and marriage," sounded so familiar. It was something her best friend would have said if she hadn't died last year.

Keara stared down at her work-worn hands, realizing why she'd confided so much to Susanna.

She was Gloria's sister. "I miss Gloria so much."

There was a long silence between them as the sound of the children laughing and playing in the garden outside drifted past the gauzy curtain.

"I've missed her ever since we were separated in childhood," Susanna said. Her voice was soft. "I know she must have been a wonderful friend to you, but I'm not Gloria. No one else will ever take her place in your heart, in mine, in Elam's, or the children's, but there is room in all our hearts for new friendships. New love."

"I know."

"If Gloria were still alive, you wouldn't be married to her husband."

"If she were alive, I'd have had a place to stay without worrying that the whole community would condemn me as an immoral woman."

"But she isn't alive," Susanna said sadly. "And it does no good to think about such things. Now you're married to Elam, and Gloria is no longer here. You have a new life to take hold of with both hands." She closed her eyes. "When I arrived here on Monday I would never have believed that on Thursday I would be saying such things to the wife of my sister's widower."

"I understood why you resented me at first."

"Well, I don't resent you now. You and Elam have a whole future and plenty of room in this house. Your new sisters-in-law saw that. It's why they kept the children out of the way so you would have a good wedding night—which I'm sorry I ruined for you."

"You ruined nothing. There wasn't anything to be ruined."

Susanna fixed her with a look. "I'm getting tired of this, Keara Jensen. Look at that mirror on the wall, and don't tell me you're too blind to see the beauty in your reflection."

"I can remember what Gloria looked like, how she behaved. It was nothing like me."

"Two beautiful women can be very different in appearance, personality, and abilities, but down deep, the character of truly beautiful women is similar. Faithfulness, caring hearts, the ability to love. I have eyes to see, and I know what love looks like. What it feels like."

Those words and the loss that echoed through them struck Keara with compassion. Here was Dr. Susanna Luther discussing romance with her, advising her, when Susanna lost her beloved husband a month ago.

"A good marriage to a solid, dependable man can be one of life's greatest pleasures and strengths," Susanna said more softly. "Elam is one of those good men. You're a good woman."

Keara felt a new sense of longing. How would it feel to be as loved by Elam as he was loved by her? And yet she had believed for so long that it wasn't to be.

She stepped over to the mirror and stared at her reflection. Mirror-gazing had never been a habit of hers. The house where she'd grown up had no mirrors. In fact, these past months, coming to the house every day to see to the children and help Elam, she'd seen her reflection in this mirror more times than ever before in her life, and it disappointed her—hair so pale, when Gloria's was so rich and black, eyes filled with shadows, when Gloria's matched the sunlit sky. Dimples that made her look like an immature child instead of a well-developed woman.

She'd decided that the mirror let her know when her hair was a mess or her face was dirty. Otherwise, it wasn't good for much.

"What's on your mind, Keara Jensen?" Susanna asked.

"The past."

"What about it?"

Keara picked up the pan of soapy water and poured it into the sink to drain. "Isn't it always the past that affects our future? Once, before I was forced to quit school to attend to family needs, I had a crush on Johnny Stark, who lived in the village of Beaver. He had dark brown hair and broad shoulders. Half the girls in our schoolhouse adored him. But when I admitted to a friend that I liked Johnny, she laughed. 'You?' she said. 'What boy would be interested in you?'"

"Then she was no friend."

"Soon, word spread through the school that silly ol' tomboy Keara McBride, who couldn't keep up with her classmates because she had chores at home—and who didn't know how to dress or behave like a girl—thought she was in love with Johnny Stark."

"How unkind," Susanna said. "That is the opposite of ladylike behavior."

"I know that now, of course, but I vowed to myself then that I would never share my heart like that again. I wasn't the kind of girl to mingle or beguile a man. I was created to care for others, and that's what I'm doing now. It's God's calling for me."

"Oh, it may very well be. But I don't believe that's all you're meant to be," Susanna said. "It wouldn't hurt, would it, to buy material that best matches your coloring, to sew a pretty dress or two like the one you're wearing, or that lovely red dress you managed not to stain with blood on Monday night, and show Elam that you believe he deserves a beautiful wife? You do know how to sew, don't you?"

"Of course."

"In that case, I need you to ride to town for me today."

Keara's gaze met Susanna's in the mirror's reflection. "I can't leave here with things the way they are now."

"The marshal isn't after you, he's after me, and if Elam's here, I'll be safe. I just want you to visit the mercantile and purchase material, some sewing supplies and lace. I can show you a few tricks of seaming that will help you show off your womanly curves to your adoring husband. You need new clothes anyway. I've inspected your wardrobe when you weren't looking, and it's definitely lacking."

Keara caught her breath and swung around. "You rifled through my clothing?"

"Oh, my! Did I say that? Must be the whiskey talking." Susanna didn't look the least bit repentant, and when Keara stalked from the bathroom and shut the door firmly behind her, she heard Susanna's laughter following her.

Twenty-Three

Elam stood on the front porch watching his father-in-law ride up the road toward the White River neighbors. The knowledge that Brute McBride was settling back into his right mind eased a nagging pain that had gnawed in Elam's gut for the past two years. Not only had he considered Brute one of his closest friends, he was also a strong man, quick thinking and quick acting when something needed to be done—a stalwart neighbor everyone knew they could count on.

His devotion to his wife had become legend along the hollow, but there was only so much one man could do to keep his farm going while caring for his wife. He'd bemoaned the fact more than once that he hated seeing his daughter swallowed up by family demands. He and his wife had both wanted so much more for her.

The dust kicked up by Brute's mount had barely settled when Elam heard the thud of quick footsteps through the house, and the front door flew inward. Keara came shoving through the screen door as if running from a fire, only she wasn't running, she was marching. Stomping. Angry.

The screen door slapped shut behind her as she rushed down the steps like a dust devil, her gaze straight ahead. She didn't even glance toward Elam where he stood staring after her from the far side of the porch.

"Of all the meddling, nosy, insensitive, bossy…" Hands fisting at her sides, she let out a furious hiss.

A few strands of long, damp hair clung to her neck, and she had rushed from the house without taking time to pull on her sleeved blouse. Her taut and shapely arms were bare from helping Susanna bathe.

She planted her hands on her hips and crossed the yard to the stone wall that protected the orchard and garden, lips moving as she muttered more quietly to herself.

Susanna was right. Keara had as much gumption as Gloria'd had. Maybe more. She was saucy and smart and spoke her mind, except for those times when her confidence failed her, such as when the subject turned to romance.

On impulse, he leapt over the half-wall of the porch and hit the ground past the flowers. He did it so silently Keara didn't hear him.

"What's she done now?" he asked.

Keara gasped and jerked around, her brown eyes nearly black with anger, her cheeks flashing rosy pink. "What are you doing sneaking up on me like that?"

"I was just—"

"Have you been eavesdropping?"

"Only for the past minute or two, but—"

"Don't I have a right to a single moment of privacy now? Did I sign all that away with the marriage contract?"

As he came nearer, he saw tears in her eyes, and as he reached for her they spilled over.

"You can have any rights you want, Keara Jensen," he said gently, his hand touching the soft, warm flesh of her arm. "Remember, you're the lady of the house."

She blinked up at him, scattering the droplets of tears with her long lashes. She had never looked more beautiful, more vulnerable, or more attractive to him. Seductive…irresistible.

He put an arm around her, tentatively, not wanting to force her to step nearer to him. When she didn't pull away, he wrapped the other arm around her and drew her forward. It was as if he couldn't stop himself. Only Keara could stop him.

She leaned into him willingly, burying her face against his chest. "Don't go messing with my mind," she said, her voice muffled by his shirt.

"I'm a husband comforting his wife. Can't a man do that?"

"A real husband can do that with his real wife."

"You're real. So am I." She felt so good in his arms. She was so very real.

Her body stiffened, and then she pulled her hands up between them and pushed away. "We aren't real." She freed herself of his touch, turned away, and stepped to the dividing wall, reaching out to touch the edge of a stone embedded with crystal.

"We can be as real—this marriage can be as real—as we want it to be." Elam didn't follow her, because he knew she needed a little distance between them right now.

And yet his heart thudded in his chest. He knew what he wanted, and it wasn't this. Not her walking away from him, rejecting the image of what a real marriage could mean for them.

"The minute word hit the air that we were to be married, everybody started trying to remake Keara McBride," she said. "Even me. I tried fitting that image of a lady I knew you'd want for your bride. And I'm obviously lacking in all the necessary requirements, including clothes."

"I didn't try to remake you."

"That's because you knew we were only getting a legal license to live together for the sake of the children and to give me a home. Bless her heart, Pen even told me how she'd longed to get her hands on me for the longest time. Like I was a hopeless waif not good enough for the likes of the Jensens. My clothes aren't pretty enough, my hair is a mess. I don't know how to behave properly."

"That's not fair. My sisters love you as their own kin."

"And then there's Susanna, who's decided she has every right to rummage around through my clothes—after all I've done to heal that shoulder of hers—and see if I have anything worth saving."

Elam's laughter came bursting forth in spite of the real danger shooting from Keara's eyes. "Those awful creatures. How dare they try to polish you up and help you look your best?"

Keara placed her hands on her hips and aimed a deadly glare at him. He continued to laugh. He even dared to saunter to her side and put his arm around her again.

"Come here." He urged her forward, and to his relief, his touch still seemed to affect her. He guided her back to the rock wall. "Remember the days you spent scouring the banks of White River, looking for just the right stones to cap this fence?"

She crossed her arms over her chest and nodded.

"You collected the prettiest ones you could find, and then you dug this one up." He ran his fingers over the jagged edges of the crystal. "You scrubbed it with a brush until all the grains of dirt were washed away, and then you set it just right so that the sunlight would catch it and make it sparkle."

"You're comparing me to a rock fence?"

Once again, his laughter echoed from the side of the house.

"Nobody's comparing you to a rock fence. I'm comparing you to a glowing crystal that tries to hide its beauty." He drew her closer, and he heard her breath go still. "Susanna caught me in the hallway earlier. She has decided you need an older sister to watch out for you, make sure you're being treated right."

"By who?"

"By me. She wants me to court you properly."

Keara's eyes widened, her lips parted, and to Elam's delight, tears once again filled her eyes.

He had seen his sisters and Gloria cry so often at so many inconsequential things that he'd long ago learned not to interpret tears as a sign of hurt or anger.

She turned away from him and stared down at that crystal stone in the wall.

He stepped up behind her. Unable to resist, he put a hand on her shoulder. As always, it was soft, resilient. "Keara?"

Her muscles suddenly tensed. "Where'd Pa go?"

He shook his head. Wasn't it just like her to change the subject? "He went to round up a posse."

She turned to him, eyes round. "A posse!"

"Maybe not a posse, exactly, but help. Support. We need our neighbors in on this thing. We know who we can trust, and we need all the help we can get right now."

She nodded.

He put a hand on her other shoulder. "Keara?"

"Yes?"

"What do you think would happen if we decided to make this a different kind of marriage?"

Again her lips parted, and he could have kicked himself. Susanna most certainly would have kicked him if she'd been listening. This wasn't at all what he'd intended to say.

"I'm sorry," he said. "Let's back up for a minute. What I should have said was that I haven't been able to get my mind off that wedding kiss. We sealed a pact with that kiss, and it didn't seem to me like the kind of pact people make in a strictly business transaction."

She didn't move from his touch. She also didn't argue with him. Instead, she blinked up at him as if mesmerized. It was all he needed.

He drew his hand from her shoulder to the back of her neck and bowed his head to press his lips to hers with all the gentle tenderness he felt for her. Her lips tasted of sassafras, and she smelled like cloves and ginger and cinnamon.

He raised his head slightly, breaking the connection as he dwelt in her golden gaze. Her eyes told him she wanted him closer, and so he kissed her again, and then his lips traveled down her cheek to the soft hollow beneath her chin.

She gasped suddenly and broke away. He once again resisted the powerful urge to draw her back.

"Keara?"

"What have I done?" She asked the question as if talking to herself, not him.

"You've done nothing wrong. This isn't a betrayal of anyone, Keara. It's a marriage. We've talked about this."

"No, we haven't." She wiped at her lips with the back of her hand then looked down at her bare arms. "Not about this." She hugged herself, hands over her arms as if suddenly ashamed of her state of undress, and she rushed toward the front steps.

"Keara, wait, please." He started after her.

She reached the front door and turned back to him. "You said that mattress was supposed to arrive at the mercantile today?"

"Yes, it's coming by train, but we're going to have family and neighbors here in a couple of hours. I'll ride to pick up the mattress. The road is too dusty—"

"Nobody needs me here for the meeting. I'll wrap Susanna's shoulder and get her back to bed then hitch Buster to the wagon and ride into town."

"I want your input on this situation when everyone arrives, Keara."

"My input? You've got my pa, Susanna, your brothers and sisters, all kinds of wise people. Why would you want my input?"

"Because you're one of the wisest of them all, Keara Jensen."

"Well…then. What are your thoughts?"

"We need to find out if there truly is trouble afoot or if we're making smoke without a fire."

"So one of us needs to overhear one of those meetings the men are having over at the farm Rod Snyder stole out from under Pa's nose."

"To do that," Elam said, "we first have to silence the watchdog. There may be more than one."

"Bribe the animals if you have to with fresh meat. I'm buying laudanum in town. That should help them sleep."

"Then once we know for sure we have a problem," Elam said, "which I'm pretty positive we do, we'll send a telegram to Susanna's brother-in-law."

"And get help here from real US marshals."

"Two will be on their way as soon as Brute gets back to the telegraph office," Elam said. "We've already discussed that."

"And someone needs to find poor Timothy, if he's even still alive."

"David's tracking him. Has been since last night. When Jael rode to town to get word to the Skerits, Kellen rode to David and Pen's and told them as well. David's the best tracker in the hollow, and he has hunting buddies in Seligman who'll be riding with him by now. From there, they could have left word for the Skerits. I filed an X on the shoes on Timothy's mount to make him easier to track when he and Frey were here yesterday. I've done that before when we needed to track, and David will remember that. I hope."

"I think you've got your plan already," Keara said. "I'll see to Susanna and ride to town."

Elam ached at the sudden shadow of sadness in her eyes, and for the life of him, he couldn't think what might have put that sadness there. "Whatever I've done, Keara, I'm sorry. I'll hitch Elijah to the wagon if that's what you want, but you'll have to cover yourself with a hood to keep from getting coated in dust. He'll pull the load better than Buster, but he'll kick up more of the road."

"I'm pretty much covered in dust all the time anyway."

"I'll have it ready for you when you're finished with Susanna."

She nodded, hesitated, held his gaze for no more than a few seconds, and then she turned and rushed inside.

* * * * *

Susanna's irritable voice continued to ring in Keara's ears as she felt the grit of dust kicked up by Elijah's huge hooves thirty minutes after helping her patient from the tub. She was already sorry she'd volunteered for this errand; by the time she reached Eureka Springs she would be just as dirty as Elam had warned.

Her lips still felt the touch of his, her face still tingled, her shoulders and arms still longed for his hands to restake their territory, but reality had slapped her hard as she stood in the yard, breathless from his kisses, longing for more than she'd ever dreamed she would want.

Confusion swirled around her as if she'd been caught in the torrent of White River after a storm. This storm had begun in her heart. After falling in love with the man who had shown such strength and dedication toward his wife, Keara now doubted him as much as she doubted herself.

When had he first felt the desire to caress her? The first time he'd even spoken of his attraction to her appearance had been the day of their wedding. It was the day his sisters had decked her out with all their artistic talents, tightened her corset to near death, and wrapped her hair in a design she'd never before or since had visited on her head.

He'd spoken to her today as if he saw her as a sparkling crystal, but she knew better. Before too many more days passed, he would realize his mistake. He had been attracted to appearance. Pa had warned her when she was a young teen that men could be dazzled by the sleight of hand a woman could wield to attract them, and when it was too late and the wedding vows had been spoken, they realized the truth.

Something caught Keara's eye as she turned a curve in the road. She glanced back toward the house and saw a flash like a mirror from the top of the bluff over White River. She pulled Elijah to a stop and watched for another flash, for movement, but she saw nothing more. It was probably a piece of glass reflecting in the sunlight... maybe even another crystal. This area was filled with them.

She tapped Elijah's haunches with the reins and he stepped forward again, plodding along as if he, too, detested the dust that kicked up from his hooves.

* * * * *

Elam left Britte and Rolfe playing in the orchard and carried Cash in for a nappy change. His baby's gleeful squeals as Elam tickled his chin drew Susanna down the stairs. Keara had wrapped her arm to hold it tightly against her body so she couldn't move it and further injure the shoulder, but had first dressed her in another of Gloria's dresses, this one pale yellow with green piping.

Braced for a scolding from his sister-in-law, Elam was surprised when she stepped across the kitchen and placed a hand on his shoulder. He recognized the scent—the same lilac and rose perfume Gloria had often worn and that his sisters so loved. The gift they'd given to Keara for her wedding had been lavished on Susanna. But he loved Keara's spicy aroma.

"If I could, I'd offer to care for him while you went riding after your wife."

"She's making a trip to Eureka Springs to pick up a mattress."

"I hope she's also purchasing the material I asked her to buy for new dresses."

"She might. With Keara, I never know."

Susanna held out a handful of photos. "I've been looking at these and grieving, as I know you've done."

He recognized the Kodak photographs, taken in Eureka Springs only three months before Gloria's death. Her face was alight with joy as she and Elam snuggled Britte and Rolfe close, her belly huge with Cash.

"Someday I'll be able to smile again when I look at these," he told Susanna.

"But not yet."

He shook his head.

"I heard you laughing with Keara earlier. What happened?"

"I just enjoy her spirit, her humor."

"I knew she was furious with me for pawing through her clothing, but I felt another emotion underlying that anger. Any idea what it was?"

"I wish I knew." He took a final look at the photographs then slid them aside and held Cash close. The squirming baby comforted him. His activity was the essence of vitality and life. "I've told her in every way I know how this week that I think she's pretty."

"What else have you told her?"

"That she's good with children and patients and horses. I admire her. She's nothing like Gloria, and yet she's so good for the children, for me, for everyone around her."

Susanna sighed, as if she, too, was dumbfounded. "I know she cares for you, Elam. A woman can see these things. She's endured much taunting and belittling in the past, and it may take time to win her over." Susanna pressed her lips together then sighed. "I don't wish to betray her trust, but I hope you understand what I told you earlier. She is worth the additional effort it may take you to draw her out of her past and into a fulfilling future."

Before he could reply, the cowbell rang on the front porch, and they turned to see Jael and Kellen, Pen, Delmar, and Brute, with yet other neighbors straggling from the barn lot where they had left their wagons and horses.

The meeting was about to begin. He only wished Keara were here to take part in their discussion.

Twenty-Four

The streets of Eureka Springs were congested with electric street-cars, horses, carriages, and tallyhos that carried visitors from spring to spring inside the city in search of cures. Keara had seen too many of those visitors cured of their diseases to doubt the claims that brought sufferers here.

She had never taken part in the huge numbers of social activities available for the people that arrived and departed on any of the six train stops during each day. She kept to herself and her own business when she came to town, though it was impossible not to encounter visitors when shopping.

Her first stop was at Welch Hardware and Furniture on Spring Street, where a muscular man in a fine white uniform loaded the box springs and mattress into the wagon. Elam had already paid for the shipment. When the man went back inside, Keara couldn't help stepping to the back of the wagon to admire the material of the mattress, the softness of it, the strength of the box springs.

It was the finest bed she'd ever seen, full-sized, much larger than those the children slept in. She was touched that Elam would give her such a valuable gift.

She closed her eyes and relived today's kisses, the feel of his lips on her skin, the touch of his hands, and his tender voice. How she longed to settle for that, to accept what he offered and be happy.

Why did she suddenly feel the need for more? She loved him. He found her beautiful. She looked nothing like Gloria, but she had been told more than once this week that she was attractive. Even if she couldn't see it for herself, couldn't she just accept it?

And yet, what happened when beauty faded? What happened when she came in from the garden, covered in dirt, hair tumbling askew, smelling of manure? She wanted to be loved as much then as at any other time.

A tallyho clattered and squeaked past, filled with finely dressed men and women, pulled by pristine white horses. People of fashion and distinction came to this town to flaunt their wealth and power and to purchase health. How they must look down their noses at people like her—a hillbilly.

She untied Elijah and climbed into the plain, wooden wagon that suddenly looked out of place here amongst the fine carriages and electric streetcars of the city. Elijah pulled his load up the hill to the mercantile two blocks away and stopped when Keara pulled on the reins. The streets were steep here on East Mountain amongst so many finely structured wood, brick, and stone buildings. She silently thanked God for Elam's act of mercy toward her. How horrible to have been forced to make a living here in this crowded city.

Though Keara thought she recognized the palomino mare and frilled surrey in front of the store, she hitched her horse to the post and went inside.

She hadn't planned to stop here, and she wouldn't have if not for Susanna. The children didn't need new clothes and there were plenty of dry goods of every sort at the ranch. But Susanna had begged Keara more than once to purchase cloth for sewing. It would take time before Susanna could easily travel, and she would need to keep her hands busy while she waited or she would go crazy, most likely dragging the rest of the family with her.

The patterns, bolts of cloth, and sewing supplies were on the far side of the huge store, and Keara headed in that direction. When she reached them, she stopped, appalled. There were so many choices, so many colors, patterns, laces, and frills. How on earth was she to decide—

"Hello, Keara."

She recognized the feminine voice behind her, and realized she'd been right about the horse and surrey outside. She turned to greet Raylene Harper, whose light brown hair was caught in a bun low at the back of her head, topped by a grass-green bonnet that matched her lace-trimmed dress.

To Keara's surprise, the younger woman's light green eyes held wary friendliness.

"What on earth are y'all doing out there on the ranch? We haven't seen hide nor hair of you all week," Raylene said.

"Just settling in."

"Well, you never came to the Springs much anyway, but it wouldn't hurt you to get out more, now that you've got a little freedom. Buying material for a new dress?"

"Uh, yes, I was just looking at all the colors." Raylene's sudden friendliness made Keara uncomfortable. "I haven't seen much of you for the past few months." At one time, when the Harpers lived downriver from the McBride place, Keara and Raylene had visited every few weeks, trading news, sharing an extra catch of fish or garden vegetables. Theirs had never reached the level of closeness Keara shared with Gloria, but Raylene was young and impressionable. Keara had never felt comfortable confiding in her.

When the Harpers moved closer to town, Raylene made friends with newcomers to Eureka Springs, which seemed to have taken all her time. Plus, Keara's friendship with Elam had apparently come between the two women.

Raylene picked up a bolt of dark red satin and held it up to Keara's face, eyes narrowed. "I've learned a few things about fashion this past year. This color looks good on you, but it's too dark." She replaced the bolt and picked up a bright yellow.

"Cynthia Lindstrom does have a certain flair for dressing," Keara said. "I suppose—"

"Pffft." Raylene scowled. "That woman has a flair for lying and back-stabbing, and I was blind to it for too long. That's what happens when a country girl tries to make friends with new people from the East. She becomes bewitched."

Keara couldn't suppress her surprise at the younger woman's words. "You and Cynthia are no longer friends?"

Raylene shook her head. "I wish I'd seen her for what she was months ago, before I confided…a few too many things to her, before I let her influence me in ways unbecoming to a lady. This yellow is pretty with your hair and eyes, but it'll show dirt too easily." She replaced the bolt and picked up another. "I made a fool of myself, tagging around after that woman like a puppy, laughing at her cruel jokes, even when they were aimed at me or my friends. This blue and purple print is perfect."

Keara examined the material. Raylene had, after all, learned a few things about back-East style from her brief friendship with Cynthia. "I saw you sitting beside her at the wedding."

"That was the final day of our friendship." Raylene set the bolt of cloth on the cutting table. She turned back to Keara and crossed her arms. "If you heard…" She looked down at the floor then across the aisle at the bolts of material. "There were…ugly rumors that…" She sighed.

"My sisters-in-law made me wear a tight corset to show everyone in the church that I wasn't in the family way," Keara said.

Raylene closed her eyes and her face reddened. "I promise you I wouldn't've ever started a rumor like that." She opened her eyes and met Keara's gaze. "I mean, I had a crush on Elam and all, and I made a couple of unbecoming remarks about your poor father—which I'm sorry about now—but I wouldn't do such a cruel thing as accuse you of…anyway, Cynthia got by with saying a lot of ugly things about a lot of people by implying I was the one telling her all these things, when I wasn't. All I told her was that I wished Elam would give me a second look, but he probably wouldn't because I was too young and because…well…you were around him all the time."

Something felt set free inside Keara. "So I have Cynthia, and not you, to blame for being forced to wear that awful corset all day?"

Raylene nodded. "I just kept hoping you wouldn't hear the rumor. She's an ugly person with a pretty face and surface charm—that's what my mama says—which helps her get away with a lot of meanness. She's still mad at her brother for dragging the family out here from back East last fall."

"Carl?"

"Yes, their father was injured and couldn't work, and Carl supported the family. He told them that in order to do that, he would have to move here. I have no idea what he does all day. He never goes to an office. He works for the government, but all I've ever seen him do is socialize with tourists and entertain dignitaries."

"So he doesn't talk about his work?"

Raylene stopped, startled, and touched her fingers to her lips, as if she thought she'd said too much. "Not that I'd know anything."

And that meant she did. And Keara knew she could get the information out of her young friend. Raylene had a tender heart, and it had become obvious over the years that the girl had a talent for spilling every thought from her lips the minute it entered her head.

* * * * *

The front of the great room was filled with ten of Elam's closest neighbors and family members, all of them seeming to chatter at once, when Jael pointed and waved toward the top of the stairs.

Elam turned to see Susanna standing there, her left arm still bound tightly against her waist, her black hair shining and loose over her shoulders. Penelope and one of the other women gasped.

"I'm not Gloria." Susanna's voice, which was slightly huskier than her sister's, carried well across the long great room as she started down the stairs. "You're not seeing a ghost. I'm most likely the reason you're all here, and Elam tells me I can trust you with my life." She glanced at Elam.

He saw the courage it had taken her to reveal herself like this, and he nodded with approval. "This is Dr. Susanna Luther," he told those who didn't know. "She's Gloria's youngest sister. She was shot in the shoulder by the man we brought you here to talk about, and she has an interesting story to tell."

"You're the reason Timothy Skerit was arrested?" Penelope asked, sounding doubtful.

"I'm the reason you all are aware of Timothy's arrest," Susanna said. "Former US Marshal Driscoll Frey brought Timothy to the Jensen home because the boy needed medical attention, and it was a good excuse to surprise the family and try to find any evidence that I had been here. Keara and Jael and Elam nursed me back to health and remained silent about me at my insistence."

"I think we should tell them everything," Elam said. "From the beginning."

Susanna was nodding just as someone knocked on the door. Elam reached for his hunting rifle, and he saw that several others reached for their weapons as well.

He went to the door and opened it a crack to find a stranger standing there. The man was young, stringy-haired, with wet clothes. He had a steady gaze.

"I just crossed the river," the man said. "David sent me. Wanted me to tell you Timothy's still alive, but that you've had a spy watching you from atop the bank across the river." He pointed to the north, where the river had carved out a tall cliff.

"Frey?"

The man nodded. "That little trick of yours? With the shoes? Made it easier to track. Fella circled all the way back around from Seligman. Just before I left, he and his poor prisoner were swimming their horses across river about half a mile east of here."

"Sounds as if they're headed for the McBride place," Elam said. "Go back and tell David to go even farther east and cross and keep watch on the road. Then find Timothy's father."

"Oh, Thomas Skerit's riding with David, along with four others. We've got us a good crew."

Elam smiled and nodded. "Need supplies before you return?"

"We're good." The man nodded and walked away.

Elam returned to his meeting.

* * * * *

Raylene had stacked three bolts of cloth for Keara to decide on and had gathered patterns, lace, and other sewing supplies to go with them. And Keara had gone along with it, more and more convinced that Raylene was telling the truth about the broken friendship with Cynthia. Raylene may have loose lips, but she had never been a liar.

"I hear there's a handsome man from Clifty who's sweet on you," Keara told Raylene after the young woman had stacked a bolt of apple-red and yellow print on the growing stack.

Raylene's green eyes danced with a bit of mischief. "Has he been talking?"

"Timothy Skerit, right?"

Raylene grinned and nodded. "You've seen him? Isn't he handsome?"

"Timothy's been shot."

All light died from Raylene's eyes. "What? When?"

"His little brother accidentally shot him when they were hunting.

The marshal who arrested him brought him to our house yesterday for me to treat him."

The pretty green eyes darkened with dread. "No! Why? Timothy never did—"

"Timothy's innocent, but the marshal isn't." Keara felt bad for being so blunt, but she needed to get information from Raylene, and she needed it as quickly as she could get it.

"I'm sorry, Raylene, but we're trying to find Timothy before anything worse can happen to him." She didn't share exactly who "we" meant. "Is there any information you can give me that might help?"

Raylene paced the length of the row of material, jerked off her bonnet, and fanned her face with it. "I can't believe this is happening. Timothy told me a few things, but he swore me to secrecy."

"Why was that?"

"Because he was warned that if he told the sheriff what he overheard, bad things would happen to…" She broke off and fanned her bonnet harder. "Oh, Keara, this is madness!"

"I know. It is. Something wicked is happening, and that marshal is part of it, I'm sure. I could tell Timothy is innocent. He's a fine young man with an excellent future…if he lives. Please, what did he tell you? It could save his life."

Raylene turned and paced back toward Keara. "That evil woman."

"Cynthia?"

"And her brother. Cynthia told Carl that I'd spoken well of Timothy, and so Carl used my name to seduce Timothy to join the little band of men at the saloon down on Mud Street." She shrugged. "They told Timothy he could make extra cash so he and I could marry. He's always kind of liked me. Used to, anyway. Trusted me, until Cynthia got her claws into him. Carl convinced him I would be glad to marry him. The rotten scoundrel."

"I heard Timothy was in a fight and was arrested."

"He overheard men talking about the best way to kill a person and make it look like an accident. Timothy was furious. Any man with a backbone would stand up to such things."

"Of course he would. What did he tell the sheriff?"

"He...couldn't tell Sheriff Nolan anything."

"Why not?" Keara asked.

"Because he was warned that if he let slip what they'd discussed, his little brother Jeremiah would suffer for it."

Keara reached out and grasped Raylene's hand. "You're sure they told him that?"

"Yes, and he swore me to secrecy, but if he's in danger—"

"He is. Raylene, this is important. Have you ever seen where Carl goes during the daytime, besides to entertain visitors and gather men to do his bidding?"

Raylene hesitated. "I...did follow Carl one day. It was when their family first came to town, and I was silly and thought he was handsome—I know better now, of course—and so I was curious about his work. I followed him through town, along Spring Street, until he arrived at Dairy Hollow. He went directly to the building where the patients were isolated when they were diagnosed with smallpox... where Gloria died."

Keara sucked in her breath. She remembered the place well. She had been there to see Gloria. "Did you see what he did there?"

"He had this tool...I think it was a microscope. He was wearing a bandana over his face, and he was collecting dirt and studying it.

Then he would place the dirt into bell jars. I thought he might be an agent from the government to see if the building was clear of the disease."

"I don't think that's what he was doing at all," Keara said. "I think he might have been collecting the contagion to infect others."

Raylene gasped. "But why would he do that?"

"Because there are some evil men in our government, and I think he's working for them."

Raylene grasped Keara by the shoulder. "I've seen Carl talking to a lot of the visitors who've come to Eureka Springs. A few of them were women, but most were men. They were the ones who started meeting. Why do you think he talked to so many people?"

"Do you think he's a good judge of character?"

Raylene wrinkled her nose. "No. I discovered that his friends were the worst sort."

"He obviously knew who to seek out."

Raylene closed her eyes once more, pressing her fingers to her forehead. "I've been such a dunce."

"You've been an innocent young woman who expects the best of people. You've just discovered it doesn't always work out that way." Keara patted Raylene on the back. "I have to leave. If we can get Timothy out of that marshal's clutches, I'll tell him to find you and let you know he's safe. Until then, I suggest you stay out of town and tell no one what we've talked about, or that you even saw me here."

Keara didn't stop to make purchases. Material was the last thing on her mind right now. She made a stop at Porch & Crook Druggists and purchased laudanum for Susanna…and for other purposes. Her next stop was at the McLaughlin Meat Market for the most aromatic meat she could find in the store. She found limburger cheese, as well, and canned fish. That should do the job Elam would need done.

Thank goodness Elijah was always faster returning home than when he pulled the wagon to town. Right now, time was running out, and she had no idea how long she and Elam would have.

Twenty-Five

The meeting adjourned, and Elam silently thanked God for his stalwart neighbors upriver. Now to do something about the one downriver.

Elam didn't like the thought of Keara being on the road with the marshal and others so close. She should be back shortly. She had never been one to linger in the city any longer than it took her to make her purchases and get back out of town, and he didn't want to leave until she made it home safely.

Penelope picked up Cash and carried him over to Elam. "I'm taking Britte, Rolfe, and this little one home with me until you get things straightened out."

Jael joined them and reached for the baby. "You have your hands full right now, Pen. I'll take them with me, at least until David gets home safely. You're going to be distracted worrying about him."

"I'll be no more worried than the rest of the family, and the cousins all love Elam's little ones." Penelope bounced Cash and grinned at him when he laughed. "You're the better shot, Jael. Why don't you stay here with Susanna while Elam and the men reconnoiter. Your children are already at our house, so everyone can camp out on the floor tonight. The older ones will be a lot of help to me."

"Keara should be back soon," Elam said, "but I don't want to leave Susanna alone."

Susanna stepped over to their little group and tickled Cash under the chin. "I don't know if the marshal will still be interested in getting to me, but I don't want my presence here to endanger anyone else."

"I don't think they're going to make an issue of it now," Elam said. "Those men gathering in town all winter wouldn't be here for you, and for secrecy alone, they won't want to raise a ruckus."

"I can ride," Susanna said.

"Not without it costing you," Jael said. "Besides, if that ex-marshal is still watching the house, you don't want to go outside and remove any doubt from his mind that you're here."

"Then it's settled," Penelope said. "I'll collect the children. Elam, where's that mixture you've been feeding Cash? I'll take a jar of it with me."

* * * * *

Keara slowed at the track that led from the road to the McBride farm. Sure, the farm didn't legally belong to her family anymore, but she still thought of it as her home. She studied the tracks that led to the trail, the horse droppings, and dog tracks as well. This trail had recently been well-used, because she'd checked on her way to town, and neither the dog tracks nor the horse droppings, nor half the other shoe tracks, had been there earlier.

The men were at the farm right now. There was an assembly taking place, may already have taken place.

She glanced at the packages on the board seat beside her. No one knew the house where she'd grown up better than she did. She had the items she needed right here with her, right now, and if she waited even thirty more minutes, who was to tell if it would be too late to find out what these men were planning? Especially if Carl Lindstrom already had the contagion and had enough men to spread it.

She climbed from the wagon and led Elijah across the road and into the forest. She tied him behind a huge boulder so neither he nor the wagon could be spotted from the road in case more men came to visit. She'd passed no one on her ride out, but there were other paths from town a person could walk if he didn't mind a little climbing.

She grabbed the cheese and the meat and left the canned fish in the wagon. She opened the laudanum and soaked the meat well with the medicine. She'd only noted a single set of dog tracks, and Elam had only mentioned hearing one dog bark the other night, but one couldn't be too careful.

She was halfway between the road and the farm when she heard the sound of a horse trotting along the road. There was too much brush to see who it might be, but she didn't want to be seen here. She left the trail and plunged more deeply into the undergrowth, where she used to pick blackberries.

No sooner had she concealed herself from the trail than she heard the sound of dogs barking. Two at least…no, there were three of them. The barking continued and grew louder as the dogs came nearer. She pulled out the limburger cheese and the laudanum-soaked meat and divided them into three portions.

Moments later, after the dogs had stopped barking and began to whine at the scent of the fresh meat and smelly cheese, they came plunging through the brush. They saw Keara and started to bark and growl again, huge animals, big teeth, but she held out the meat for them, one by one.

It didn't take long, with gentle talk and good food, for the ferocious-looking dogs to settle and start licking her hands for the remainder of their treat. She prayed she hadn't given them enough to kill them, but that she had added enough laudanum to calm them down long enough to get in and out.

If she'd brought twine, she could have tied and muzzled them, but how could she have guessed at the upcoming day's events when she left the house?

Only a half mile up the way, Elam and the others had probably ended their meeting. She only hoped she could overhear something helpful and get back to Elam quickly enough for him and the others to make their move.

* * * * *

Elam and Kellen were in the barn saddling Moondance when Elam heard a horse-and-buggy pull up outside.

He stepped to the door and then groaned.

"What is it?" Kellen asked.

"Miss Harper."

"Raylene? What's she doing here?"

Elam shook his head. With that girl, there was no telling. "I'll be right back."

"I'll finish with Moondance."

Raylene guided her horse, Honey, to the hitching post beside the barn and stepped down from her fringed surrey. "Hello, Elam."

He nodded. "Raylene."

She reached into the surrey for a paper-wrapped package. "I

brought Keara a gift of apology. I've turned my back on a good friend to go trailing after a wolf in sheep's clothing, and I think Keara will look beautiful when these are finished." Raylene looked toward the front porch. "Is she in the house or in the barn? With her, it's hard to tell where she'll be. I swan, that woman will work her fingers to the bone if you don't stop her."

"Keara isn't here right now," Elam said. "She went to town for supplies."

"Yes, I know, I saw her there at the mercantile, and she left me halfway through our material selections to get word to you about what we were discussing." Raylene looked around the ranch, eyes darkening with alarm. "At least, I was sure she was coming back to you. She wouldn't have lingered, she was in a hurry. Do you think she might have gone to the sheriff instead?"

Elam took a slow, deep breath. Young Raylene had always had an excitable streak about her. One of the reasons her parents allowed her to have so many animals was because the animals tended to calm her.

"What did the two of you discuss?" he asked.

"Timothy's arrest and that crazy marshal and Carl's silly snooping through the isolation building for the smallpox victims last—"

"She told you these things?"

"Well, I told her about Carl's snooping. She told me about Timothy's arrest, and when she left the mercantile like a fox after a rat, I thought she'd come straight here. I was so grateful that she forgave me—well, we didn't actually have time for the whole forgiving and hugging and pledging to never do anything like that again—anyway, I went ahead and bought the materials we looked at, plus one more that I think will suit her coloring, and—"

"You didn't see which way she went when she left?"

"No, I just took for granted she was coming back here."

"Frey."

She blinked. "What?"

"Marshal Frey arrested Timothy. Word has it that he's between here and your home. Raylene, I'll have to apologize to your father later, but I can't let you go home right now. It could be dangerous."

"For me? But why? I rode here without being stopped."

"But you came here. To my ranch. If Frey realizes that, he—"

"May stop me to torture me for information!" Raylene's eyes widened with both fear and excitement.

Elam rolled his eyes. The child had a lot more growing to do. But what was he going to do with her right now? Let her in the house so she'd see Susanna? If his guess was right, this whole mess would be over with today, but what if it wasn't? Raylene had no sense of secrecy whatsoever.

Raylene gasped. "You think that awful marshal has Keara?"

"I don't know, but I'm going to need help to confront him. There are quite a few men at their new hideout."

"Where's that?"

"The old McBride farm. Raylene, I'm going to unhitch Honey and put a saddle on her. I need you to ride to each home upriver and tell them I'm moving in. The men will know what to do." And it would keep Raylene from entering the house until she returned from her mission.

* * * * *

Keara had known the barn would be the best place for a bunch of people to meet, and she heard the voices from inside as she drew near. She knew just the place she could listen, and even watch.

Pa had built an indoor toilet and bath for Ma when she was first paralyzed, but the outhouse connected to the barn was still there, and at Keara's demand, it had been used when anyone was working outside, in order to keep the house cleaner.

When she reached the outhouse she pulled open the door slowly to keep it from squeaking. Stepping inside reminded her why she'd been so happy to have an indoor toilet. Ugh.

Still, she eased the door shut behind her and pulled the lock down in case anyone was crazy enough to try to use this instead of the indoor toilet.

There was enough light coming in from the sun-moon cutouts at the top of the tiny building that she could see her way to step up on the toilet seat ledge and peer through the knothole into the barn.

Light filtered in from several open, glassless windows, and she counted at least twenty men seated on makeshift board benches in a semicircle, with the marshal standing in the center, facing them. Carl Lindstrom stood to his right, as if he was the second in command.

"…recruited a good team," Frey was saying, "and though we had hoped for twice as much help, we don't have time to screen more men. Your pay will come after you've done your jobs, and though your names will never be mentioned on lists of praise for valor, you will always have the satisfaction of knowing you've served your country in this silent war. The enemy will be thwarted with these containers instead of bullets, and you will survive because you've been inoculated."

Keara felt the ice of dread as he continued to praise these killers for what they were about to do.

He began to call out names, and as he did so, each man stepped forward to receive his utensils—a canning jar, apparently sealed, and a stack of terrycloth towels. Carl gave each man a map.

They were going now! They had to be stopped today. Keara had to get to Elam, to the sheriff. They had to call for help.

She unlatched the door and eased it open, eased it shut, and turned to run.

She'd gone three steps when someone grabbed her from behind and threw her to the ground. A big man with beefy hands and a red face leaned over her.

"I saw what you did to the dogs." He raised his fist, and all went dark.

Twenty-Six

Elam rode beside Kellen toward the McBride farm while Delmar rode ahead of them on his way to find David and his team. Delmar had the fastest horse in the county. He was a little too proud of that fact, but it came in handy at a time like this.

They needed to be organized for this, and right now they were scrambling around the woods like mice tossed into the swirling river. But Elam couldn't waste time. He couldn't wait for David and his men to catch up with him, not if what he suspected had actually happened.

Instead of following the usual wagon track to the farm, they rode to the forest trail that led from the road to the back of the McBride barn and tied their horses in the woods.

That was when Elam heard a familiar nicker at the far side of a house-sized boulder. He plunged through the blackberry thickets and found Elijah still hitched to the wagon, his neck looped with a rope and tied to a sturdy tree.

"Kellen."

"Coming."

Elam caught a whiff of something ripe.

Kellen stepped up behind him. "What is it? That Elijah? Phew, what's that smell?"

Elam knew exactly what it was and that put the fear into him. "Limburger. Keara and I discussed distracting the watchdog and getting to the house to find out what the men were up to."

"Think she's decided to do it by herself?" Kellen asked.

Elam wanted to wring her neck. "She was going to buy laudanum for Susanna. She probably used a dose of it on the dog. I'd bet she's already at the farm." But why would she do something so dangerous?

Kellen glanced at the trail entrance and pointed. "That could be why."

There were horse droppings, dog tracks, boot tracks of all kinds. A meeting was taking place at the McBride farm, and it was happening now.

"Well, what are we waiting for?" Kellen asked. "Let's get there."

Together they crossed the road and kept low as they raced down the foot trail. Elam prayed that they weren't already too late.

* * * * *

Keara smelled manure. She heard the deep sounds of unfamiliar men's voices blending together in the distance, and a vicious snake bit her over and over again in her cheekbone. She groaned softly, but she could barely hear herself past the pounding in her head and the murmurings of the men.

Something touched her left shoulder. She jerked away and tried to get up. The darkness whirled around her. Her stomach twisted into knots. She was going to vomit.

"Mrs. Jensen?"

Her eyes opened in the darkness. That wasn't an unfamiliar

voice. As her head continued to spin, she tried to place it. Young man. In pain. Frightened, but trying to act brave.

Another touch. A hand, gentle but insistent. "Mrs. Jensen?"

She didn't vomit. In spite of the spinning darkness, she pushed herself up and tried to focus. Someone helped her, and the touch was still gentle. As she straightened, her eyes became accustomed to the gloom, and she saw thighs encased in Elam's old work pants. One of the thighs had extra thickness beneath the material.

She finally placed the voice. "Timothy?" she rasped.

"It's me."

Her surroundings came into better focus, and she saw that they were in a stall in the barn. "I know this place."

"You do?"

"I used to live here."

"In a barn?"

Goodness, he was as young as Raylene Harper. "No, but we kept a mean bull in this stall. I think I know how we can get out of here."

"It's been reinforced. One of the men nailed a bunch of boards up high, so we can't even climb out."

"Where are the men?"

"They've gone outside."

"All of them?"

"Yes. Mrs. Jensen, you did fine work on my leg."

"You can call me Keara. Have you heard what they're planning?"

"Sure have. The marshal tried to convince me to join them. Said I'd make enough money that my folks would never have to work again."

"I take it you turned him down."

"Do you know what they're up to?" His voice rose with obvious outrage.

"Shush. Don't draw attention."

"I'm sorry, but—"

"They're planning to cross the border into Oklahoma Territory and murder more Indians."

"You know about it?"

"We're digging up details in bits and pieces. When we get out of here, you need to look up Raylene Harper."

"Raylene? She's in on this."

"No, she's not. She just got tricked. She's worried about you."

"I don't think we're going to get out of here alive."

Keara sighed. This young man had a bad attitude. Perhaps he wouldn't be a good match for Raylene, after all.

When Keara's head stopped pounding so wildly, she inched her way past Timothy to a particular portion of the outer wall. "Did I mention we kept a mean bull in here at one time?"

"Yes."

"We've kept nothing in here since."

"Why not?"

Keara pressed her ear against the wall. She heard no one talking. It sounded as if the men were all at the barn entrance on the other side of the building.

She pressed her fingers against the boards. Sure enough, no one had noticed. "Because the bull kicked the boards loose here." She pushed harder to allow daylight in.

Ma died and Pa lost his will to live about the time the bull kicked out the boards. Keara had her hands full corralling her brothers, and no one had seen fit to nail the boards back in place. They were as loose as a latchless door.

"Can you help me with this?" she asked, keeping her voice soft.

Timothy moved immediately to her side and reached for the boards.

"Quietly," she said. "It won't help us if they catch us again."

"I'll push the boards back and you climb out," he said. "I'll follow."

Timothy had just crawled behind her into the shady side of the barn when they heard an outcry and a bellow from within the gang of men mingling in front of the barn.

"What's that?" Timothy asked.

Keara couldn't help thinking of her husband. She knew he'd planned to come to this place soon, but now?

She pressed her finger to her lips and led the way around the side of the barn. She saw a crowd of men shoving two men to the ground, kicking them, punching them.

"No," she whispered.

"That's Mr. Jensen!"

Keara glanced back the way they had come, where one of the windows stood open. "Come and boost me back inside."

"But why?"

"I need a gun."

"But they'd have all taken theirs."

"My pa left a hunting rifle in the barn all the time." She led the way back around the side of the building. "Said a fella never knew when he'd need to shoot a snake or other varmint." She'd been so angry with Pa when she'd been forced to move that she'd left his rifle in its hiding place. If Snyder hadn't found it, she might have a chance to use it.

With Timothy's help, she climbed into the barn through the

window, felt through the shadows until she clutched the reassuring handle of Pa's rifle, and handed it out to Timothy. She shoved her toes into a slat in the wall and heaved herself back through the window. Timothy caught her with a grunt.

She checked the rifle for ammunition and was relieved to find it fully loaded. They had to hurry. "Let's go."

Timothy didn't balk at facing down a crowd of angry men. He walked at Keara's side, reached for a sturdy limb, and rapped it against the palm of his hand. "I thought I'd die, anyway. This will give us a better chance."

Keara cocked the rifle, aimed at one of the men kicking Elam, and squeezed the trigger. There was a cry, and the man fell over, grabbing his shoulder. She shot again as the men grew silent and stopped their attack on Elam and Kellen. Another man fell.

She cocked the rifle again. "I have a few bullets left. Who's next?"

"Mrs. Jensen." It was ex-US Marshal Driscoll Frey stepping toward her through the crowd.

She took aim. "Good. You're the one I wanted."

He stopped and held his hands up. "Wait!"

She held the rifle steady. "Give me one reason why I should."

"We aren't going to kill your husband."

"I know that, because I'll kill you first."

Nobody moved.

"And yes," she said, "I know there aren't enough bullets in this rifle to kill all of you, but I'm one of the best shots in the county. Ask anyone who knows me."

"She is." Elam pulled himself up, blood dripping from his cheek as he reached down to help Kellen. "I know her well."

With Keara's bead on Frey's head, Elam and Kellen stepped through the frozen crowd of men. Elam didn't attempt to take the rifle when he reached her. The men didn't need any distractions.

"Your secret is out, men," Elam said. "Not only do we know you're planning to murder innocent US citizens, but we know your names. Driscoll Frey may have told you he's a US marshal, but he's not."

As Elam spoke, the brush behind the crowd parted, and out stepped David Pettit with his band of men. One of the men saw Timothy and rushed forward.

"Pa," Timothy said softly.

David and his men trained their pistols on the crowd from behind.

The sound of horses reached them from the wagon track, and all but Keara looked to the side to see who was coming.

"Anybody messes with my daughter will have to face me, and I've already been in jail once for killing a man."

Keara did look then. "Pa!"

Sheriff Nolan joined Brute McBride. "We've more lawmen on their way. Anyone who tries to get away will be shot. McBride, looks like your daughter has already begun the process."

Pa slid from his saddle and stepped to Keara's side. He grasped the rifle and took it from her. "Darlin', I've never been prouder of you."

He turned back to Frey and his men. "You thought you'd make war against legal US citizens? Those tribes own that land, and they've got as much right to live in this country as you. Fact, I think they've got more rights. They haven't been planning to murder anybody by spreading disease."

Elam dabbed at the blood on his face and took a step forward. "There was a cry of outrage by citizens all across this country about the horrors of the forced march. If you think that cry was loud, wait until they hear about this. And they will."

The silence was broken only by the groans of the men Keara had shot.

As the sheriff took over and ordered the crowd to drop their weapons, Elam drew Keara aside and caught her in his arms.

"I thought I might lose you," he whispered. "When you didn't return to the house, and I found Elijah in the woods..." He pulled her close. "Keara, don't you ever do anything like that again."

Keara hugged him, and when he lowered his lips to hers, she kissed him with all the love she'd tried to conceal in her heart, though she winced in pain.

She smelled like manure, she was covered in it, and her hair fell around her face like a squirrel's nest. Her final question had been answered, and her heart was home at last.

Twenty-Seven

Keara lay in the tub until it seemed she'd soaked nearly every drop of hot water into her skin. Her fingers were wrinkled and she felt relaxed down to the bone.

Someone knocked on the door. "Have you drowned in there?"

She smiled. It was Susanna, who had been the one to insist on this luxury in the first place. "Still working on it."

"Well, I'm coming in. I brought clothes I want you to wear when Elam returns from town with Sikes."

"Is it the blue and purple?"

"No." The door unlatched and Susanna stepped in. "Don't worry, I'm not making you wear fifteen pounds of undergarments."

Keara raised her eyebrows at the pieces of silk and muslin her friend carried over her arm. "Are you sure? You shouldn't have done all that work. I could've—"

"Yes, but you wouldn't've," Susanna said, mimicking Keara. "You'd have worn your old, stained brown things until they fell apart. I, on the other hand, love to sew when the neighbors aren't trying to set up a practice for me, and the movements are helping my shoulder heal more quickly. Hurry and dry off. I want to get these clothes on you and get your hair dry in the sun so Elam can see the final result."

Keara did as she was told. She'd learned that there were certain things Susanna would simply not back down on, and the remaking of

Keara Jensen was one of them. The two women had exchanged a few heated words over it, but as Keara had learned to stand her ground with Gloria and remain friends, the same worked for Susanna.

Sadness weighed Keara down for most of the week, once they received the news that Susanna's brother-in-law was on his way here by train to pick her up and take her immediately back home.

"I'd still like to observe a few more procedures before you have to leave." Keara had followed Susanna's instructions about new herbs to collect and dry, but several of the patient treatments—mixing certain powders for pneumonia, testing for blood diseases, breech births—hadn't come up in the daily routine of seeing to patients who lived in the area.

Once folks found out about Susanna's medical degree, the Jensen parlor, which was set off from the great room with fancy French doors, had many days become a regular medical practice.

"When is Sikes planning to leave with you? Can he at least spend the night?" Keara pulled on the first layer of soft underwear. It wasn't scratchy.

Susanna sighed. "He doesn't want to stay and visit. Typical of the man. He plans to catch a later train back today. He has sleeping berths for both of us, so it should be a lot more comfortable returning than it was riding out here. But he has business to get back to and he can't linger. His words exactly."

"We'll take good care of Duchess while you're gone." Keara pulled on the second layer of underwear, eyeing the rest. Too bad Susanna had gone to all the trouble of sewing two extra layers that Keara would never wear—at least not in summertime.

"I get the impression you think I'm coming back this way." Susanna held up a beautiful silk chemise, blue eyes sparkling.

Keara caught her breath and reached out to feel it. "It's lovely!"

Susanna handed it to her to pull on. It fit perfectly.

Keara frowned at Susanna, however. "You are coming back, aren't you?"

Her friend avoided her gaze. "I have patients who need me in Blackmoor, especially with Nathaniel gone. You know, you're a lady of means now. You could easily afford a train trip to Pennsylvania to visit with me…perhaps learn a few more procedures."

Keara's spirits brightened. "I could travel back to Blackmoor with Duchess on the train."

"About that—"

"And then you could travel back with me."

Susanna gave a soft sigh, as she often did when she wanted to communicate that Keara was being as bullheaded as Brute McBride. At last, however, she held up the dress. It was the apple-red and yellow patterned material, snug around the midriff and tapering out from the hips. It had Georgian sleeves and a neckline that wouldn't embarrass Keara to wear, and yet it most certainly wouldn't choke her, either.

"Try it on."

Keara did as told, and as it slid down over her hips, she knew it was a perfect fit. What couldn't Susanna Luther do?

The mirror image of Keara in the dress was…

"Stunning," Susanna said.

Keara could only nod.

"The bright yellow brings out the gold in your eyes. And that's with wet hair. Wait until we get it fixed."

Keara stared at the reflection of the two of them. So different on the outside, and yet she'd begun to see so many similarities between them. Perhaps it was because she'd grown to love Susanna as she had Gloria.

And then the tears came. Keara couldn't help it. She'd been more teary-eyed these past few weeks since the capture of the killers, sometimes for no reason whatsoever, but now she knew why she was crying.

"Susanna." Her voice was husky with an effort not to burst into sobs. "Are you sure you can't just stay here?"

"Oh, my dear." Susanna placed her arms around Keara and held her close—a gesture of affection she wouldn't have been able to make before her shoulder had been given all these weeks to heal. "Nothing is ever set in stone, you know."

Keara nodded and cried.

"You have Elam's love. That's a wonderful gift."

Keara nodded, sniffed, cried harder.

Susanna released her and stepped back, and Keara saw tears coursing in a healthy flow down her friend's face. "I hate leaving," Susanna said. "As this day has drawn near, I've dreaded it more with each hour."

"Then why?"

Susanna took her by the arm. "Come, let's step outside into the sun and start drying that hair along with our faces."

Keara went with her. The front porch steps were totally cleaned of bloodstains now, and the late spring breezes carried with them scents of clover from the fields. A rain last night had settled the dust, and the wind was warm enough for drying hair.

Susanna stepped over to the stone wall, where Elam had once chosen the embedded crystal to show Keara what he felt about her beauty. "This place has become like my true home," Susanna said softly, looking out across the orchard where the children were weeding, interspersed by much play with their wandering baby brother. "After all these years of resisting Nathaniel's pleas for me to listen to him about his faith in God, his belief in following Jesus Christ, I've only recently seen that faith in action in a whole community. Maybe because I wasn't looking before." She touched Keara's arm. "It's in you, in Elam, in his lovely sisters."

"You're a part of the community now."

Susanna smiled. "I'll always be a part of the Christian community now, and I have your example to thank for that. As for the future, we'll wait and see. I have to return and make peace with my past."

As she spoke, they heard the sound of Elijah's trot and looked up to see Elam returning with Sikes Luther.

"Your hair!" Susanna cried. "It isn't finished."

Keara chuckled. "You can stop worrying about my appearance now. Elam made it clear the day he found me covered in manure with my hair looking like a crow's nest that he doesn't see me from the outside."

Susanna winked. "Oh yes he does. You know those times you aren't watching, and he can't keep his eyes off you? When he's working Freda Mae in the corral and loses concentration when you step out on the porch?"

Keara felt her face grow warm. "We've been lingering on the front porch after everyone else has gone to bed."

"I know. Why do you think I've started putting the children to bed early? How do you think I've found the time to sew your dresses?"

Keara felt the tears again. She blinked them away as Elam and Sikes approached the house. "Come back to us, Susanna," she whispered. "Please come back to us."

Susanna placed an arm around Keara's shoulders and walked with her toward the arriving carriage.

* * * * *

Elam saw Keara and Susanna walking toward them, and he couldn't take his eyes from Keara.

"That's your new wife?" Sikes asked.

"That's her."

"A lovely young woman."

"Her beauty begins in the heart and radiates outward." Elam didn't care if Sikes thought him a besotted fool, but he believed the man would understand. They'd shared quite a bit of correspondence since the incident with Marshal Frey, and Elam had found Sikes to be sincere, methodical, and dedicated to his career.

Elam climbed from the carriage and resisted the urge to go to Keara and take her in his arms. They only did that in private. He'd kissed her a total of five times since the day of Frey's arrest, and it frustrated him to move so slowly. But he trusted Susanna's advice.

After so many weeks of watching his wife's kindness on a daily, nightly basis, Elam realized that her love had been lavished on his children since long before Gloria's death. Keara was a gift from God for him and the children.

He thanked God for her every day.

After introductions, Sikes gave his apologies. "After our correspondence, Elam, I had so hoped to be able to spend more time here and get to know you better."

"You are welcome to stay as long as you wish."

"I had planned to do so," Sikes told him. "But a special meeting has been called about legislation to prevent this kind of travesty with the Indians from happening again. I don't want to miss that meeting."

Elam understood. By the expression on Susanna's face, he thought perhaps she was beginning to.

"You know, Elam, that you and your courageous wife, as well as your family and neighbors, share the legacy of heroism that Susanna has earned in her quest to get the truth out about the barbarians who met in Eureka Springs to murder innocent people." Sikes gave his sister-in-law a nod of respect.

Elam could see the surprise on Susanna's face, and he smiled. She would be sorry for speaking ill of Sikes in the past.

"Perhaps when you have a longer break," Elam said, "you could come back out and visit us. There are luxurious hotels in town if you're concerned about comfort."

Sikes chuckled. "I've been on hunting trips with our president. Theodore Roosevelt is not always concerned about comfort. He keeps his eyes on his goals."

"As do you," Elam said.

"Please, do come visit us," Sikes said. "We will roll out the red carpet for our Arkansas heroes."

* * * * *

Keara remained teary-eyed as she helped Susanna prepare to leave. There wasn't much to pack, as Susanna had not been able to carry a lot with her on Duchess, but Penelope was almost exactly Susanna's size, and since her girth was growing daily, Pen had no use for her usual wardrobe. She sent several ensembles for Susanna's travel.

The time came far too quickly for Kellen to drive Sikes and

Susanna to the station. In the short few hours Keara had been in the company of Sikes Luther, she was reassured that he would see to Susanna's safety and comfort on their trip back to Blackmoor. He would also see to it that the sheriff of that town would not be able to throw his weight around to make life uncomfortable for Susanna.

As the buggy disappeared over the hilltop, tears slid silently down Keara's face. Elam turned to her, and he reached for her.

"Oh, sweetheart, I know you're going to miss her."

Keara could only nod.

Elam put his arm around her and walked with her to the orchard wall, where Britte and Rolfe had run to the far end, waving at the carriage. They, too, would miss their auntie Susanna.

"She hasn't left you alone, you know." His voice was tender, and Keara looked up at him, enchanted by his gentleness.

"We still have Duchess," he continued, grinning.

Keara returned the grin, but she couldn't laugh.

"Susanna wants us to keep the mare for breeding stock."

"You mean I won't be able to ride the train to take Duchess back home?"

He touched his forehead to hers. "You and I can ride to Blackmoor together for a visit."

"You know, of course, that Susanna and Sikes will never be a match, no matter what you're thinking."

Elam smiled at Keara, his dark eyes filled with love so powerful she could feel it. "You never thought that you and I would make a true match."

Keara swallowed, took a deep breath. "I might not have dared think about it, but I did dream."

Elam grew still. "You did?"

She glanced toward the children playing around a tree. She swallowed again. "Cash will be toddling around soon, getting into everything. Don't you think he's going to need a younger brother or sister to teach him responsibility?"

Elam's breathing stopped for a moment. He cupped her chin with his hands. "Keara, do you mean it?"

She smiled through drying tears, and she nodded.

He caught her up in his arms and swung her around and then placed her on the ground and kissed her. "Keara, how long have I loved you without knowing it?"

Her laughter joined the laughter of the children in the orchard. She wrapped her arms around her beloved husband's neck and brought his face back down to hers. "I don't know, but you're going to love me for a long time to come."

Life truly could be filled with joy again. And it all began with a kiss.

Author's Note

I love Eureka Springs, Arkansas! There's something about this town-on-a-hillside with curving streets, trolley cars and horse-drawn carriages that beckon a person into the past. The Victorian homes that line those shaded streets are colorful and breath-taking. It makes one think of simpler times—when there were no cell phones, computers or even automobiles. The healing springs drew Native Americans to the area long before white settlers arrived, and though the neighboring tribes would engage in combat, when they came to the springs for healing, they put down their weapons in peace.

Something about that resonates with me, and I hope it resonates with you. Our spiritual healing comes from another source—from Jesus Christ. When we come to the foot of the cross we need to focus on the truth of God, on healing ourselves and one another. At the foot of the cross, may we lay down our weapons in peace.

—Hannah Alexander